To Joan

best wishes

Pan Douglas

THE MAY INCIDENT

by Pamela Douglas

authorHOUSE®

AuthorHouse™ UK Ltd.
500 Avebury Boulevard
Central Milton Keynes, MK9 2BE
www.authorhouse.co.uk
Phone: 08001974150

First published by AuthorHouse 10/4/2010

ISBN: 978-1-4520-6667-7 (sc)

This book is printed on acid-free paper.

PROLOGUE.

It is an extraordinary thing, but, whenever anyone asks me about my life's history, I can rattle off an amusing set of anecdotes from my early childhood, through the war years, school, Art college, adolescence and marriage etc, etc, and my memory will completely exclude "the May incident".

I do not do it intentionally; my biography flows wittily off the tongue, innocently passing over the whole affair. My brain has blotted it out, temporarily. A few hours or sometimes days later, I think "it's happened again!" The whole experience was clearly traumatic enough for my subconscious to protect me from the memory; and yet, when I do think about those four years, it is not with distress, Rather with sadness and regret. I suppose it is just my brain doing it's job of protecting it's host.

I have never had occasion to discuss it with a psychiatrist, but I would imagine he or she would have a professional explanation for it.

However, be that as it may, I feel that it is time to do a little therapy of my own and clear out the cobwebs, dust it off and clear my mind of it once and for all and give the whole experience the full treatment.

I believe in the premise that we are what our parents have made us; a happy home makes a happy child. It is generally accepted these days that a person who experiences abuse as a child quite often becomes an abuser. Or, blame or bless the genes, if that is the way you see it.

So then, it requires that I contrast the background and characters in May's life as well as my own, as far as, at least two generations.

But, truly my driving force is my desire to pay tribute to the strength of my parents love for each other.

I have also decided to write it in the third person. This way I hope to keep the events in perspective.

NEWSPAPER HEADLINES FROM AN EVENING HERALD MILLENIUM SUPPLEMENT

Jan 24 1901. Halley's Comet was seen from Plymouth.

Feb 16 1902. Marconi made the first trans-atlantic wireless communication from Lizard.

May 15 1903. Joseph Jacobs of the Barbican fined 30s. for speeding with horse at 18m.p.h. fined 30s

June 1904 Actress Ellen Terry played in Much Ado and The Merchant of Venice in the Theatre Royal.

June 8 1905 An A8 submarine sank off Plymouth Sound losing 15 men.

June 27 1906 Devon felt earthquake tremours a few weeks after the San Fransisco Quake.

Feb 21 1907 The Prince of Wales opened a new Dockyard extension.

May 1908 a poll was held on whether the three towns should be amalgamated.

Jan 1909 the Plymouth Workhouse Infirmary & new nurses home in Greenbank Rd was opened.

May 1910 Edward VII died.

Oct 1911 Captain Robert Scott's expedition set off to the Antarctic.

April 15 1912 Emmeline Pankhurst, suffragette leader arrested in Plymouth arriving from the USA

May 5 1914 Amalgamation of Plymouth, Devonport and Stonehouse to be known as Plymouth.

Jam 1915 Kitchener called for 1,000 men from Plymouth to enlist.

June 191 Many Plymouth men died at the battle of Jutland when 333 officer died.

May 1917 the Royal Naval Air Station Cattewater was founded in Plymouth Sound.

Nov 11 1918 The Great War ended. Thousands marched and sang to celebrate.

May 31 1919 Rat catchers offered 3d per rat in naval buildings & ships in Devonport.

Oct 4 1920 French sailing vessel Yvonne crashed into the Breakwater. One man drowned.

Ded 1921 5,500 men and 500 women reported registered as unemployed.

Aug 19 1922 Mrs Patrick Campbell and Paul Robeson appeared at the Theatre Royal

Feb 20 1923 Captain Scott Memorial to be placed at Mount Wise overlooking Hamoaze.

April 1 1924 Plymouth's five toll gates were closed.

Feb 12 1925 Captain Amundsen Noewegian explorer visited Plymouth.

May 18 1926 General Strike violence in Old Town St. protesters arrested.

March 1 1927 Charles Lindbergh's Spirit of St. Louis spotted flying over Breakwater

Oct 17 1928 The King decreed that Plymouth would be a city.

Oct 1929 Wall Street Crash spawns depression in Plymouth.

August 7 1930 Two Million out of work.

July 29 1931 Mayor Clifford Tozer opened new Central Park at Milehouse.

Jan 1932 30 Plymouth Policemen go to Dartmoor prison to help quell a prison riot.

Nov 30 1933 Three Plymouth Hospitals announced plans to amalgamate.

July 2 1934 Plymothians were warned to conserve water during a heat wave.

May 18 1935 A Banquet at Guildhall to celebrate the bestowal of Lord Mayoralty.

Jan 28 1936 St. Andrews Church to mark funeral of King George V

May 12 1937 Coronation of King George VI marked with service on the Hoe

May 28 1938 Empire Air Day was held at Roborough Airport.

June 5 1939 BBC bought Ingledene in Seymour Rd to convert to studios.

Feb 15 1940 Crowds welcome HMS Exeter after fight with German Graf Spee

July 1 1940 German forces invade Channel Islands.

March 20 1941 The Plymouth Blitz begins.

April 1 1942 A small number of oranges arrive to be issued to children.

April 27 1943 Plymouth compares devastation on Coventry

April 25 1944 Plans for regeneration of the city displayed in the museum.

May 8 1945 Plymouth greets the news of Allied victory in Europe.

Nov 2 1946 Food shortages set to worsen after worst harvest for years.

Oct 28 1927 King and Queen visit Plymouth to see plans for rebuilding.

Jan 17 1948 Plans for new housing schemes for Plymouth unveiled.

Dec 1949 Randolph Churchill was adopted as prospective candidate for Devonport

Feb 24 1950 Labour wins General Election slender margin of five seats.

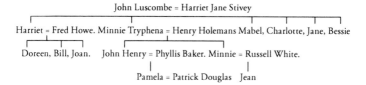

John Luscombe = Harriet Jane Stivey

Harriet = Fred Howe. Minnie Tryphena = Henry Holemans Mabel, Charlotte, Jane, Bessie

Doreen, Bill, Joan. John Henry = Phyllis Baker. Minnie = Russell White.

Pamela = Patrick Douglas Jean

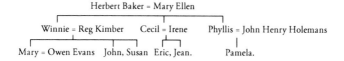

Herbert Baker = Mary Ellen

Winnie = Reg Kimber Cecil = Irene Phyllis = John Henry Holemans

Mary = Owen Evans John, Susan Eric, Jean. Pamela.

(Guernsey)

Paul Garonne = Martha

Eloise (Ellie) = Sidney Evans

May.

CHAPTER ONE.

Plymouth City did not exist at the dawn of the 20th century. The three towns of Plymouth, Devonport and Stonehouse did not become a single entity until 1914. From the earliest days Devonport was made up of villages such as Pennycomequick and Millbridge. On the highest point of the town stands the village of Stoke which retains it's village character even today.

It was in the early 18th century that this family's forebears came to live in Stoke, in Penlee Road, in the third of a row of four cottages named Mayon Cottages. We shall not dwell on these early days here, but take up our story on the 12th of August 1907 with the birth of John Henry Holemans. He was the first male to be born into this household for two generations to parents Henry John, a naval officer and Minnie Tryphena, nee Luscombe, the second eldest of six sisters who all idolized him. Having no brothers of their own, a nephew was someone to spoil. But although they bought him sweets and items of new clothing, or toys, young Johnny was not actually a spoilt child in the accepted sense. Far from it; he was a lively, cheeky and full of fun little chap who plagued the life out of his little sister Minnie. "Hey sis, I'll bet I can sing with my mouth open wider than you!" he would challenge, as he took a very deep breath and prepared to sing. "No you can't!" cried Minnie, rising to the bait. "Show me then!" grinned Johnny, slyly., and poor Minnie opened her mouth really wide to sing,

1

as Johnny popped a cake of soap into her mouth, and ran! "Maa! He's done it again Maa!" Minnie wailed once she could speak. "Oh, Min," sighed her Mother, "You know what your brother is like, but you always get caught! When will you learn? You are silly!"

He didn't mean any harm, of course, and took his punishment bravely; what was called punishment was never harsh for their Mother loved them both dearly. She was the sort of woman who would never hear a bad word spoken about anyone., a very gentle kindly angel. She was a home loving body who worshipped her husband and fussed over him whenever he was home from sea.. She was only four foot nine in height; in fact all her sisters were small in stature like herself. They had all been born in number three Mayon Cottages, in the big downstairs front bedroom as had Johnny and his sister, as did their grand parents and great grand parents before them.

The middle three of Minnie's sisters had flown the nest and married more or less as soon as they were old enough and came home to visit occasionally. The house was semi-detached double fronted quite large for a cottage, with a small stip of garden each side at the front and another square patch of garden at the back. The main part of the house had a parlour at the front opposite the main bedroom and two large bedrooms directly above with a small box room over the front door.

Along the central passage a turning to the right led to the rear end of the house which was single storied, and consisted of the diningroom leading on to the kitchen, above which was a tiny attic room where Johnny slept. The outside door of the kitchen led on to the wash house where thert-was a huge copper with a fire underneath on wash days. At the end was the outside toilet. The house would have no bathroom for many years yet.

The two spinster sisters, Charlotte and Mabel, shared the two large upstairs frontrooms and young Minnie slept in the boxroom.

Mabel was a dedicated school teacher; Charlotte, the eldest had worked in a shop after finishing school, for a short time before it became her duty to tend the elderly and sick of the family, and in time, devoted herself to making life comfortable for Mabel and helped Johnny's Mother keep house. She was always there for everybody.

Whenever Johnny's father was home from sea, life was predictable. The household revolved around him. Henry was a mildly eccentric man who had a habit of doing things on the spur of the moment. He was once sent to town to the market one Christmas to purchase a turkey and came back with a rocking horse!

He built his own crystal radio set on which he loved to listen to music, especially Opera., and when it was on, no-one dared to speak. He was not fierce about it; he just was master in his own house and Minnie so loved him that his slightest wish was granted. So he would listen in peace, then all of a sudden he might jump up, switch off the set, and say, "Right! Who wants to go to the pictures?" and he'd put on his coat and hat as he walked out the door, not waiting for anyone! If those wishing to go did not hurry and catch up with him they would be left behind.

He wrote and produced pantomimes for the sailors in the barracks at Christmas time. One year he himself was to play the dame; so he decided to buy himself a pair of corsets for the part. But not content to pick up a pair at a second hand shop, he made up his mind to shop for them in the poshest department store in the city, Pophams. Where lady shopwalkers in the underwear and lingerie departments strolled around silently overseeing their domain, dressed in long black elegant dresses and wearing a flower. One can only conjecture at the distress and indeed horror he caused when he waltzed in asking quite calmly to be fitted with a pair of lady's corsets! It is best that we draw a hasty veil over the scene. Suffice it to say that he came home with the corsets; but that was Henry! He probably smiled through the whole thing.

Johnny was always delighted whenever his Father came home. When he was little Henry would often take his son out on a Sunday morning down to 'the lines'. This was a parade ground in Granby Barracks where the Royal Marine Band would march up and down playing the rousing marches as only a Marine Band can. Johnny would march up and down beside them, with his tin trumpet in seventh heaven.

Then suddenly, Henry would be gone again, back to sea, and the home would return to it's quiet, female run routine; except for the odd pranks Johnny would find to play on poor gullible Min.

Charlotte enjoyed helping her sister keep house; if ever she had had a sweetheart or ever desired to be married, she never said. Mabel, on the other hand, had had a sweetheart who was a sailor in the first world war. She had many affectionate postcards and letters from him from all over the world, each one ending with the endearment, "Dinna forget." But he died of the fever in the far east aged only twenty two, and she never ever wanted another.

Other than that, little about the first world war seemed to effect the family. Henry was of course involved in some sea engagements but he never referred to it at home as he knew how it would distress his sensitive wife, and as no-one else was of the age to serve in the Army then they were more fortunate than many families who lost loved ones in that great conflict.

Johnny did well at Stoke Damerel Junior School, with

Mabel's coaching at home, he eventually had no trouble passing his exams at aged eleven and earned himself a place at the Devonport High School for Boys, a highly respected seat of learning throughout the county. He made many friends, especially two who were to remain his closest friends for most of their lives.

The first was Frank Pinnicker who later traveled the world with the civil service; and Fernley Adams, whose Mother was Jamaican. His Father was in the Merchant Navy. Fern was not quite as dark skinned as his Mother, Ada, but had a mop of black curly hair and sparkling dark eyes. He was later to become a Naval tailor specialising in Naval dress uniforms.

These three were inseperable, and their greatest love as young men was Scouting.

Although Johnny's family had always attended Stoke Damerel Church to worship, unfortunately it did not have a scout troop, so they joined St. Micheal's Church troop in Albert Road, Devonport, in the next parish. Scouting was their passion. The outdoor sporting life of it filled their leisure days well into their working lives. Camping and boating photographs filled the family albums.

Now Johnny as a young man is called Jack by all his friends. Though why John should become Jack is rather a mystery, in fact he wrote a little ditty about it which began, "Once upon a time there was a little boy named John, They used to call him Jack for short because John was too long.

He used to like to sing and dance and tried to write a song,

But that's another Mother's tale."

Not far away, no more than a mile or two, on March 25th 1908, Phyllis Gwendoline Baker was born.

The youngest of three, all redheads like their Father's family. Herbert Baker had been born in London, one of twenty one children. When he was a young man the family moved to Devonport where his father started a livery business in Albert Road. Stabling horses and carriages for the gentry. He married Mary Ellen, who lived at Dartmeet on Dartmoor, and he would ride or walk the fifteen miles to court her on Sundays. The story goes that the first time he was invited to take tea with the family he fell into the river whilst crossing over the rocks on a short cut to the house and turned up on his future Mother-in-law's doorstep soaking wet.

Herbert became an employee of the Army and Navy Stores which later was to become the N.A.A.F.I. After they were married they lived in a terraced house near the Dockyard, where their children were born. Winifred, or Winnie as everyone called her; she was an elegant dainty girl who grew up wanting the finer things of life. She would not get dirty like her young sister Phyllis, whose carrot coloured hair earned her several nicknames including "copperknob" and "ginger", but her Father called her "Pickles" because she was always in a pickle. Her Mother despaired of ever keeping her neat and tidy like Winnie.

Their brother Cecil, the middle child, like many boys in a Naval Town only ever wanted to be a sailor. But Pickles was the apple of her Father's eye; he loved her spirit and took her with him on business whenever he could. It was from him that she learnt all her skills which would make her a shrewed business woman in later life.

After leaving school her personality earned her an interesting job of demonstrating products such as polish, on stands in large stores and trade fairs. She, like Jack's Mother, was under five foot tall; a small round bundle of energy and spunk which made her popular, especially with the lads.

Living as they did off Albert Road, they attended St. Micheal's Church, where the vicar was modern thinking and keen to cultivate the youth, especially the Boy Scouts and the Christian Fellowship, regularly holding social evenings after evensong.

It was here that Phyllis and Jack first set eyes upon eachother. All the lads would gather at one end of the hall and eye the girls, waiting for the music to began so that they might approach them and ask for a dance., and there were many who tried to catch the eye of the jolly little red head and would compete for her partnership. Jack knew, the moment he set eyes on her that she would be the girl for him., but he was going to bide his time.

On Sunday afternoons the young people used to stroll around the band stand in Devonport Park. just a short step from Albert Road. Indeed, for generations this had been the place to meet and pair off. Mabel had many tales to tell of when she too was young and strutted there with her friends.

Phyllis was never short of a boyfriend to walk her home after the Sunday evening socials, but often wondered why that handsome Jack Holemans had never tried to be one of them. Jack had been working since he matriculated, as an apprentice for W.H.Hodge & Son, a large wholesalers in The Octagon, in Plymouth. They supplied hardware and hairdressing sundries, toys and china to many retail shops in the South West. When Jack had served his two years apprenticeship in the store he would become a traveller for the firm, visiting their shops in Devon and Cornwall taking orders. Fortunately, Jack had done well at school in French and it caught the attention of his boss when he volunteered to translate letters from a shop keeper in the Channel Islands., and impressed them even more by successfully replying to them and securing an order.

This earned him an unexpected bonus and the offer of a small car to begin his work as a trainee Travelling salesman.

On reaching this position in life, Jack decided that it was time to start things in motion with a view to begin courting Miss Phyllis Baker.

At the following Sunday evening social, Jack asked Phyllis to dance, twice, much to her surprise. She was flattered, as he had always been a boy whom she had not been able to entice with her charms before. She had seen him watching her but he had never before made an advance, until now. Jack was different. He was certainly very handsome, not more than five foot seven but trim and athletic. His straight black hair smoothed back neatly, shone with a touch of Brilliantine but not as much as his wonderful smile.

It warmed all who saw it, showing two rows of strong white teeth and a pair of the blulest eyes that Phyllis had ever looked into. She knew at once that he was the one, but she wasn't going to let him know it just yet. Besides, she enjoyed her freedom and certainly had no intention of giving up her merry times with all the other lads who always sought her out for dances and the right to walk her home. But tonight it was Jack's turn for that honour. Phyllis was not haughty or vain, she just liked enjoying herself.

They met in the park the next Sunday and strolled along chatting and laughing. Jack could be jolly company she found; and at the social that evening they danced together several times; so much so that his sister Minnie chided him for neglecting her. "You are supposed to be here with me brother Jack not flirting with that ginger huzzy. She's too popular by half!" "Now then Min, don't be so jealous. You dance with other boys too don't you?" replied Jack. "That's not the point!" she retorted, "Mother wouldn't like her anyway, she's got red hair and you know how Ma hates people with red hair!" This was the first thing that shot into her mind to use as a weapon but actually she had hit a mark.

Their Mother, though always gentle and kind natured in all things had an unreasonable 'thing' about people with that coloured hair. There seemed to be no known reason for it but she held firmly to the opinion and never wavered. Jack frowned to himself. This could well be a challenging problem if he was going to marry the girl, as indeed he had set his heart on it.

Jack took Phyllis home again that evening with his young sister dragging along behind, for he was responsible for her of course. She scuffed her feet and muttered to herself, but Phyl and Jack were too engrossed in eachother to notice.

When they returned home Min could not resist the urge to run to her Mother and spill the beans, making a great point of how disgustingly red Phyl's hair actually was. Mother received the news with quiet dismay but realized that if Jack was really in love with this girl then red headed or not there was nothing she could do about it but hope that she was a nice girl and worthy of her darling boy. The following weekend Jack was not able to attend the social as he was traveling too far from home to get there. Of course Phyllis only felt disappointed for a few moments. The lads soon clustered around vying for her attention, and it was another who walked her home. The following Sunday Jack found that Phyllis had promised another boy that he could escort her home, so he had to be content.

Jack thought about this situation a lot through the ensuing week, and when Sunday came round again he had made up his mind as to what must be done. After having a couple of dances with her, during the interval Jack took Phyllis aside and asked her why she had let another chap take her home. "I don't want you to take me for granted Jack Holemans." She replied. "I am not your property." And then Jack answered, "But if we are going to get engaged I didn't expect you to walk out with anyone else!" For the first time in her life Phyllis was speechless. She had met her match. She thought quickly to herself that if she wanted this boy she was going to have to mend her flighty ways and give up her favourite past time of flirting. But still, he was taking a lot for granted wasn't he talking about being engaged. "I don't know where you got the idea that I would get engaged to you! You haven't asked me yet anyway!" "Well, I will as soon as I've spoken to your father". He replied. "Never mind my Father, it's me you need to ask! Honestly! "Inside she was delighted and confused at the same time. She wanted him to ask her properly in the moonlight, but when he took her home it was drizzling with rain and Min was moaning at him to hurry up as she didn't want to get any wetter, so the romantic moment would have to wait. There was just time for a quick kiss before he was gone for another week. Next time she'd be ready and she hoped that he would be too.

The next Sunday Minnie was in bed with a cold so Jack knew that this would be his best chance to settle things between them. They met in the park in the afternoon and when they found a quiet spot with a secluded bench they sat down. Jack took her hand and told her about his prospects with his company and said that there was noone in the world besides Phyllis that he wished to share his life with. He kissed her and told her he loved her. Phyllis was so happy and hugged him hard as she whispered "Yes please." In his ear. They made arrangements for her to come to tea at Mayon and meet his family, all except Father of course as he was away at sea.

So, the next Saturday they did just that. Charlotte laid on a big spread of sandwiches and cakes like never before., and Mother, despite her aversion took to Phyllis at once admitting that she was a lovely girl. Min was expecting an explosion and was quite disappointed. Little did she know that she too would marry a redhead named Russell White in a year or two.

During the week Jack bought the ring and plans were made for him to come to tea at her home so that Jack could formally ask for her hand.

Recently, Phyllis's Father had left the N.A.A.F.I. and taken the job of Head Park Keeper of Devonport Park which included the large brick building in the centre of the park, with an ornate veranda running all round it as well as a similar balcony outside the upper floor. The back quarter of this building housed the Park's tea rooms with a children's playground at the back.

The Sunday afternoon of Jack's important visit, he decided to impress his future Mother-in-law with a conjuring trick. One of Jack's friends, Desmond Leach, had taken up collecting tricks and the two of them would go into town every Saturday morning looking at new tricks. Desmond intended to take conjuring up seriously and hoped one day to become a member of the Magic Circle. As Jack was now contemplating getting married he did not feel that he could continue to spend his hard earned money on this hobby any more, but wanted to perform this one time with his newest trick involving a pint of milk. He had practiced this trick until he could perform it confidently, without mishap and decided that it would be just the thing to impress Mrs Baker.

The trick was to take the top off a bottle of milk, stir it using a knitting needle, replace the lid then turn it upside down, remove the lid and amaze the audience by stirring it once again, this time up side down before restoring the lid and bringing the bottle of milk to the upright position.

Jack set off for the park with his trick in his pocket, minus the milk of course.

The more important task of asking Phyllis's Father if they might get married, uppermost in his mind; everything went well. Her Mother liked his warm smile and father approved of his employment prospects with Hodges and Son. Father had a chat with Mother and when tea was over they both gave the happy couple their blessing, with the stipulation that they wait a year because Winifred was getting married in a few months time and they could not be expected to afford two such events in one year. Especially as Winifred was marrying into a somewhat wealthy family so no expense was being spared. Indeed Winifred would not have it any other way. She was well aware that her family were not as posh as the Kimbers and did not want to be thought cheap or beneath them socially even though they were.

This being agreed, they relaxed and tea was cleared away. Jack decided it was time to perform his trick. Phyllis, Winifred, Cecil and Mother and Father were asked to sit in a semicircle and Jack asked if he might borrow a pint of milk in order to perform a little trick. Mother nervously agreed; Phyllis fetched one from the kitchen and Jack stood in front of the hearth facing his audience.

"You won't spill any on my new hearth rug, will you young man?" said a concerned future Mother-in-law. "No, no it's quite safe, leave everything to me." Said Jack confidently. After all, hadn't he done it five times last night for his own Mother? "Oh dear." Muttered sister Winifred, sensing disaster. Jack successfully reached the stage of removing the cap on the inverted bottle of milk. Everyone held their breath as he stirred the upside down milk bottle without mishap. He withdrew the knitting needle and tucked it under his arm, took the cap out of his pocket ready to replace it on the bottle. This too he did successfully and everyone sighed with relief. But, just as he was about to return the milk bottle to the upright position, disaster struck! The magic cap fell off allowing the milk to gush out all over the new hearth rug!

Poor Mrs Baker screamed! Father, who was just returning, exploded with rage and Jack was instantly evicted! He felt sure that all his chances of marriage had been washed out with the milk! But, of course, wash out it did, with no real harm done to the rug, thanks to Phyllis's quick action. But it was a few weeks before Jack dared put his nose around the door of the Park Keeper's lodge. When Jack and Phyllis next met, however, he was relieved to hear that once Mother knew that no harm had been done to her precious rug, they had all actually seen the funny side of the incident, especially when Father was reminded of the day when he had arrived on his future Mother-in-law's doorstep soaking wet all those years before. All except Winifred, who thought it all very vulgar and degrading and threatened her sister never to let Jack perform any conjuring tricks in the presence of her future-in-laws.

The evening when Jack gave Phyllis the ring, she said that she would wear it for ever. They parted at her back door; sadly Jack was going traveling for at least ten days. He hoped to be back in time for the following Sunday social. Unfortunately, he did not return until the following Wednesday when some friendly gossip lost no time in telling him that Phyllis had been taken home form the social by one of her old beaus and had been seen walking in the park with another.

So on Thursday evening Jack called on Phyllis and they walked around the band stand in the park. When they sat on a park bench he confronted her with the gossip. When asked if it was true, she replied that it was; and that she saw no harm in some company whilst he was away.

With that Jack took hold of her left hand and removed the ring.

"If you are going to marry me, then I don't expect you to go out walking with other fellows." Began Jack softly, holding her hand. "But I only…" Phyllis began, but Jack interrupted her saying, "If you don't see the harm, then you can't wear my ring until you do." Phyllis had not stopped to think how Jack would feel and was very sorry, but coax as she might, he would not give the ring back. "You can do without it for one week, to teach you a lesson not to be so flighty. I love you and I hope you love me, so think carefully and I'll ask you next week if you want it back."

Without talking they walked back to the house in the park; Jack left her at the steps to the front door, kissed her gently on the cheek and walked away. Tears flowed down Phyllis's face as she pondered on how serious it was to take Jack's feelings lightly. He really loved her and she was shocked at the shame of it. She had been showing off her ring to all her friends all week. However would she explain it's absence? Phyllis was not a girl to be at a loss for long. She decided to tell them that it was at the jewelers being altered as it was a bit loose.

Jack's affections were clearly not to be trifled with. She really did love him and wanted to marry him so she resolved to be good and prove to him that she would be his and his alone.

At the end of the week they made it up and Jack gave her back the ring. They swore never to lie to eachother or ever do anything that would jepordize their life together ever again.

They were married on July 20th 1930 at Stoke Damerel Church where all of Jack's family had been baptized, married and buried for six generations. It was a beautiful bright sunny day and the church was filled with all their friends and relations. They spent their honeymoon in Salcombe as they both loved the sea. Then they set up home in a little flat off Albert Road.

Fernley's Father owned moorings at Admiral's Hard under Halfpenny bridge. He came across a bargain which he thought Jack might like to buy. It was a twenty two footer with an inboard engine. Jack and Phyl were delighted and bought it, naming it the "Pickles". They spent many happy weekends around Plymouth sound, Bovisand and Cawsand bay.

The following summer Minnie married the red headed Russell White and they lived at Mutley.

Jack and Phyllis did not live in their flat for long. That winter was hard and Jack's Mother caught Influenza and sadly died. At the request of Jack's father they moved into 3, Mayon Cottages with Mabel and Charlotte. Henry bought them a baby grand piano as a late wedding present and it looked wonderful in the corner of the front parlour which Phyllis loved to play. They were very happy and content in their home together.

APRIL 1930   GUERNSEY.

Martha stood at the window of her parlour and wiped away the tears. Father Peter stood quietly by the mantelpiece with his back discretely turn away from her, giving his old friend some time to compose herself.

Martha's daughter Eloise had got herself into serious trouble this time, and no mistake. He pondered over the girl's life wondering how many times she had reduced her saintly mother to tears. But Martha was thinking more of her husband, Paul. It was all his fault. Even the conception of their daughter was a violent bad memory; a night she had often tried to forget, but could not.

They had been married just a year, and Paul had been employed as a gardener for the St. Claire family since leaving school, but on that day he had received the sack. Why, she could not clearly remember, but it must have been associated with his erratic bursts of temper, no doubt.

He had come home in a surly mood, needing to punish someone, anyone, saying that if he had not married her he would have gone to England and worked with his brother on the Devon estate where Phillipe was doing so well.

That night he became drunk and aggressive and forced himself upon her, violently. Eloise had been the outcome. Martha was convinced that her daughter had inherited her father's temper, joined with her own willfulness, though she had, herself lost any will to express it during the fifteen years she had lived with these two volatile people.

Father Peter recalled the pretty child he had baptized and watched grow up, running wild along the cliff tops, constantly being reprimanded for missing school, preferring to scramble around the rock pools on the sea shore. A wild spirit with an quick temper, often fighting with the boys who teased her. She hated all the other children, he recalled, always happiest alone. She had been punished for stealing, often. Only trifles, like apples or eggs, and once, a puppy belonging to a neighbour's child, just to upset her.

But when she was fourteen it was time for her to find work. Her Mother's cousin was the housekeeper at the St.Claire manor house and arranged for Elouise to work as a kitchen maid there. Fortunately the dismissal of her father several years before was long forgotten and it was agreed that she should work there.

Paul had managed to make ends meet doing odd gardening work and maintainence for the town Mayor who, for some reason, got on quite well with him. Perhaps the fact that they had been boys together at school had something to do with it.

Unfortunately, the other servants at the manor did not like Eloise, Lizzy, as they insisted on calling her, much to her annoyance.

Mary Rose, the parlour maid simply refused to speak to her, though Susie, the scullery maid was too simple minded to care. Eloise's aunt, Elsie Brooks, did her best to get Eloise to keep her place and tried to teach her jobs, but it was an uphill struggle. The child just wanted to be off, out of doors running wild when work was to be done.

The boot boy, Clifford, was her own age; he preferred to call her Ellie, which she liked. Unfortunately, he encouraged her willfulness. They often ran off to the orchard together, climbing the trees and chasing the pigs when they should have been at their tasks.

He was the first real friend she had ever had and they enjoyed running running off through the woods at night, catching rabbits.

But the inevitable happened. At fifteen they discovered their sexuality when swimming in the pond at the back of the woods. Ellie's shift clung to her small breasts and Clifford could not resist reaching out and touching her rosy nipples that pressed through the thin wet fabric. It felt like an electric shock shooting through her body. They both saw too, the effect it had on his body. After a frozen few moments they began slowly to explore one another and, during the days and weeks that followed they discovered the delights of physical contact until there came the ultimate result. In their ignorance they had not known that Ellie would become pregnant.

Martha wiped her tears and turned to Father Peter. "What are we to do Father?" she asked him with such sadness in her voice that he tried his best to sound hopeful. "He must marry her of course." "Oh, no! That's impossible! Clifford is only a boot boy; he could not possibly support a family."

At that moment, Paul Garonne burst into the room having heard his wife's declaration. "There's only one thing to do with Eloise, send the child to the nuns. I want nothing more to do with the little slut! She's not staying here and that's my last word!" He slammed the door as he went out again, cursing under his breath.

Father Peter crossed the room and put his hand gently on Martha's shoulder. "Perhaps your husband is right, my dear. My sister is a nun at St. Peter's in Plymouth. I'm sure they would take her. Theirs is not a closed order, in fact the sisters of St. Peter's are very much community workers. They step in as 'Mother' when a poor family has their own Mother in hospital or confined to bed, and they take over the day to day running of the family until she is well enough to return to the fold. They tend the sick and raise money for the poor selling their needlework. They also take in unmarried mothers and help them have their babies adopted. I'm sure Eloise will not be the first young unmarried mother my sister has taken under her wing."

And so it was agreed that Father Peter would write off at once to Sister Josephine, his own dear youngest sister and ask her to take Eloise in. Clifford was packed off to the other side of the island to work for his uncle on his potato farm.

Before the week was out, Eloise's small bag of belongings was resting on the top step of the quay side where she and her Mother waited for the Ferry boat to leave. There would be no prolonged hugs or even tears; they had long since dried up, leaving a strained silence. Father Peter watched from further down the quay side almost out of sight, not wishing to intrude. He knew that there would be no knowing when Martha would see her wayward daughter again. Of her Father, there was no sign. He had been drinking steadily for days.

The Ferry whistle blew and the last of the passengers boarded the boat. Without a single look back, Eloise stepped up the short gang plank and vanished from sight. Almost immediately the boatman cast off and the steamer chugged slowly out of the harbour into the channel. Martha turned away and set off up the main street towards home with a purposeful stride as though her body said, "Well, that's that. There's nothing more to be done about it but get on with life as best we can." Neighbours turned discreetly aside, not wishing to add to her troubles, thinking, there but for the grace of God go I. Several could be seen whispering together and crossing themselves as they went indoors.

It was Father Peter who sadly watched the boat until

it was a tiny dot on the horizon. He knew, at least, that Eloise would be in good hands; his sister Joanna, now Sister Josephine, was the gentlist, kindly woman on this earth and he felt confidently optimistic that that whatever was to happen to Eloise and her new born child, his sister would be her devoted guardian angel.

APRIL 1930

Sister Josephine re-read her brother's letter as she waited on the dockside at Millbay in Plymouth. It was not the first time the sister's of St.Peter's had been asked to take in an un-married mother and see them through this difficult time. This dear child was just fifteen and far from home. Everything would be very strange to her after the smallness of island life.

Her brother had described Eloise as having dark blonde hair in pigtails, and wearing a brown long coat. It was the first coat that Eloise had ever owned, she had only ever had a shawl. Father Peter found it in a second hand box of clothes in his vestry the day before she was to leave, and thought she would be glad of it in the cold early spring mornings ahead.

Eloise held it closely around her as the boat approached the dock. She had had some time to think on the journey and decided that with this new life, she would throw away the old name and call herself Ellie from now on. It would remind her of Clifford whom she was missing terribly.

As Ellie descended the gang plank she had no trouble picking out the distinctive black and white figure with the warm smile, waiting on the quayside. Ellie remembered her Mother's words of warning to be polite and obedient, so she stopped and gave a bobbing half curtsy with her head bowed, before the welcoming figure.

"You must be Eloise Garonne. I hope you had a pleasant

journey my dear. My name is Sister Josephine, but I expect my brother told you that." she said.

"Yes, thank you, he did, and thank you, I enjoyed the boat journey. I am never seasick, and I would prefer it if you called me Ellie please sister." Ellie stopped speaking quickly, realizing that her words might already be sounding boastful and rude. But Sister Josephine took her arm and said, "Of course, my dear, if you wish." And lead her away towards the gates with no sign of anything but pleasure that she had arrived safely.

"It's not far to walk to Wyndham Square," she said, " if you're not too tired when we get there, there'll be time for some tea before I take you to your new home."

Ellie had been wondering all the way across the waters of the channel, what it would be like in Plymouth and where she would live. Would she have a nun's cell in a convent? Would she be expected to scrub the chapel floors to earn her keep?

As they walked along, Sister Josephine kept chattering to her about the town, and the community around the Cathedral. Ellie did not listen much, she was too busy looking all around her. The dock area was very large and full of warehouses and machinery. Lorries and cranes, all working at a great rate. On the mainland, it would seem that there was so much for everyone to do, that it must be done at full speed.

Clutching her bag firmly, Ellie and Sister Josephine dodged in and out of the busy thoroughfare, as they came to the Octagon, an eight sided 'square'crossing Union Street they had to weave behind a brewers dray pulled by two enormous horses, delivering beer to the many public houses along this road. There seemed to be one on every corner, frequented by many workmen and sailors standing about in the doorways. The noxious smell floating out from these doorways hit Ellie in the face as she passed, like a shock blast from an open blacksmith's furnace.

They traveled along King Street, turned right up a steep hill with a very high wall on one side, which Sister Josephine explained was the wall surrounding the Royal Naval Hospital. At the top of the hill they reached yet another pub on the corner of Wyndham Square. The Cathedral stood at it's centre with the tall spire pointing high into the sky above the city. It was surrounded on three sides by terraces of large attached Victorian three storey houses with railings along their frontages.

Circling the cathedral, on it's far side they came to one of these houses which Ellie rightly guessed to be the convent of the Sisters of Mercy. As they entered, two sisters came out from the farthest doorway to greet them and they were ushered into a large warm refectory where more than a dozen nuns were enjoying tea and buns and chatting merrily.

Ellie was astonished. She had always thought that nuns in convents went creeping about whispering or not even talking at all! Sister Josephine saw Ellie's expression and guessed the reason. She laughed and explained that the sisters were taking a quick tea break before rushing off to work amongst the families of the parish when the children came home from school shortly, to prepare their meals, as well as share their troubles and their joys; and although the sisters spent many hours in prayer, their time was mainly spent in service.

After Ellie had been given a large mug of tea and a bun she was taken through to a corridor which lead to the Mother Superior's office, where Sister Josephine explained that if the reverend Mother approved, she would take Ellie around to Mrs Murphy's right away before returning to her own pre-arranged tasks.

Mother Superior smiled and nodded and said a few words of welcome, gave Ellie her blessing and said that they would talk again tomorrow when she would give Ellie all the details of her new life here in Plymouth.

Sister Josephine then took Ellie back out through a small passage way which came out at the back of the convent. The narrow lane led to a row of tall thin terraced houses facing the backs of the grander houses on the square. She was not to be staying in one of those then., she realized. Nothing so grand for a girl in disgrace.

These narrower houses were probably servant's houses in Victorian times. They were rather drab and neglected looking and had the odd bush or weed growing in the front, pathetically trying their best to brighten up these narrow strips of gardens.

The door of number seven stood open. Indeed, Ellie would find that the door was never closed in all the time she would be living there, for this indeed was the home of Bridie Murphy, a large, plump, unkempt lump of an Irish woman who met them in the doorway, which she filled, beaming with several teeth missing.

"There ye are Sister, with another of your little lambs, I shouldn't wonder. Come in, come in."

Sister Josephine hurried Ellie inside, not wishing to discuss the child's problems on the doorstep for all the neighbours to hear. A few heads had popped out as they arrived, she noticed. They would, no doubt, hear about her soon enough, for Bridie Murphy was the gossip queen of the whole parish. She loved to tell her friends how kind she was to give her rooms to these poor girls who were in so much trouble. Had'nt she been a midwife all her life and knew just what these poor girls needed? She never mentioned the fact that she was well paid by the convent for her services.

The gushing welcome continued as she led them into

her front parlour divesting Ellie of her coat and baggage, sitting herself down on a chair while Sister Josephine gave Bridie the necessary details written down for her by the Mother Superior. Bridie studied the paper briefly before putting it down on the mantelpiece, weighed down by a statue of the Virgin Mary.

"That'll be fine Sister Josephine, you won't need to worry about her at all, so you won't. Haven't we done it all before then? Mary McCarthy has gone back home this very mornin' so this one can be havin' the same very room."

Sister Josphine looked at the mantle clock and gasped. "The children will be home from school any minute, I'm down with the Wilson family this week, I must be off." "Ah, the poor soul. Did her appendix burst or were they in time Sister?" Bridie asked and looked almost disappointed when Sister Josephine called back as she was leaving that Mrs Wilson was on the mend. She turned back at the door and said to Ellie, "you'll be all right here with Mrs Murphy my dear., she has a nice room for you and will give you some supper later. Have a good nights sleep, and I'll be back to get you in the morning about nine o'clock to take you back to see Mother Superior." And was gone before Ellie could thank her. Ellie bobbed a curtsy at the vanishing back of Sister Josephine which made Bridie burst out laughing. "Sure and you've no need to curtsy every whip and while to herself. Save that for the priest or perhaps Mother Superior, else you'll be bobbin' like a puppet all day long!"

Another great laugh shook her belly as she grabbed Ellie's coat and baggage and pushed them into her hands, and lead her through the passage to the stairs.

"Come along and I'll be showin' you yer room. It's all clean and fresh for you., but you'll have to keep it so for yourself mind. I can't be climbin' these here stairs more than I can help."

They went up two flights of stairs, Mrs Murphy puffing and slowing down as they rose higher up the stairs, pulling herself by the banisters like the hoist Ellie had seen on the dock side. Bridie needed all her breath to climb, so said nothing but pushed a door open to the left of the second landing and pointed the way.

Ellie entered the room which was to be her home during the next several months. It was small with a brass bed in the centre and a chair and a wah basin with a jug, and an old chest of drawers by the window. The view was of the walls of the back gardens of these houses which looked even more unkempt and neglected than the fronts. There were washing lines draped with grey sheets and two pairs of trousers which looked as though they would not stand many more washes before falling apart. The floor of the room was of rough bare wood with a scrappy crocheted mat by the bed. Two blankets, two heavily mended sheets, a pillow and a towel lay in a pile at the foot of the bed.

By this time Mrs Murphy had recovered her breath. "Put your things away and have a wash if you want one. I'm off downstairs to start the supper. If you're not too tired I'll be glad of a hand with the tatties. Mary was a good help in the kitchen". She didn't wait for an answer but turned and puffed her way back downstairs.

Alone at last Ellie sat on the chair inside the door, her eyes drawn to the large picture above the bed which she had seen so many times in Father Peter's study. It was the Sacred Heart. It made her feel very homesick and she felt the rush of tears begin.

After a few minutes she stopped herself, determined that nothing was going to make her cry. She was on her own and must not show any weakness. All that was happening she had brought upon herself and must be strong. Life was going to be very different here. Her Mother would have been pleased with her behaviour so far, but she didn't know how much longer she could keep it up.

Looking in the mirror in the hallway as she came back downstairs Ellie fancied she could see her waistline beginning to thicken, but that was probably imagination, although she did feel different some how. Three of her 'curses' missed now, so she began to wonder what was ahead.

"Is that you girl?" Mrs Murphy's shout broke her thoughts as she hurried into the kitchen where the Irish woman thrust a pinny and a sharp knife in her hands and pointed her towards a bucket full of potatoes. There was a huge saucepan beside it. "There'll be seven of us for supper tonight so you'd better fill it up." She said pointing to the saucepan and passed her a bowl of water. "I've the four sons who work in the Dockyard. They have appetites like hogs so they have, but as long as there's tatties they are happy, bless 'em! They have both the two back rooms on the first landing, mine is the one at the front, and the other room across from yours is Catherine's for the present. She's another such as yourself, expectin' in five months I reckon. Doctor says four but I know different. Haven't I been a midwife for thirty two years? Sure I can tell at a glance, so I can. You now, well, it's early to tell, but you've a long ways to go. So, how many 'shows' have you missed now?" "Three." Muttered Ellie shyly. "Ah well then, another six months for you then. You'll be goin' off like Guy Fawkes, I shouldn't wonder.!" And she laughed loudly at her own joke.

Mrs Murphy chattered on about her experiences as a midwife, non-stop as they both worked preparing for the meal. Ellie thought the huge saucepan would never fill, and her fingers began to wrinkle in the cold bowl of water. At last she was finished and the pan was lifted on to the big black range by Mrs Murphy as though it was as light as an empty jug. She then set Ellie to scraping a heap of carrots and cutting them into yet another saucepan whilst Mrs Murphy pulled out a bag of sausages from the larder and cut them apart, pricked them and put several on to the largest frying pan Ellie had ever seen, even back at the Manor house as home she had never seen one so huge!

After being told to slice up a large loaf of bread and pile the pieces on to a plate she was told to set the table.

Mrs Murphy decided that it looked like rain so while the supper was cooking she and Ellie went out into the back yard and took in the washing. After it was sorted and folded, the sausages were set on the stove. Not long after, as they were sizzling merrily in the pan, there was an almighty noise as the four sons arrived home from work on their two huge motor cycles.

Their shouting and laughing was deafening as they crashed into the house, pushing and shoving each other good humouredly. Mrs Murphy shouted above the noise, "Will yes quiet down now! Do ye want to frighten our new lodger out of her wits?" They all stopped in the doorway of the kitchen, jamming it up as each tried to get in before the other to take a look at her. "And take yer caps off, have ye no respect for the house?!" their Mother scolded. "Stand forward and be named." She commanded. "This is Patrick, my eldest", she declared, as she pulled a giant of a young man into the room. His grin widened as he winked at Ellie. "And this is Sean, and this is Shemus, his twin." The two red heads close together left this fact in no doubt. "And this is my darlin' baby boy, Mick." She said as she patted the last one's cheek. "Ah, Mam! Will ya stop callin' me yer baby now! I'm twenty two for Christ's sake!" he said blushing. "None of that language in this house my son or you'll feel the back of me hand, as big as ye are!" replied his Mother. "Ha, Ma, but you'd only reach his elbow me darling." Said Sean, They all laughed as she aimed a blow in their general direction. "Get off to the yard and wash yourselves before I lose me temper, so I will!" she shouted. "But Ma," said Mick, "You haven't told us who this gorgeous creature is! And her fillin' the kitchen with her beauty!" Ellie blushed as she tried to hide her smile. "You behave, young Mick, I want no hanky-panky with this one like the last! This here is Ellie Garonne and she's come over from the Channel Islands, so she has." "To have a babe, I shouldn't wonder" whispered one twin to the other.

"Enough I said!" shouted their Mother, "be off with yes!"

They crashed out slamming the door as they went along the passage to the back wash house, joking and shoving, making yet more noise.

"Sure, but the house is never quiet when they're in it!" laughed Mrs Murphy, returning to the stove. Well, that must be the understatement of the year, thought Ellie. She wondered what their Mother had meant when she mentioned 'hanky panky'. Before she had time to think on it, the door of the kitchen opened again and as quiet as a mouse, a young pregnant girl crept in, placing two shillings on the table and slumping into the nearest chair to rest herself with a sigh.

"And this is our Catherine I was telling yes about before." Introduced Mrs Murphy.

"So, how was your day Cathy?" she asked.

Cathy groaned and held her belly with both hands. "God, it's getting tiring workin' in that shed; and she won't let us sit down for two minutes together; and I fell sick all the time! Jesus!" "None of that language now girl, or I'll put soap in yer mouth!" Catherine looked across at Ellie and asked, "And who is this poor sod? Another one to join our merry band? Mary's gone now, I suppose?" "yes, she's gone this mornin', back to her Mammy if she'll have her back, that is." Said Mrs Murphy, turning the sausages in the pan. "the baby's gone to the orphanage so that's the end of her, and this here is Ellie with a good six months to go."

"Oh, I'll be done and gone by then pray the Lord!" replied Cathy. "Are you going to be working at the shed with the rest of us?" she asked. "I expect she will, though she's not been told yet. She's to meet with Mother Superior in the morning"" replied Mrs Murphy. "God help her then!" said Cathy, wincing s she rubbed her aching back.

"God! I'm in agony!" she moaned, "just you wait till it starts kickin'!" laughed Mrs Murphy. "That son of yours is goin' to give you a good beltin' from in there, so he is!" "Welcome to our happy home, we'll have a chat later." Cathy said to Ellie as she began to rise.

Catherine hoisted herself up, swearing under her breath at Mrs Murphy and went out to the yard. As she passed the men they could be heard making obscene remarks which she returned in equal measure.

Not long after that, the supper was ready and they all crammed into the small kitchen to eat, but not before their Mother made the boys wait for Grace which she asked Ellie to say for them. After a moments embarrassment she took a deep breath and rushed one off. It was hardly 'Amen-ed' before the boys fell upon the food. It vanished a lot quicker than it had taken to prepare. Ellie noticed that Cathy had very little appetite. She herself picked at hers as she was extremely tired. But she was expected to help clear up before she was permitted to slip away to her room.

Cathy was at her door as Ellie climbed the second flight. "I'm getting to come up them stairs puffin' like the old lady herself!" Cathy laughed as she leaned against her door jam. "You look like you've had a long day too. Perhaps we'll chat tomorrow." Without waiting for an answer, Cathy turned into her room and shut the door.

The next morning Ellie was awakened at six thirty with the noise of Bridie's sons getting up to go to work. They argued and squabbled and laughed their way down the stairs where their Mother called them for their breakfast. She knew there would be no work for her this day so Ellie snuggled down, away from the frosty draft which came under her door and she yawned sleepily. What seemed but a few minutes later, there was a knock on her door and Cathy's voice was calling her to get up and come down to eat. She hurriedly washed and dressed herself, then descended the stairs meeting Cathy at the bottom.

"The boys wake you up at an unholy hour, don't they? Dockyardees start at seven o'clock. Did you hear them start their motorbikes?" "No." replied Ellie, "I missed that. I must have fallen back to sleep quite deeply if I didn't hear that." she smiled. "Good for you, girl. You'll need to learn to be immune to them four as quick as you can!" Cathy retorted with a laugh.

She lead the way through to the kitchen table, still cluttered after the brother's breakfast. "You can clear that lot for me and make room for yerselves". Was the greeting they got from Mrs Murphy. They had bread and porridge; not very tasty and a little burnt, but filling none the less.

At nine fifteen, after Cathy had gone off to work, Sister Josephine arrived to take Ellie to see the Mother Superior once more. It was a dank, foggy morning and as they crossed over to the convent Sister Josephine kept chattering away about the weather for the time of year and how April Easters were usually much warmer than March ones. Ellie had quite lost track of time lately what with everything happening so fast, and had forgotten that it would be Easter Sunday this weekend. Today being Maundy Thursday, things would be in full preparation for the extra services in the Cathedral. They passed through the convent to the office of the Mother Superior. Before they had time to knock, the door was opened from within and they were greeted by the tall somber figure of the Reverand Mother who gave a small nod of acknowledgment as both Sister Josephine and Ellie genuflected to her.

"Sit down my child." She said indicating the chair in front of her desk. "now, we must talk of your future." She moved to the big chair behind her desk and sat, whilst Sister Josephine took one, tucked away in the corner behind the door where she waited silently, until she would be spoken to.

"Now then, a few details." Began the Mother Superior, as she took up a pen and a pad. "Your parents are both in Guernsey, let me confirm the address." Ellie nodded and helped fill in the other relevant information. "You will need to see our Doctor later this morning so that he can confirm your expected date of your confinement and ,of course, check on your health. The previous girls who have come to us find that Mrs Murphy is an excellent midwife and many of them have given birth here in our infirmary of our convent, if not in their own rooms. We will explain to you later on in more detail about our usual arrangements for after the birth. But there is plenty of time for that."

Ellie did not really take this in, as she had hardly had time to think further ahead than this day. She was experiencing so many changes all at once.

"Have you anything more you want to ask me, child?" said Mother Superior, kindly. "Will I be going to work like Cathy, Sister?" she asked. "Ah, yes. We must see to that Sister Josephine. Perhaps we could arrange for her to start in the factory after Easter, do you think? That means you'll have until Tuesday to settle in and get to know your way about the town. I expect it seems very large to you, after living on an island." "Yes, Sister." Replied Ellie. "Come along then, Ellie." Said Sister Josephine, as the Mother Superior stood, signaling that the interview was over. "Let's get you to the Doctors. I'll come back and give you his report afterwards, shall I Reverand Mother?" said Sister Josephine. "that will do very well, Sister Josephine. You'll find me in the church, for there is much to do in there today. If you have the time later come in and help, Sister. I'm sure another pair of hands would be most welcome, especially as we have many extra offices. No doubt I shall see you, young lady, at Mass. Mrs Murphy always brings her household along; she is a good Catholic woman."

"Go along now, and see Doctor Joseph. You'll find him very kind and understanding."

Sister Superior stood and Ellie and Sister Josephine bobbed once again, and after the Mother Superior gave her blessing, they turned and left the room. Out into the street, they turned left to the far end of the square passing a large shed-like building at the corner.

"That's where you'll be working I expect, along with the other girls. We'll call in there on our way back." Said Sister Josephine.

The Doctor's surgery was in a large elegant house at the end of Seymore Avenue, a few minutes from the Cathedral square. They walked straight in and knocked on the first door on the left with the Doctor's name plate on it. It had several letters after his name.

A voice called for them to come in and so they entered a small room with a desk and some chairs around the walls. Behind the desk sat a bespectacled woman in her forties. She had a very turned down mouth and looked extremely severe. Ellie was at once intimidated by her, and when told to sit, sat in the nearest chair very stiffly, whilst Sister Josephine spoke softly to the receptionist.

The appointment had previously been made, so it was

only about ten minutes before the doctor's door opened and a very tall grey-haired man came out, leading a pregnant woman by the elbow. "You'll not have to wait long now Mrs Barker," he said to the short but very plump woman of about thirty. "We'll be getting the signals from your baby that he wants to arrive, in about two weeks, I shouldn't wonder." He said kindly. "Keep drinking plenty of water and you'll be fine. Goodbye." Doctor Joseph smiled warmly as he saw her out, then turned back and, after closing the door, stood in front of Ellie.

"Well now, Sister Josephine, have you brought me the young lady from over the sea?" he asked soothingly, taking one of Ellie's hands into his large warm one, putting her immediately at ease. "Yes, Doctor Joseph, she arrived yesterday and is lodging with Bridie Murphy. She has the room that Mary O'Donall had." said Sister Josephine. "Ah, yes. Poor Mary" he sighed, then brightly, "well now, lets have you in and take a look at you."

He led Ellie into his sanctum which was a light airy room, all painted cream and it had a high examination couch under the window covered with a clean sheet. She was instructed to undress behind a screen and lie on the couch. The Doctor gave Ellie a thorough examination after which, when she had dressed again and sitting in the chair in front of his desk, he called in Sister Josephine.

"Well, Sister, she's a fine healthy girl, though a trifle thin. You need to eat for two now you know." he told her. "Plenty of Bridie's 'tattes' and drink lots of milk. Now Sister, I presume the arrangements will be as usual. I'll see Ellie once a month to start with. I should put her date due, about October the twentieth. It's not easy to be sure because we know next to nothing about the - ahem - history. Quite. So if there's nothing more, I'l give her a prescription for some iron tablets and see her next month."

Sister Josephine thanked him and whisked Ellie out into the reception room where she made an appointment for May.

"There, that wasn't so bad, was it?" she asked as they left the building, returning the way they had come. "No. He was quite nice to me, thank you. But, I'm confused about having the baby. I don't know anything about what happens, I mean. My Mother never told me about it." Said Ellie, softly.

Sister Josephine tutted to herself. then said, "Oh, don't worry my dear, if you have any questions you must ask Bridie Murphy. There's nothing she doesn't know about having babies."

They walked back to the corner of Wyndham Square and turned towards the side road leading to what Cathy had called "The Shed". Farther along the road could be seen, and smelt, the back entrance to a large brewery. Sister Josephine explained that there were several breweries in this area and that the little factory, called Thomsons made the metal tops for beer bottles. They walked down to the side door and were immediately hit by the noise of the metallic clatter and the pungent smell of oily machinery.

The old watchman in the cubicle by the door stood up and touched his cap when he saw Sister Josephine. "Mornin' Sister; got another of they waifs for us 'ev'ee?" he laughed and patted Ellie on the cheek. Mister Thomson's in 'is office, you go straight in." "Thank you Tom," said the sister, "and how are you?" she asked him. "Tolerable thank 'ee" he replied, as he scratched his thinning hair before returning his cap at the favoured angle.

At the other side of the passage was a frosted glass door with E.Thomson Manager printed in gold letting. Sister Josephine knocked and a loud deep voice declared "Come in!" so they did.

Within, the office was very brown. Brown furniture, brown carpet and two tones of brown peeling paint on the walls devided by an even darker brown dado rail. The whole officesmelt of tobacco smoke. There was paperwork everywhere, especially on the side table where a typewriter stood with filing cabinets bulging on either side. The chair at this desk was vacant for the moment, but behind the large central desk sat the man with the loud voice. He was a huge man; bald headed and red nosed with fluffy side whiskers. He wore a collarless striped shirt with stretch arm bands and a shiny black waistcoat from which hung a large watch and chain, attached to the pocket across his enormous belly, which drooped as he stood up.

"Good morning Elias" Said Sister Josephine smiling, "how is business?" "Tolerable" replied Mister Thomson, echoing Tom's opinion of the state of things in general. "Please, have a chair" he invited. "This is Ellie Garonne lately come from Guernsey and is staying with Mrs Murphy for a few months. Have you a place for her Elias?" she asked. "We are grateful for your compassion towards our young women." "Ahem, yes, well, one does one's duty as the Lord tells us to do, Sister." He replied, Ellie thought that this was said as the done thing to say rather than with any true feeling. In actual fact these girls were a source of cheap labour and indeed money was always Elias Thomson's main concern in life. "That's very good of you Elias, I'm sure your reward will await you in heaven." She smiled. "As it is coming up to the Easter weekend I assume you will be closed on Monday? So if it is convenient, shall we send her along with her room mate Catherine Miller on Tuesday morning?" "Fine Sister" replied Elias. "The usual rates of pay of course. One shilling a day to start with then, when she's up to speed we'll increase it to two shillings."

"Very well, if that is the present wage I'm sure it will

be agreeable." Said Sister Josephine, as she stood. "May I let Ellie take a quick look into the factory so she can see a little of what the girls do?" "But of course" said Elias as he stumbled to his feet again. "you'll excuse me if I don't come with you, I am expecting a colligue shortly." "No, no don't trouble yourself Elias, you have been more than helpful. Good morning to you and God bless you." Sister Josephine raised her right hand in a blessing as Elias bowed his head and coughed with embarrassment.

As they left the room, the secretary who had obviously operated the typewriter, returned with a pencil behind her car and carrying two cups of tea. She smiled and held the door open with her elbow and as they passed through Sister Josephine said, "Good morning to you Maisie, is your ear-ache better dear?" "All gone now thank you Sister." She replied as they moved away down the passage to a set of swing double doors at the end.

Sister Josephine pushed one open and let Ellie inside. The noise here was much louder of course. Ellie saw that it was indeed a huge shed with machines at one end where four men were working dressed in overalls and aprons with rolled up shirt sleeves. The centre of the room, coming out of the back of the machinery were two shoots, spilling out metal caps down onto two conveyor belts either side of which stood four rows of young women, six each side.

They wore shabby clothes covered with huge aprons and grey white caps covering their hair. Beside each girl was a large box on her right side and a pile of empty ones on her left. As they stood there, she heard one girl shout "Boy!" and immediately a tall lad appeared with his trolley and wheeled the box away to the back of the shed where two men were closing and labeling them before stacking with others for delivery. When the lad had stacked it away he returned to the girl with an empty one. Just at that moment

Ellie caught sight of Cathy, who on seeing her waved briefly and smiled. She was instattly shouted at by a very tall thin severe looking woman who was pacing up and down between the rows. "None of that Miller, you'll lose count!" she snarled sarcastically; then turning around said, "Good morning Sister," "Good morning Mrs Willis." Replied Sister Josephine." Have you brought me a replacement for Mary McCarthy?" asked Mrs Willis, giving Ellie a stern looking over. "Yes, I've just seen Mister Thomson and everything is arranged for her to start next Tuesday." Informed Sister Josephine. "Her name is Ellie Garonne. She's living with Mrs Murphy along with Catherine Miler." "So I gather". Retorted Mrs Willis turning to glare in the general direction of Cathy.

"And how long will we have the pleasure>" she asked caustically. Sister Josephine winced at the over directiness of the question; after an intake of breath, answered, "The usual I expect, Mrs Willis. I won't keep you longer; but Ellie will come at seven thirty on Tuesday. Good morning to you."

She turned on her heels holding her emotions in check as she guided Ellie back through the double doors. That was one woman she really did not like having to deal with. It strained her Christian patience to the limit.

They stepped out into the bright light of the roadway where the sun had at last decided to break through. "Now then, it's Maundy Thursday and I must be at the Cathedral service all afternoon so I really must get back. It's not yet ten thirty" she said as she looked at the large clock over the workshop doors. "Would you like a little time to explore the neighbourhood before you return to Mrs Murphy's? I should grab the chance if I were you. Once Easter is over you won't have much time to yourself." "Oh, yes! I'd like that. Things have been happening so quickly I would like to be on my own for a bit, thank you." Replied Ellie with some relief. "Of course, my dear." said the sister, "and you can't get lost because you can see the spire of the Cathedral for miles." She patted Ellie on the shoulder and asked her if she had any money. "Yes I have, thank you." Ellie replied. She had five shillings in her pocket that Father Peter had slipped into her hand at the quayside before she boarded the ferry. Was that only two days ago? Sister Josephine was disappearing around the corner giving a backward wave, as Ellie pondered which way to go.

She decided to carry on down the road, away from the Cathedral, passing the brewery on the corner. She remembered seeing the beautiful enormous cart horses pulling a dray on her way from Millbay Docks on the morning of her arrival. They were magnificent beasts with flowing manes and brass ornaments decorating their bridals. There were two in harness just coming out of the tall brewery gates, pulling a cart loaded with barrels and boxes of bottles which tinkled and rattled as they moved off towards Union Street. Perhaps some of those bottles had tops on them made at the Shed.

As she reached the corner Ellie found herself in King Street. On the opposite corner stood a shop with the most delicious smell pervading from it's open door. She crossed over to find that it was a fish and chip shop which also sold faggots and meat pies. Although it was not yet dinner time the delicious smells made Ellie feel extremely hungry, she was not to know that the presence of the newly growing child might have something to do with it, so she could not resist the urge to spend some of her precious money. She entered the shop and was greeted by a jolly young lad who called her "my lover" and served her with a fat round pie in a brown paper bag and took her tuppence with a saucy grin. She smiled back as she turned out of the shop and began to stroll along King Street nibbling at the edge of the very hot pie.

She walked contentedly along, under a railway arch, past pawn shops and a barber's shop where several men were sitting on a bench waiting on their turn in the chair. One of them called out to her,"Give us a bite!" in a friendly fashion. His mates joined in the laughter. Everyone seems extremely friendly in Plymouth, she thought as she passed an old woman with a basket of bunched flowers who gave her a smile and called, "Good mornin' my lovely." As she went along her way.

A little further and the road widened out. Ellie stopped in her tracks to stare. Of course living in Guernsey she had never before been in a city, but she was not prepared for the sight before her. On her left was the Odeon Cinema with it's marble steps going up to wide glass doors, not yet open, with glass cases on the walls displaying a picture of a man on a horse waving his hat in the air with letters in bright colours saying 'STAGECOACH" and some pictures of Indians giving chase. Though Ellie didn't know anything at this time about cowboys and Indians, she hoped that she would soon be able to go with Cathy perhaps.

Ellie then stared in wonder at the COMING SOON posters on the other side of the entrance showing a man holding a different sort of gun, looking extremely frightening with the title of "SCARFACE" slashed across it. She stared wide eyed as she munched on the last fragments of her meat pie.

Turning around to look across the junction, Ellie was once again astonished at the size and grandeur of the enormous shops. Not cheap dingy little shops like the pawn shopes and barders she had passed earlier. Suddenly, here were elegant glossy, tall buildings given over to the most beautiful clothes draped on slim poised manakins in windows so large, they would have encompassed the whole of her Grandmother's house in them, she was sure.

The road forked here, so she took the left hand one which led up to a huge building marked THE CORN EXCHANGE. An emposing fascade with a row of grand windows flanked by tall columns, above a pair of huge open gates beneath. Inside this gigantic entrance stood row upon row of stalls, selling everything one could possibly need. Fruit, vegetable, flowers, toys, materials, pots and pans, and so much more.

The more she walked between the rows the more she saw. The place was buzzing with people chatting as they purchased their wares from stall holders who called out their most tempting bargains. "Roll up! Roll up! Fresh today! Lovely crabs, straight off the boats at the Barbican! Bought 'ere by yours truly this very morning'! Up at five I was to get the best one for you lady! How about it?" said the man in the striped apron and a straw boater calling encouragingly to a lady standing in front of his stall. His banter did the trick for she bought the crab and six fresh herrings as well, leaving both parties well satisfied.

All this was so new to Ellie, she spent most of her time staring with her mouth open. As she passed a paper boy he shouted, "You'll catch a fly if you don't shut yer gob maid!" She laughed back at him and moved along to look at a stall so tempting she had to stop. There was a sweet shop at home, of course, but nothing like this. It was arranged with rows and rows of jars of sweets. Every colour, shape and size, the like of which Ellie had never seen; from little dolly mixtures to enormous lollipops and sticks of rock. She used a half penny piece for a scoop of what the stall holder called sherbet dabs, thinking she would share them with Cathy this evening.

At the end of this huge indoor market building, the

path led outside where even more stalls with stripy awnings stood, displaying yet more things of every description. Eggs, chickens, pet foods; the variety seemed endless.

Finally, reaching the end, she came to several busy roads and was uncertain which way to go. The thoroughfare was very busy and she was reluctant to attempt to cross so she stayed on her side of the road and walked towards some gardens she could see a way off. The street was buzzing with cars, open topped buses, bicycles and trams running on metal ruts in the centre of the road.

Ellie came, at length, to the gardens which were outside a large church with seats along by a low wall. Carefully crossing the road to the church she sat on a seat and tried one of the sherbet dabs. The frothy fizziness took her by surprise and she coughed for a moment until she was accustomed to this new experience.

She sat there for quite some time watching the world go by. Everything was a complete new world to her. After a while she got up and decided to look inside this lovely church. It said ST.ANDREW'S on a notice board by the entrance. It was such a cheerful looking building she wandered inside. It was certainly the largest church she had ever been in with beautiful stained glass windows and carved furniture. She sat in a pew and stared slowly around her not wishing to miss a thing.

Time slipped by until she heard a clock strike two. Perhaps she should start back, Ellie thought; as she came out into the sunshine. The building next along the road was the elegant structure of the City Guildhall. Tall and majestic with a tower and a statue of an Elizabethan gentleman standing in the square.

Ellie looked for the Cathedral spire as she walked along, but after several false turns she asked an old man sitting on a bench if he could direct her. He pointed across to where there was another railway arch, so heading that way she soon caught a glimpse of the now familiar spire between the houses and shops.

It was almost three o'clock by the time Ellie found her way back past the 'Shed' and into the back lane leading to number seven St.Peter's Lane, where she entered Mrs Murphy's house through the ever open door.

As she opened the kitchen door, Bridie turned and on seeing it was Ellie shouted at her, "Where the hell have you been all day? Out galivantin' round the town was it? You never thought about me here waitin' fer a bit a'help. Oh no! You girls are all the same. Yer think everybody's goin' to wet nurse ye through yer little troubles like it was no bother to anybody else. Well, let me tell you my girl. It is a bother! And you'll pull yer weight here! While ya stay under my roof ye'll earn yer keep; so grab that apron and start on that bucket of tatties!"

Ellie had the sense to see that Bridie was angry enough not to be argued with, so she mumbled an apology, took off her coat, hung it up behind the door and put on the apron. When Ellie had been working on the bucket of potatoes for a few minutes Bridie had calmed down enough to ask her about her visit to the doctor. Ellie told Bridie that Sister Josephine had told her to get some advice about what happens when you have a baby from herself. Bridie roared with laughter. "God Almighty! Not another who thinks babies come from under a blessed gooseberry bush is it? Dear Heaven! Do your Mothers teach you nothin'? Well, it's a long story so we'll save it for a better time than over the tatties. Did you go to see about yer work?"

"Oh, yes." She replied. "We went and met Mister Thomson and he said I was to start when they open on Tuesday and I would get one shilling a day to start with."
"One shillin'!" roared Bridie. "The mean old skinflint! And

he'll hold back the two shillins' as long as he can, I shouldn't wonder!" She turned to the table and looked down at Ellie and pointed at her with the wooden spoon she was holding. "Now understand this, my girl, every day, you'll get paid one shillin' when you leave work, right?" Ellie nodded, pausing the peeling to pay attention. "You bring that shillin' straight to me, and put it on this table. That's for yer bed and board, understand?" "Oh but…" began Ellie; "No 'Oh buts'" said Bridie. "It costs more than that to feed yer and when ye go up to two shillins' a day, on that Friday I'll be givin' yes a whole shillin' fer yerself now. That's what all the girls do, so there's no point in arguin' about it. If you can find a way to be earnin' any money fer yourself besides," she said winking, "Well, that's your business though I'll not have you bringin' any men in yer room, understand?"

Ellie did not understand that last part at all but thought she would ask Cathy when she had the chance. She also decided she'd better be careful with what was left of her five shillings if she wasn't going to see any of her wages for some little time.

As soon as she could slip out, she took her coat to her room and hid her money away in a drawer with her few belongings, then returned to the kitchen where Bridie kept her busy until the men came home from work. They crashed in the house creating havoc just like the day before, making suggestive remarks to Ellie and getting back-handers from their Mother. Yelling and laughing at her, they stumbled out through to the back yard for their strip washes just as Cathy came home from the 'shed'.

She slumped down on to a chair as she slammed two shillings on the table, keeping her hand over the money. Bridie advanced, reaching out to take the coins but stopped short on seeing Cathy's hand firmly covering them. "Well," said Bridie, waiting for an explanation. "It's Easter weekend and we don't work again now until Tuesday. Do I keep my shillin' now?" she asked in a determined tone., expecting, or at least hoping, for no argument. But she reckoned without the stubbornness of Mrs Bridie Murphy, who burst into a fit of sarcastic laughter. "You've got a nerve, Cathy Miller, to ask it! What do you think's going to pay for your keep? Why, you'll be two days short this week and a day short next week. And this one here," shaking her thumb in Ellie's direction, "not bringing in a penny 'till Tuesday!"

Ellie paused as she stirred the stew on the stove to see what would happen. "Well, its my shillin' by rights" complained Cathy. "By rights is it?" shouted Bridie. "the day you got yourself up the spout you gave up any rights young lady! Be thankful I put the food in yer belly every day of the week, wages or no!"

"You wouldn't if Sister Josephine didn't give you a months money regular for lookin' after us girls. Oh, don't think I don't know! You'd not do it for love nor a shillin' a day that's for sure!" grumbled Cathy.

Mrs Murphy smirked and folded her arms. "Are you thinkin' of doin' somethin' about it then?" she challenged. "Just remember it's me that'll be havin' the care of yes when yer time comes." With that obvious blatant threat, Cathy knew when to back down. She gave glare for glare, then pushed the two shillings towards Bridie and she left the room and climbed the stairs.

"I hope you were payin' attention there, Ellie." Smirked Bridie as she scooped up the coins from the table. "You pull yer weight and pay yer way here or ye have yer babies in the gutter for all I care!"

Ellie knew from past experiences with her Father's temper that there's always a sensible time to say nothing.

After they had all eaten and, just as the men were to leave the table, Bridie called them all to pay attention.

"Now then, let's get things clear here. Tomorrow is Good Friday and we'll all be going to eight o'clock mass." "Ah, Mam!" the boys began to moan. "Shut your mouth and do as you're told! We'll be going to mass I said, and then, no doubt, you boys will be goin' to the pub." "We'll be goin' to the pub right enough, then we're off to the Brick Fields in the afternoon! There's a team comin' up from Redruth to play our boys, so it should be a good game!" declared her eldest son. "So, you'll want yer supper a bit later then?" asked Bridie. "Sure, that would be fine Ma, thanks." he added. "You go off now then, to yer Billiards as it's Thursday, I guess that's where you're off to now." "Right enough Ma," they all said at once and stood. "Off you go then, but give me yer wages packets first!"

Grumbling, they pulled them out of their pockets and waited for Bridie to open them and dole out one pound to each of them. "And you'd better make that last the whole week now!" she shouted as they scrambled out the door.

The girls were just finishing clearing the table when she said, "And the same goes for you two. Eight o'clock mass then back here, you can give me a hand with the floors for the rest of the day. Then on Saturday we'll be changin' the sheets in the boys beds, if the weather lasts, that'll be a good job done too."

It was quite clear to Ellie that Bridie Murphy always got as much free labour out of any girls unfortunate enough to fall under her, so called, 'care'. Finally the kitchen was cleared, the dishes done and put away, so that Ellie and Cathy were allowed to slip off upstairs as Briedie settled down for a nip of Gin in her favourite chair by the stove.

By unspoken agreement, the girls settled in Cathy's room to talk. "I saw you come into the 'Shed' this morning; you got the job then." began Cathy. "Yes, I met Mister Thomson. He seemed very nice". Ellie repleied with a shrug of her shoulders. "And his secretary, isn't she thin!" "Yes; He's O.K. but watch your bum when he goes up the lines. He's a pincher." she laughed. "Oh, dear. I didn't like the look of that woman, Mrs Willis?" said Ellie. "The old dragon, you mean. She's a right sod! I bet she won't let you work near me. She'll be sure to keep us apart. You mustn't let her get you down, that's all. She can be a real bitch if she thinks she can make you crazy." There was a pause whilst Ellie digested this daunting prospect.

"Oh, I forgot; I went exploring this morning and bought some of these." She put her hand into her pocket and took out the sherbet dabs. "Help yourself" she said as she opened the bag on the bed. Cathy's face lit up as she reached forward. "Hey! I love these, thanks! Where did you go?" she asked as she began to suck noisily. "I'll tell you later; first I want to know about work; what do you do?"

"Well, you saw Fred, Bob, Jo and Larry on the stamper." began Cathy, "Every mornin' they take delivery of sheets of metal which have been rolled out at the reclaiming metal yard at Catdown. They stack 'em at the end of the shed, and they feed 'em into the machine."

"What does the machine do?" asked Ellie.

"Well, every Brewery has a different cap for their bottled beer and it's made with a Die. That's a sort of stamp they set into the wheel, and when the machine is started, it cuts up the sheet of metal into small circles and they are stamped and shaped into caps. They come down the shoots on to our conveyor belts."

"Yes, I saw that." said Ellie beginning to get the picture.

"well, it's our job to count'em and pack'em in boxes of one thousand each."

"Goodness, we don't have to count to one thousand do we?" said Ellie, sounding quite alarmed at the prospect.

"No, of course not silly. I don't suppose any of us could count that much anyway. Certainly not without a mistake. No, you'll have ten wooden pots in front of you and you count ten into each one, that gets you to one hundred. Then you tip them into the box on your right and move a red marker along on the wire above your head. When you have done that ten times, that's one thousand, see?

That's when you push a white disc across and shout 'Boy' and the floor boy comes over with his trolly, closes the box and takes it away and stacks it with the other boxes for the Brewery. Then he brings you back an empty one and you start all over again!' "Simple really." Laughed Ellie, taking another sherbet dab. "The old dragon marks down your shout on her board." "well, it doesn't sound so hard." Smiled Ellie passing the bag of dabs to Cathy. "It's hard on your hands, them caps are very sharp. We wear leather shields like gloves, else there'd be blood everywhere!"

"So. What does 'up to speed' mean?" asked Ellie. "Well, you're only going to be getting' one shillin' a day to begin with because you won't be able to do it very fast. If you drop one you have to stop and pick it up, and that takes time too. So, to be worth two shillins you have to fill four boxes every hour; and we work from seven thirty to twelve thirty, then one 'till five, that's a five and a half day week."

"Gosh! That's thirty boxes a day!" Ellie gasped after some quick thinking. "Clever girl! It's not difficult after you get used to it. If you do more than forty you get an extra shillin' bonus. But if you're off work you don't get paid at all! The four girls next door, that's Sandra, Viv, Julie and Maggie, they'll walk with us to work. You'll like them, though I don't suppose Sandra will be working much longer. She's eight months gone and enormous!" declared Cathy grafficly.

I don't know anything about having a baby. Cathy."

said Ellie rather embarrassed. "The Doctor told me to expect to have it in October, but Mrs Murphy says I'll go off like Guy Fawkes! That seems a long time, how about you?"

Cathy laughed, "Guy Fawkes? That woman knows, believe me! Mine's due at the end of August. I haven't told Mrs. M but he's kickin' already." They both looked at Cathy's tummy jerking vigorously and when Ellie put her hand on it to feel it, it kicked, and they both laughed heartily. "Mine doesn't do that." Said Ellie. "No, it won't yet. But believe me the day it does you'll know it!" replied Cathy reaching for the last sherbet dab.

Ellie spent the next hour asking Cathy questions, mainly about having babies and of Mrs Murphy's role in it all. She was told that a girl called Mary had had a hard and bloody labour which Cathy had assisted with, but she saw no point in relating the details to Ellie; she looked worried enough as it was., taking in all this new information.

At last they both began to yawn and wishing each other good night, went to their beds.

After the girls had finally satisfied Mrs Murphy with the chores, this Saturday afternoon, they were free to do as they chose. The men had gone off to watch Argyll play football in Central Park and Bridie was preparing to take an afternoon nap, so they went next door to find the other four girls that Ellie would be working with.

The house was owned by Mrs Hilda Hooper who was somewhat dim and mindless at first impression, but was inclined to slyness and not above theft if the opportunity arose. She was never seen in anything else but a wrap around apron over a non-discript skirt and jumper, thick stockings and very shoddy shoes. Her hair was thin and scooped together in a rough knob on the top of her head. She was neither fat nor thin but scrawny and scruffy looking.

As the two girls approached her front door, which, like

Bridie's always stood open, Mrs Hooper was just coming out. "I'm just poppin' round to number thirteen, Grace's youngest 'as got croup again. The maids is up in Maggie's room, go on up." She walked off down the road as the two girls entered. As there were four girls in number nine, Sandra and Julie shared the large front room on the first floor, Mrs Hooper preferred the back bedroom and Viv and Maggie had the rooms on the second floor, equivalent to those of Ellie and Cathy next door.

The girls upstairs heard them and called for them to hurry up. They were laughing at Julie's baby kicking. As they entered, seeing what was going on, Cathy said, "I don't think it's anything to laugh at, my bugger gives me jip!" "So does this blighter!" said Julie, "but it's playing football at the moment, I think!" "Perhaps he knows Argyll's playing at home today!" laughed Viv.

They were introduced to Ellie and were soon chatting about their expected events. Ellie told them some of her background but only enough to briefly cover the subject.

Julie, who was next to be giving birth was not really very big considering she was due some time in May. "My Mum said she hardly got big at all when she was having me, so she said, so I suppose I'm going to be like her."

"Lucky you!" groaned Cathy. "I've got months to go and I already feel top heavy!" They all stood in a line in front of the old mirror attached to the wardrobe door and went into fits of giggles at their various shapes. After all the hilarity had died down they began to plan what they were going to do over the bank holiday.

"Well, I'm just about broke" said Cathy. "Old Mrs Meany drawers wouldn't let me have my shillin' cos we were goin' to be workin' less this week!" "Why don't we pool what we can each spare and see what we've got eigh?" suggested Maggie. Ellie said, "Shall I go up and see what

I can find?" "I'll come and bring what little I've got." Said Cathy "Though it won't be much." They both slipped quietly back into next door so as not to disturb Bridie, and went to their rooms. Ellie decided that one and sixpence should be enough for her share as she needed to be careful. That would leave her about three shillings for herself, perhaps for a rainy day.

Back in Maggie's room at number nine, they each tossed some money down on the bedspread. Maggie shuffled it all about so no one could see who had put in what, then began to count it up. "Eight shillings and ten pence half penny." She declared with satisfaction. "Goodness! We're rich!" cried Sandra. "That's for six of us remember. Not much really for two whole days." moaned Cathy. "Well," said Sandra, "That's about one and six pence each so if we take six pence each tomorrow, then save the shilling each for Easter Monday, we should be able to have a grand old time!" "Right, that's agreed then?" asked Julie. They all shouted "Yes!" and danced about as though they had won a fortune.

"So, said Viv, what are we going to do with all this great wealth? Any suggestions?" Sandra then said, "Well, I think, tomorrow it's Sunday, we'll all be going to Mass as usual, then back home for our cold lunches, also as usual, then after, why not take Ellie up on the Hoe and introduce her to the seamier side of our lives? I mean, of course, the boys on the Belverdere!" "Then we could go on the pier and have an ice cream or something!" suggested Sandra. "We might even find some fellers who'll buy them for us!"

"You just been lookin' at our figures darlin', do ya honestly think we are goin' to pick up any blokes?" laughed Cathy. "Only if they got thick spectacles!" screeched Maggie. Once again they were falling about laughing. They all knew full well what local girls thought of them. They tried to keep their boys away from what they called "the banged up bunch of St. Peters" or even "the Catholic puddings" by others.

And so the Sunday passed in jolly mood with the sun shining. Ellie was most impressed with Plymouth Hoe and it's wonderful view of the sound and Drakes Island. No one managed to pick up any fellows but they had a great day with three pence three-farthings left over at the end of the day. Ellie thought that they were a great bunch and couldn't remember ever having such a good time. It was her first experience of friendship with girls of her own age. They strolled home laughing together as the sun was setting.

By mutual consent on Monday they walked along Union Street and caught the Cremyl Ferry from Hap'penny Bridge and went for a walk around Mount Edgecombe Park, which stretched out into the sound along it's western side. The big house in the park had belonged to the family of Mount Edgecombe for many generations but since the great house had burned down the park had been opened to the public. It was often used by the Plymouth citizens for weekend picnics.

When they got tired of walking they lay down on the grass by the water and had their pies and bottles of shandy which they had purchased earlier from the Inn on the quayside. For this one moment in time they were content, each knowing that come Tuesday the old reality would return with very few days like these to come, in each of their foreseeable futures. When at last they reached home, they stopped for a moment at their gates and gave eachother a friendly hug before going indoors.

On Tuesday morning, Ellie and Cathy got up at six thirty, just as Bridie's sons were leaving for the Dockyard on their motor bikes. Bridie yelled to them to come to the table as the porridge was getting cold. They filled up with a good bowl full each, and a thick slice of bread and dripping. Then, after helping with the dishes, went up to their rooms to make their beds.

They met the other four girls at a quarter past seven outside, in the drizzling morning mist and hurried round the corner to the 'Shed'. Inside they showed Ellie where to hang her coat and scarf and how to clock in. then they went through the doors into the workshop where she was shown the rack of overalls and caps for their hair. In the pocket of the overalls were a pair of leather mittens to protect her hands from the sharp metal caps.

As Mrs Willis approached, they whispered "Good luck" to her and scurried away to their places as she said, "Now then, there's work to be done if you don't mind ladies." She emphasized the word 'ladies' In a very sarcastic manner which made all the other workers smirk and giggle. The local maids were always glad of a chance to jibe at the pregnant ones.

"Now then, Garonne, is it? What sort of name is that pray? Is it French?" asked Mrs Willis staring down her nose at Ellie. "Yes Madame, it is." replied Ellie, "but my Mother came from Devon." "Well, well. I hope I am pronouncing it correctly then!" said Mrs Willis with a sneer in her voice which brought on even more laughter from the chorus. "Yes thank you Madame." Said Ellie feeling embarrassed." Oh my dear! You don't need to call me Madame! We are not in France here! Thank the Lord! Mrs Willis will do very nicely. Now, you'll work here in the second row at the end of the belt. You'll be collecting caps the others leave behind. Especially the ones that fall off on to the floor. Now, I assume you can count, can you?" she asked. "Yes Mrs Willis." Replied Ellie. "Right then." Mrs Willis proceeded to explain the process by which Ellie would collect and count the caps into the pots and boxes. Ellie was glad that Cathy had already explained it to her because Mrs Willis deliberately gabbled through these instructions with the intention of confusing the new recruit, but Ellie concentrated and followed without too much trouble. "We shall see how many boxes you can fill shall we?" "Yes Mrs Willis" replied Ellie politely. Just then the machinery started up and the head man shouted, "Are we ready Mrs Willis?" "Thank you Fred; stand by girls!" The machinery changed gear and with a metallic roar the metal caps came rattling down onto the belts.

For the next ten minutes Ellie struggled to get the hang of picking up the caps with the leather mittens on and counting them into the pots. Of course she dropped several and had to spend time picking them up. She was sure that the grinning girl next to her was pushing some off the belt deliberately. She was certainly having a giggle at Ellie's expense. Although it was noticed by Mrs Willis who came around behind the girl and clipped her ear. "You will fall behind with your own quota if you mess about, Hawkins." She sneered.

Once Ellie had filled her first box and shouted for the boy, as she triumphantly pushed the white counter indicating her first thousand, her friends cheered her. Mrs Willis shouted "Enough!" and they quickly got on with their work., but the encouragement lifted Ellie's spirits and she filled the next box much more confidently. Of course she was very slow compared to the others but she was determined to get it right despite the cuts on her fingers where the mittens did not seem to protect them.

The four hours till lunch break seemed to take forever, but at last twelve thirty came and the machinery was shut down. They all stood still until Mrs Willis gave her permission for them to go. Hurrying outside in the passage, Ellie met up with Cathy. "How are you feeling?" she asked her anxiously, when she saw Ellie's bloody hands. "Rather sore but I don't care, I'm getting used to it." "Well done kid!" said Viv, "I vote we buy her a pie for her dinner. We've a couple of pennies left from yesterday's outing."

Outside the 'Shed' they all sat in a long row on the wall. Several of the girls had run down the street, including Viv to the corner Fish and Chip shop that Ellie had found on her day exploring the town. Viv was soon back with several hot pies and Ellie tucked into hers as though she had never been so hungry in her life. Just before they went back into work, the girl called Liza Hawkins who stood next to Ellie at the belt, gave her a shove as they were going in the door. Instinctively, Ellie grabbed her hair from the back and pulled. Liza screamed out and Ellie said, "Oh, I'm sorry! I thought I was going to fall and I grabbed at the nearest thing, I really am so sorry!" Her friends laughed, "Good for you girl!" said Viv, "She had that coming. I don't think she'll bother you again."

It was several weeks of hard grind before Ellie was finally told that her quota was high enough to receive two shillings a day. It was with pride on that day that she stood in the line at the door at five thirty to receive her two shilling pieces. And even more proud when she took them indoors to Bridie and stood beside Cathy as they both slammed down their money on the kitchen table.

Bridie stood with her hands on her hips and growled, "About time too! It took you long enough. By the by, you have a six o'clock appointment with the Doctor so get wahed up and go over there. I'll keep yer supper hot 'til yer get back."

Ellie had been in Plymouth for two months now, and it was time for her third check up with Doctor Joseph. She arrived at the surgery and rang the bell before entering. The receptionist smiled at her and told her to sit and wait.

After a few minutes Doctor Joseph was ready to see her. As usual he checked her pulse and blood pressure and asked if she was taking her tablets properly and drinking plenty of milk. Ellie nodded, though actually getting plenty of milk out of Mrs Murphy was not easy. You had to catch her in a good mood before you dare to ask.

Then he weighed her on his scales and wrote down the amount on her chart., then he sat in his chair and looked at her. "How have you been feeling? Any sickness?" he asked. "No. None at all. "replied Ellie. I can feel my tummy getting a little bigger and I'm always hungry but I feel fine." She smiled. "That's good, good." Said the Doctor. "You are standing all day at work, I know. If it gets too much for you, you are to ask Mrs Willis for a stool, do you understand?" "Yes Doctor." Said Ellie. She knew that one or two of the others had stools, especially those close to their time; but Mrs Willis made a great fuss about it and the other girls called them 'sissies' and such like names. Doctor Joseph wrote out a note for her to give to Mrs Murphy, the date of her next appointment was made and she hurried back for her supper.

Bridie had set it out with her pills and a glass of milk. She must be in a good mood thought Ellie as she put the note on the table. The next morning Bridie said, "I had a message to say you are not eating enough, so I'm to send you off with a packed lunch each day, if you please!" You'll get bread and cheese and an apple, like it or lump it! If you want more you'll have to spend your own money. I give you a shillin' a week now, so you can afford it."

"A shilling doesn't go far and I need some new shoes." Responded Ellie. "Then get'em from the second hand shop in King Street, that's good enough for the likes of you my girl."

That night after Ellie had finished writing her weekly

letter to her Mother, she had hardly gone to sleep when she was awakened about one thirty when she heard a lot of bustling around. Julie Lethers, next door had gone into labour. It was June the tenth. She was at least two weeks over due, Bridie said, and was likely to have a bad time of it.

Nobody slept any more that night. All the girls gathered in Viv's room at the top of the house and listened from the open doorway as Mrs Hooper and Bridie dashed in and out of the front bedroom where Julie lay sweating and moaning. Her contractions were irregular and violent and the poor girl screamed a lot.

Bridie called Ellie to carry some hot water up from the kitchen for her and things came to a head about five o'clock. Doctor Joseph had been called and after much more rushing about, Julie finally stopped screaming. It was all over. Julie's baby was born at five minutes past five and at twenty past the baby was pronounced dead. It had never even cried.

"Well, at least the poor maid won't have to go through the agony of giving her baby away." Mumbled Viv to the others.

"What do you mean? Give it away?" asked Ellie.

"We don't get to keep our babies, didn't you know that? The Sisters find good homes for them and we go back home like nothing ever happened." Viv informed her. Ellie had had no idea that this was the way things were organized for them; their babies taken away and adopted. She wasn't sure how she felt about it. She hadn't really thought about the baby at all as a person, so far. Would she care? Julie may well have. How did Cathy and the others feel? At this distressing time it was certainly not the moment to ask them.

They were all told by Bridie that there was nothing more they could do and they'd better get washed and dressed, it would soon be time to go to work. Fortunately it was Saturday so they only had to work for half a day. Not many men liked working Saturday afternoons because they mostly wanted to go to football or some other sport. The season for football was coming to it's end and the league tables were all the men in Bridie's house could talk about.

Work over, they hurried home to see how Julie was. She was, in fact, very ill indeed…Mrs Hooper didn't think she would live. They were not allowed to see her yet, and Sandra went upstairs to sleep in Viv's bed with her. Though she cried most of the night.

That evening Ellie added to her letter which she had begun the night Julie went into labour and told her Mother about it and of the arrangements the Sisters made for babies to be adopted. She told her Mother that she didn't know how she felt about it. She hadn't even thought whether she would be returning home after she had her own baby. She felt confused and just to confuse her still more, her baby kicked for the first time.

Sunday morning they got up as usual to go to Mass and were met by Sister Josephine who had come to their houses to be the one to tell them that Julie had died in the night. The Mass would be said especially for her and her baby. No one spoke the whole day. Neither did they feel like eating or going out. They were all in a state of shock. Only Sandra cried. Bridie said that the others would cry too when the shock wore off.

They worked on the Monday almost in total silence. Even the local girls were quiet in respect for their loss. No one really noticed but Mrs Willis let them alone to work and grieve in their own way. On Friday they watched as Julie's body was driven away in a hearse followed by her family, away to the cemetery near Mutley Plain. They could not afford to take her back home to Nothern Ireland. Julie's uncle and aunt, who lived at Mutley assured her parents that they would tend her grave until they could come again. Mr. Thomson had kindly given the girls the half day off so that they could attend the funeral.

In the weeks that followed, Sandra still fretted and worried for it would not be long before it would be her time to go into labour. The whole experience had left her terrified, and her health began to suffer. She was taken off work and Doctor Joseph insisted that she rest as much as possible. Her baby had stopped kicking so much and that made her more worried in case it should be too weak to be born, as Julie's had.

Bridie was very good with her and then when the day came on the second week in July, all went off surprisingly smoothly, only taking two hours. To everyone's relief she was none the worse for the experience, but needed her friends support when Sister Josephine came to take the baby away. "Now don't worry about him, my dear. I can tell you now that the couple who have been waiting for your baby are really nice, good Catholic people and they have a wet nurse all ready to take on the feeding of this wee fellow." Sandra took a last look, clinging to her friends. She had a good cry before falling into an exhausted sleep.

Ten days later, Sandra's father arrived to take her home to Newton Ferris where friends and neighbours had been told that she had been away helping to nurse a sick relative. They all hoped that the embarrassment of her pregnancy had been well hushed up so that she would pick up the threads of her old life once again and no one the wiser. Such was the service that the Sisters with Mrs Murphy's help, were able to provide.

The experiences of these two girls pregnancies left a marked impression on Ellie. She now saw plainly the situation that they were all in, and she felt angry. Angry at the boy, Clifford, for making her pregnant in the first place;

angry with her parents and Father Peter for sending her away, and angry with the nuns for insisting they give up their babies. But most of all she was angry because everyone made sure that these girls would feel shame and disgrace if people knew. Her views and her moods changed almost daily. The anger sometimes changed to sorrow, with each passing thought about their plight she felt certain that it could somehow be resolved in a better way but she did not know how. "But what else do you expect?" argued Cathy when Ellie expressed her feelings one night before bed. "According to everyone we are harlots! Scarlet women! To be hidden from view! Never mind who put us up the spout in the first place! No one's going to beat my Dad the length and breadth of Plymouth Hoe, are they?!"

"Your Father?" Ellie asked in astonishment. "Don't look so surprised. There's plenty of families off Union Street what's got Fathers and Brothers and sisters and Aunts all mixed up so you don't know whose is whose!" laughed Cathy, surprised that Ellie had no idea such things went on. "But your own Father?" Ellie said softly. "I can't believe it." "My dear girl, my Mother told me that in her day in Ireland, the local priest or the Lord of the Manor expected to have the right to take a young girls virginity." Said Cathy with great worldly knowledge in her tone. "I don't believe you, you're joking; aren't you?" stammered Ellie. "So it has always been my friend, and it is always the poor pregnant girl who is made to feel the wicked one. Daughters of Eve and all that stuff. The trouble is, by the time we are wise enough to know what's going on it's too damn late!"

That night Ellie learnt a great deal about the facts of life from Cathy. Facts which added to the accumulation of anger that was building up. She pondered all these new facts over the next few weeks and came to a few conclusions. After this, she was going to make sure that she didn't get caught a second time. Men would pay for their bigotry. Oh, yes, men would pay. She'd see to that.

On Sunday after Mass Sister Josephine called Ellie into the convent garden for a chat. "Ellie my dear, I have had a letter from my Brother. He says that your Mother asked him to write to me. It seems, after reading your letters to her, she doesn't want you to give up your baby if you don't want to, that is. She says if you send it back to Gernsey, your Mother will bring the child up as though it were her own. Your Father won't have you back, but he is reluctantly agreeable to your Mother's suggestion. It will, after all be her grand child. The decision will be up to you of course. I do not recommend you even think of keeping it yourself, you will find it hard enough to earn a living on your own, without trying to look after a baby. That is why we always find good parents for adoption. It is better for the child. I'm sure you must see that. Give it a lot of thought and pray for guidance. God will tell you what is best, I am sure. We will talk again in a day or two."

Ellie went back to the house where she found Cathy waiting for her. "What was all that about then?" she could not wait to ask. Ellie indicated that she would tell her upstairs away from flapping ears. Once in Cathy's room, Ellie told her about the letter.

"Well," said Cathy, "I can understand how your Mother feels. You're lucky to have a Mother who wants to love and care for her grand child. I wish mine was. I'm not the first daughter who's been sent here you know. My sister Maisie came two years ago. She's working in the kitchens of a hotel in Torquay at the moment. Her little boy was took off to be adopted. She says she often wonders about him and has a little cry. Especially now that she's going to be getting married. She can't make up her mind whether to tell her fella about it. He might not want her if he knows, you see."

"Dear God! It's all such a muddle!" cried Ellie. "I don't know what to tell Sister Josephine." "You're lucky," Cathy said, "to have the chance, I haven't. I've got to get back to my job, if I can still have it. I was working in the hardware department in Tozer's. Me Mam told them I had to go into a convalescent home'cos I had pleurisy, so I'm going back there to work, I think, but I'm not going home to live under the same roof as that bugger ever again! That's for certain!"

"Where will you live?" asked Ellie. Well, Bridie says there might be a room at number five down the road. There's a girl there what's leavin' to get married in the autumn. Well, we'll see anyway."

A few days later Ellie went to find Sister Josephine on her way home from work. She told her that she wanted to keep the baby and have it brought up by her Mother until she could look after it herself some day. Sister Josephine smiled and said, "Very well, my dear, I will write and tell my Brother and we will arrange everything for you." Ellie felt a lot better after that and slept well for the first time in ages.

In late August Cathy had her baby. Two weeks later Maggie had twins. Much to the delight of the couple who had been waiting particularly for someone to have twins. They were both girls which suited them very well. Cathy had a little boy, she was almost glad to see the back of him as he looked too much like her father for her liking.

Two other girls had come to live next door, but Cathy didn't feel like making new friends with them for so short a time. But it was hard to say 'goodbye' to Maggie. She had been the jolliest of their group. When she went home to Torpoint at the end of two weeks she promised to keep in touch.

It was good news for Ellie to hear that Cathy might be

living nearby, at least she wouldn't be loosing all her new friends. She was startled when she got home from work the next day to hear Cathy calling her. She clambered slowly up the stairs for she was very large now. "Quick Ellie! Good news!" she called from above. "Hang on do! I can't come any faster!" cried Ellie. She flopped down on the end of Cathy's bed to regain her breath. "Good news, good news! My Mum's been to see me and she says I've got my old job back and I'm going to have that room down the road! The girl is moving out tomorrow! I've been thinking, why don't I get you a job with me in Tozers when you've had yours, then we can share that room! It'll save money, what do you say?"

Ellie did not hesitate but agreed gladly and smiled happily at her dear friend. They chatted away like two birds in a tree until Bridie yelled up, "Will ye not be comin' down for yer supper, Ellie girl, or will I give it to one of these hungry great sons of mine?" "Coming now!" shouted Ellie and after giving Cathy a great hug and a kiss, hurried as best she could down the stairs.

The following week Viv Cox took the two new girls in her house to work at the 'shed'. Watching them, Ellie couldn't believe how clumsy they looked which made her aware of how fast she herself had become during the last two months. In fact the day before, Mrs Willis had given her a bonus shilling for the third time.

Ellie decided to stop off on her way home at the shop on the corner of the square and buy something for Cathy. There was a nice little purse in the window for five pence so she bought it and hurried back to the house with it. Cathy was delighted. Her own purse had not been fastening properly for some time. "but you shouldn't have Ellie, you worked hard for that bonus." Said Cathy. "Don't be silly, I wanted to, so there." Laughed Ellie.

When Cathy was up and about she went along to Tozers and was delighted to meet up with all her old mates who asked her if she was better now? Of course she said she was fine now and looking forward to coming back. The manager also said that he would be willing to take on her friend next month but only in the stock room. Cathy felt sure that Ellie wouldn't mind; anything rather than the 'shed'. Cathy moved into her new room at number three at the end of the week. She had the large first floor front which was light and airy. Ellie found Bridie's house very strange without Cathy.

Then, only a few weeks later, one Friday just before Mrs Willis was about was about to call the lunch break, Ellie's water broke and two of the girls were sent with her to walk home. She collected her wages, put on her coat and left the 'shed' for the last time. Bridie met her at the door and thanking the girls, helped Ellie inside the kitchen.

"Shouldn't I be going to bed?" asked Ellie. "What ever for?" laughed Bridie, "Have you got any pains yet?" "Only a twinge just now." Replied Ellie. "I thought it would all begin quickly." "Well, for some it does. Young Sandra now, sure she hardly had time for any pains at all before it was all over. Then there's others, well they have pains nearer and nearer together and after a long time they come close enough to finish the job."

Just then the first real contraction took Ellie by surprise. She gasped with shock and held her breath. "Don't be doin' that now! Or you'll make it worse. It's better if you breathe in and out slowly 'till it's gone. Sure it'll only last a minute." Explained Bridie. Sure enough by the time Bridie had said that, it was indeed all over. "We'll see how long it is before the next one, then we'll know if it's time to go to bed or not."

The pains slowly came closer together and by the time

Cathy had come home from work Bridie was ready for putting her to bed. They helped her up the stairs together and then Cathy went off to tell Doctor Joseph that Ellie had gone into labour.

When she came back she said, as she walked into Ellie's room, "Do you know what date it is?" "Oh, my Lord!" said Ellie, "It's Guy Fawkes day tomorrow! Bridie will be cock-a-hoot when she sees she was dead right about my time." "I heard that !" said Bridie as she puffed into the room with a glass of milk for Ellie. "You shouldn't be surprised I was right. I'm nearly always right, I'll have you know! Haven't been a midwife for neigh on thirty years? If I don't know thing like that by now, well, I just don't think I'd know anything'!" They all laughed, then Ellie stopped laughing suddenly as another contraction came.

It was two o'clock in the morning on Saturday November the fifth that Ellie gave birth to a healthy seven pound dark haired baby girl. "Ah, sure she's a sweet wee babbie, so she is." Said Bridie, "And we didn't even need Doctor Joseph to get out of his bed. Sure you were no trouble at all, at all, were ye darlin'?" she cooed at the baby as she wrapped her up and put her into Ellie's arms. "And you're really goin' to keep her then?" asked Cathy. "Oh, yes. My Mother would have broken her heart if I'd let her be given away. Sister Josephine says she's to stay with me for three weeks, then she'll be old enough to travel. My Mother and Father Peter are coming over to collect her. She'd like to take me home too but my Father won't hear of it. He feels the disgrace badly, so she says, and she had enough trouble persuading him to take…her."

"Yes, her. What are you going to call her then?" asked Cathy excitedly. To get to name a baby was a real novelty amongst these girls who dare not personalize the experience.

"I've been thinking about that. My Grandmother was called May. I thought it would please my Mother if I called her May Eloise. That's my proper name you know."

"Oh, that's lovely, Ellie. And will she be baptized before she goes away?" "I expect so. It would be nice if we could do it here. Father Peter can do the service. Would you like to be her Godmother, Cathy? And you Mrs Murphy?" "Well I never!" exclaimed Bridie. "Of all the girls I've seen through their troubles, you're the first one to ask me to do that! Well, would you credit that?" she smiled countentedly. "Well, enough of all this chat, you get some sleep. Sister Josephine will be in to see you in the morning and you, young Cathy, get off to your own house now!"

Three weeks later Ellie's Mother Martha, and Father Peter landed at Millbay docks. It was a fine Autumn day and Ellie had pushed the borrowed pram with May tucked up warm inside, down through the Octagon to the docks to meet them.

There were tears of joy and lots of fuss made of the baby who slept soundly through it all. Then Ellie led the way back up the hill to St.Peter's Square where they were to stay in Bridie's house. But Father Peter said that he would be given a room in the convent and after a cup of tea, left to go and find his sister.

Those few days with her Mother went too quickly for Ellie. She knew that each hour drew her nearer to the time when she would have to say 'goodbye' to her baby daughter. She had begun to love her most dearly and it was going to be very hard to part from her.

The Christening went off without a hitch and May just seemed to watch everything that happened to her with her large brown eyes with great interest. Bridie cried most of the time especially when it was time for her to make the God parent's responses. Cathy tried not to giggle but couldn't take her eyes off the sight of Bridie in her new hat! It was brown and quite ugly with one feather at the front which bobbed all the time. Bridie even made her sons come, they were all dressed up with suits and ties and their hair slicked down.

The tea afterwards was also Bridie's treat and very lavish it was too. Her sons had never seen a spread like it; so refined too, they said. Unlike their Mother's usual table. Even a white tablecloth which Sean noticed was really one of Bridie's best sheets. The next day it was all over and May and her Grandmother and Father Peter were gone.

For the next few weeks Ellie and Cathy settled into a routine of working in Tozers and coming home together to live in their spacious room. They had their own little stove and wash stand with an indoor toilet downstairs, quite a treat after Bridie's outside loo. They enjoyed preparing their own evening meals; now that they were keeping all their wages, they felt quite well off and revelled in their independence. Bridie's two younger sons Patrick, nineteen and Sean twenty one, often took them to the pictures or for walks on Sundays on the Hoe. In the back row of the Odean or the Royal Cinema, Patrick would slip his arm around Ellie and sometimes give her a little peck on the cheek in the romantic films. In the darkness it was odvious by Cathy's giggles that Sean was giving Cathy a good cuddle as well.

One evening after they had been in the pub on the way home and had a Shandy or two, and the boys their draught beer, Patrick whispered in Ellie's ear something to the effect that he'd like to do a lot more than just kiss and cuddle her. Ellie reacted violently and slapped his face hard.

"No man's ever going to get something for nothing from me Patrick Murphy! So you can forget such ideas." "and she stormed out and headed for home. The others caught up with her as quickly as they could. Catching up,

Patrick shouted, "I'm sorry maid! I didn't mean to upset you now!" When Cathy came up beside her she said, "Ellie, slow down for Gawd's sake! He's not doin' anythin' different to what all fellas do! They all try and push their luck as far as they can." "Sure and you can't blame us for tryin' with two beautiful girls like you for company!" Sean said with such a sad look on his face that it made Cathy laugh. But not Ellie. "Just don't ever, do you understand?" she said as she stared Patrick squarely eye to eye. Patrick was by now rather cross and said without thinking. "Well, if it's payin' ya want, I'll give ya a pound, how's that?" This earned him another slap which made them all laugh and then they went home together with no harm done to their friendship.

The girls spent Christmas day with the Murphy family, they all went to Mass and both girls particularly prayed for their babies. Bridie cooked them a great Christmas dinner and the girls mucked in preparing the vegetables. It was a fun day, for they laughed and sang a lot and went out to the corner pub in the Square in the evening, all getting quite drunk with the festive spirit.

CHRISTMAS 1932

Almost the last thing on anyone's mind was celebrating Christmas. It was certainly an unusual time in their family. Both Father, Henry John and son, John Henry's wives were expecting at the same time. Phyllis and Jack had been married two and a half years; six months before Henry's wedding. He had been widowed a short time before marrying his 'other woman' Ethel as some of the family referred to her. And so it was that both wives became pregnant about the same time. Henry and Ethel were then living in Ethel's house in Somerset Place, just around the corner from Mayon.

During the Christmas festivities, which they did not celebrate together, but kept in constant touch, curious to see who would go into labour first. As it happened, it was Ethel, Henry's wife, who was admitted into Devonport Maternity Home shortly after New Year's Day., as she was expecting twins and being older, having a daughter in her late teens, could not have a home birth as Phyllis was preparing to do. On January the sixth Ethel gave birth to two lovely girls whom they called Betty and Joan. Soon after, Phyllis began to get the urge to walk. She walked around the garden, the block, the park quite tiring everyone out who insisted on keeping her company. At last things began to look as though her time had come.

Meanwhile, at three Mayon Cottages, Phyllis and a very dear friend and midwife, Nurse McGuirk, arranged the home birth in military fashion. Everything Nurse Mac did was precise and orderly. Early in the morning of January the ninth, all was ready. She packed Jack off to work, then dosed Phyllis with castor oil to get things under way. Jack left reluctantly but was re-assured that he could pop back at lunch time if he wished., and as his office was not far down the street, he left them to it. Aunt Charlotte was put in charge of the kitchen to prepare clean linen and later, hot water as required, whilst her sister, Mabel, left for work at Devonport Junior School. Both they and their sisters had all been born in that downstairs bedroom, as had Jack and his sister Minnie, as well as their grandfather before that. So it was very important that this baby be the fifth generation to be born in this very room.

The Doctor dropped in about nine o'clock but was sent packing by the intrepid Nurse Mac as 'not needed on this voyage'. At twelve o'clock Jack shot back through the front door and was ordered to sit on the stairs and keep out of the way. Without any trouble at all, and would anyone dare do otherwise for Nurse Mac? a few minutes later the baby slid gracefully into the world. A quick slap, a cry, and it was all over.

So on January the ninth nineteen thirty three, Phyllis gave birth to a bouncing baby girl whom they named Pamela Phyllis. The Holemans clan had increased by three in one short week. Poor Jack had to wait outside for another ten minutes before Nurse Mac would let him in, then the three of them were met together for the first time, which would prove to be the start of many happy years together. Mabel came home from school at half past four, declaring that she was never around when any of the exciting things happened in the family!

Shortly after Pammy was born, Phyllis was given an Airdale bitch by a cousin and she was called Biddie. She was so gentle with the baby and appointed herself guardian. When Pammy was stretched out on a rug in the back garden Biddie would stand guard and not mind at all if the baby pulled at her coat. As time went on Pammy learnt to pull herself up on her feet by clinging to Biddie's hair and indeed took her first steps stumbling along beside the dog who moved forward slowly and carefully, easing the child down to the ground again if she began to stumble. So everyone gave Biddie the credit of having taught Pammy to walk.

These early days of marriage were full of happy times spent out on 'Pickles' in and around Plymouth Sound and it's beaches, accompanied by many friends and relatives and such family gatherings on the sands with picnics and games. Cousins and Aunts and friends sharing these halcyon days.

Pammy was a chubby child with a bright smile just like her Father's and a head a soft blonde curly hair. Amongst so many friends and relations she could well have been spoilt but Phyllis was determined not to let that happen. She looked forward to giving Pammy some brother or sister soon. Charlotte and Mabel adored her. It was like having two Grandmas instead of one. Of course there was Grandma Baker too although she had already got a grandson, Eric who was Phyllis's brother's first child. He then had a sister shortly after Pammy's first birthday and she was named Jean. Phyllis's sister had a daughter too about this time. Mary who was soon followed by brother John and later, sister Susan. And so the families grew.

AUGUST 1933

To celebrate Ellie's eighteenth birthday, and Cathy's engagement to Sean, they all went out with Patrick to the Palace Theatre and saw a great variety show starring Wee Georgie Wood. They had a most enjoyable evening and after the show they crossed the road to the pub called The Red Dog to have a celebratory drink or two. Sean and Cathy were planning a Christmas wedding and would be moving into their new home on New Years Day. An old chap who worked in the dockyard with the boys had recently lost his wife. He lived in a small terraced house in Stafford Place about half a mile from St Peters; he was dreading living alone so he suggested that if he moved into the downstairs front room the newly weds could live in the rest of the house for a small rent if Cathy agreed to cook for him and do his laundry. It was a marvelous opportunity for them and as they got on very well with old Mister Porter, they agreed.

Ellie was delighted for them of course, but she wasn't looking forward to living by herself. She was getting fed up with her job as well, being stuck in the stock room all day long and not really working with Cathy as she would have liked.

Just as she had finished telling Patrick this, he said, "Well why not have that job?" pointing to a notice behind the bar which said,

WANTED YOUNG LADY FOR BAR WORK
ACCOMMODATION INCLUDED.
NO EXPERIENCE NEEDED.

Ellie read it and laughed. "I don't know anything about bar work! Anyway I'm too young aren't I?" "Of course not." Said Sean. "You're eighteen now aren't you silly?" "Well, there's no harm in asking is there?" Cathy added. "I'll have to think about it." She replied. "Well, don't leave it too long or the job will be gone."

That night Cathy was full of her chatter about her wedding so she wasn't really listening to Ellie's remarks about changing her job. Finally Cathy stopped talking and went to sleep, leaving Ellie to consider her future. The following day was early closing so she told Cathy to go on without her as she had an errand she wanted to do. Then she walked along Union Street to the Red Dog public house. It was almost two o'clock and there were only a couple of people finishing their drinks before closing time. She went up to the bar and asked to speak to the Landlord.

A tiny middle aged lady came out from the back and said, "Hello, my dear, can I help you? I'm the Landlady of this pub. My old man's the sleeping partner, literally! He's sleeping right now, as usual!" She laughed a thick smokers laugh that developed into a cough. "Oh, well," said Ellie, tentatively, "my friend and I saw your notice when we were in here the other night. You need a live in bar maid, and I wondered if I might do." "Well, you're pretty enough to draw in the customers, I'll grant you that. And with my scrawny looks this pub certainly need some!" The coughing laugh came again. "I think you should know, I've never been a barmaid before, but I could learn. I've been working in the stock room at Tozers so I'm strong." Ellie said. "Have you had the sack dear?" asked the Landlady. "Oh no!

I haven't even given in my notice yet!". "Well, then I see no reason why we shouldn't give you a try. It's not very hard to learn and once you get the hang of pulling a good pint it's easy. Just so long as you don't try to cheat the till." "Oh, I wouldn't do that, really." Exclaimed Ellie.

"All right then. My name's Ethel Stone, Eff to all my regulars, but you'd better call me Mrs Stone for now. My hubby's name is Sid. He works in the Palace Theatre back-stage, scenery, so he gets home late and sleeps most mornings. Now when can you start?" she asked. "I'll have to give a weeks notice, so the end of next week I suppose." Said Ellie. "I'd better show you the room before you make up your mind, hadn't I" said Ethel.

It was two thirty as Mrs Stone followed the last customer to the door and locked up. Then she led the way through to the back. The Red Dog public House was a large building on a corner plot, of three stories. The outside was covered in dark green tiles with the main door set at it's corner and a side door with a glass panel marked "SNUG". Mrs Stone explained as they climbed the stairs that the snug was the popular haunt of the 'Theatricals' who came to perform at the Palace Theatre opposite. "We get all the big stars in here, you know. We've had Lupino Lane, and Sid Fields. You'll see their pictures on the wall in there, all signed 'to our darling Eff!" At the top of the first flight of stairs Mrs Stone pointed out her rooms at the front and three back bedrooms usually let to actors; then up to the next landing where there were three more letting rooms and a bathroom, and at the back she showed Ellie into a smaller room over the back yard. It had been freshly cleaned and was simply furnished with a cosy looking bed, a wardrobe, a chest of drawers, wash stand and two chairs. Pretty curtains blew gently at the half open window.

"Well, will that do you love?" asked Mrs Stone wheezing,

with a fag in her mouth. "Oh, yes. It's fine, thank you." She felt relieved. She hadn't expected such a neat little room.

"You'll find this back bedroom quieter than the rest, though them theatricals do make a lot of noise when they come in late, so keep your door locked, mind." They chatted about a few final arrangements as they descended to the now empty bar, and as she let Ellie out she said, "I'm sure we'll get on fine together, don't you? I'll see you after you've worked out your time with Tozers, cheerio!"

Ellie returned to the square to find Cathy busy ironing. She lost no time telling her all about her new job. "Well I never!" said Cathy. "You made up your mind quick didn't you? And you never said a word!" Ellie looked at her astonished. "Never said a word?" she exclaimed. "All you've got in your head is wedding bells! Last night I couldn't get a word in edge wise. Anyway I didn't want to say much until I knew if I wanted the bloomin' job!" "I'm sorry Ellie." Said Cathy, "I am a bit full of me own plans aren't I!" They laughed and talked through the rest of the day over housework and cooking. Going through all the new things that would be happening to them both.

Ellie worked her last week at Tozers and on the Sunday, packed up her belongings. Patrick helped her carry it all down to the pub in the afternoon. Mrs Stone welcomed her in and she found her way upstairs to what was to be her new home. Patrick gave her a peck on the cheek and left her to it. Mrs Stone called up, "When you're ready you can come down and I'll start teaching you the pub trade."

Within a fortnight you'd have thought Ellie had been born in a pub. She took to it like a duck to water and was very popular with the customers. Mrs Stone told her to buy herself a blouse and a skirt.

"Something frilly to show off your bosom dear! And a skirt to cling to your nice round bum. And get some fancy shoes and stockings, that'll be the ticket. Don't get me wrong dear, I don't mean to turn you into a common slut! I just think you should make the best of your figure. After all it's good for business to have a pretty eyeful behind the bar."

When the Murphy boys came in one night to see how she was doing, their eyes popped out of their heads. Patrick said, "Cor! I knew ya was a pretty maid, our Ellie, but you looks like a film star with yer hair tied up with a velvet ribbon and lipstick and all! A proper 'It' girl, eigh Sean?" "She certainly is!" gasped Sean. "Good for trade is she Mrs Eff?"

Mrs Stone gave her wheezy laugh and rolled her fag to the side, nodding as she pulled their pints. "Oh, yes! She's like a pot of honey and here come the bees!" she laughed as a bunch of her regulars burst through the door all wanting Ellie to serve them.

On Boxing Day, Cathy and Sean got married at St. Peters church and Ellie was her bridesmaid, of course. The reception was held at Bridie's house. It quite rivaled the christening two years before except that this time there was a beautiful wedding cake which had been made by Bridie herself much to everyone's amazement. The happy couple did not go away for a honeymoon, they just couldn't wait to set up house in Stafford Place.

1935

Shortly after Pammy's second birthday, Phyllis was taken ill with Rheumatic Fever. For some months she could hardly move about the house without a stick or the aid of a nearby chair to sit on whenever she felt the need to stop and rest. Doctor Reeves was very worried about the possible after effects. It certainly took a lot out of her. Fortunately Charlotte was there to make life as easy as possible for her, looking after Pammy and getting the meals. The fever slowly abated but not without a cost. Phyllis's lovely red hair was never so full bodied or as richly coloured ever again; and she had to wear spectacles as it affected her sight. But the saddest thing for her was that she had to tell Jack the doctor said she would never be able to have any more children.

In a few months she was back to her old self, determined not to let this setback spoil their lives. After out growing her cot in her parents room where Pammy was born, she was given the box room over the front hall which used to be her Aunt Minnie's room when she was a girl. It just held a single bed, touching the walls at head and foot and resting against the windowsill, with just enough room for a bedside locker and a tiny clothes cupboard. it must have been no more than six feet by four, but Pammy loved her own little room.

Once when she had to stay in bed with the measles, her father brought her up a present in a shoe box. He set it down carefully on her bedspread. "Oh, Daddy, what's inside? I can feel something moving!" "You'd better open it then sweetheart". He replied, with a wicked smile on his face. She scrabbled with the lid and squealed when she saw what was inside. "Oh, Daddy! They're lovely! Thank you!" she said as she lifted out two tiny kittens. One ginger and one black and white. They mewed softly as they wriggled to be put down. She laid them gently onto her bed and watched them look for a nice spot to curl up. "What are you going to call them then?" asked her Father. "Now let me see. I think I'll called them Tibby and Toby like the kittens in my story book!" She was allowed to keep them in her bedroom for just the one day then she was able to get up and come downstairs and look after them.

That Christmas was spent in the Lodge at the centre of Devonport Park where Grandad Baker was now the Head Park Keeper. A bed was made up of two large armchairs pushed together end to end for Pammy in her parent's room. On Christmas eve she was so worried that Santa Claus wouldn't know where to find her that she would not go to sleep. "Now you mustn't worry darling. Daddy wrote to Santa and told him where we would be spending Christmas so he'll know where to come." said her Mother kissing her. "I want to stay awake and listen for him, shut your eyes tight mind!" warned Phyllis as she turned off the light and half closed the door. Eventually Pammy dropped off to sleep.

At some point in the night she awoke to a strange sound which she was convinced was Santa landing his sleigh in the park. So she shut her eyes tightly and waited. Undoubtedly she dropped off to sleep again because the next thing, it was dawn and as she opened her eyes she saw shapes beside her bed. One in particular was tall and had four legs. Later when she was allowed to open her presents this strange shaped gift turned out to be a small basket on legs with tiny dolls clothes hanging all round it and inside lay a tiny baby doll dressed in only a nappy. It was a toy she would love for many years and she told everyone that she had heard Santa arrive in his sleigh. Probably it had been the sound of a train passing through the nearby station but Pammy was convinced otherwise.

1935

Two years slipped quickly by, Ellie was almost twenty and she had grown into a good looking, though some might say, a rather common blonde. For she learnt early in her barmaid's career to enhance the lightness of her hair with peroxide. Her figure was well rounded and she naturally attracted a lot of attention from the male customers. Though she always managed to keep them at bay when they got fresh.

Mrs Stone, though a tiny woman, was extremely effective in dealing with troublesome customers. She kept a big rolling pin underneath the bar and was not above laying about any man with it if they got too drunk or refused to leave, and if any of them tried to lay hands on Ellie she soon gave them a taste of her tongue, which was nearly as bad as a whack of the rolling pin, so, jokingly said her regulars. Now and again a lodger of the theatrical variety would press his advances upon Ellie, but she became very experienced at repelling them. She sometimes got a couple of free tickets to the Palace Theatre and once took Cathy to see "The Student Prince."

Ellie was earning a fair wage in the pub and quite a lot in tips, so not surprisingly she began to enjoy the pleasures of shopping for nice clothes and smart shoes. The higher the heels the better. Cathy didn't know how she managed them, she said that she felt sure she would turn her ankle if she wore them. But then, Cathy did not have Ellie's shapely legs to show off.

1936

By the time she was twenty one she had had several proposals of marriage from customers and sailors, even a few actors. But none of them interested her until Sidney Evans came into her life. Sidney was a sailor on H.M.S. Hermes and he and his three friends, fresh off the ship, were working their way along Union Street on a pub crawl. As many sailors liked to do. They were all very loud and getting very drunk. Sid was not. Mainly because it was his turn to keep sober and get them back aboard in a taxi before ten thirty. That was the arrangement these four friends always made. One to be 'Mother' as they called it and hold the money.

It was about ten o'clock and Sid was worried that they were going to be late, if they didn't stop drinking soon. "Come on boys, enough for tonight eigh? Come on. Drink up and let's go." "Don't be a spoil sport Mother!" shouted the one named Pete. "Get yourself a drink and shut up can't you? I want a piece of that barmaid before I go anyway." He said catching sight of Ellie. "Oh no you won't young fella me lad!" said Mrs Stone, "Or you'll taste me rolling pin!" She came round from the bar bradishing it and slapping it in her palm of her hand.

"Ooh! Look at the little dragon boys!" shouted another of the sailors. "Let's sit her up on the bar!" Two of them advanced intending to lift Effie up, but Sid stepped between her and them and said, "Enough! Enough! Now lads. I can't let you be disrespectful to a lady. Your Mothers wouldn't like that now would they?" "Ah, but you're our Mother, Mother!" said Pete. "I want a kiss from the pretty darlin' over there." "Oh Lord! I'm sorry Miss, Madam, but I'm going to have to do some rough stuff." declared Sid. With that he banged two of their heads together sending them sliding down on the floor amongst the sawdust and he pushed Pete into a chair which tipped back against the wall.

"Could you please get me a taxi Mam before they get up again?" Sid asked. There were always taxis cruising Union Street so it only took a whistle from Ellie for one to pull up at the door.

By the time it parked, Sid was ushering them out of the pub and with a quick apology, bundled his pals in and they drove off singing, down Union Street towards the Dockyard.

"What a nice lad," laughed Effie; "so gallant and so polite. He must have a lovely Mother." "He's handsome too." Said Ellie, impressed with the way he had come to their rescue. Though they were both used to drunken sailors and many a night the naval police had come in and broken up fights, especially if soldiers and sailors got drunk in the same bar and fell out, they seldom encountered a service man with such caring manners. It wasn't very often that a young man like Sidney behaved in such a nice way. Ellie wondered why he had not been drinking too. Little knowing that for Sidney, too much drink made him uncontrolably violent.

A few nights later, they were back, but with Sidney in charge, they came in quietly and were fairly sober; they had come to apologise. Effie and Ellie laughed it off saying they were not the first sailors to be threatened with the rolling pin. Pete said he was mighty glad she hadn't used it on him as it looked more dangerous than a navy policeman's truncheon.

Reg, one of the other sailors saw the piano in the corner and it wasn't long before they and many other customers were singing to all the songs Reg could play. They leant over the back of the instrument swaying their glasses of beer giving their tonsils full reign.

But Sidney was more interested in sitting at the bar gazing at Ellie. Whenever there was a break from her serving drinks he would engage her in conversation, making his shandy last as long as possible. After they closed the pub that evening Effie said to Ellie that she hadn't failed to notice the attention that Sidney had paid to her all evening. "Yes, he wants to know if he can take me to the pictures on my night off." Smiled Ellie. "And are you going to?" asked Effie. "I might." She winked and laughed as they cleared up.

For the next two weeks whilst Sid's ship was in port, they saw a lot of each other. Pictures, walks on the Hoe and even a visit to the skating rink at Millbay. Ellie had never been roller skating before and had a lot of fun trying.

All too soon it was time for his ship to sail. On their last date he took her to pictures and they kissed and cuddled in the back row. "Can I write to you Ellie?" Sid asked as he said 'goodnight' on her doorstep. "Of course you can Sid, and if you write nice letters I may answer them" she teased. They laughed and kissed, then he called a taxi and that was that; leave over.

Ellie took a last look and imprinted the picture in her mind so she would remember him with his black wavy hair and brown eyes, his tall strong frame. Not all that good looking, until he smiled then his face lit up and he looked really handsome.

During the next six months Sid wrote to Ellie about

once a week. Letters from exotic foreign places with photos of him and his mates by Pyramids in Egypt and lots of places around the Mediteranian. He asked her to send him a picture of herself when next she wrote. So, the following Saturday she went into town and found a photographer's shop and had a couple of pictures taken. She thought that she would also send one to her Mother so that she could show baby May. Ellie did not want May to grow up not knowing her Mother. Many times in her letters she would ask her Mother if she mentioned her to May.

As time went on, Ellie began to feel guilty for not having told Sid about her baby. By his letters he was clearly looking upon her as his steady girl. That evening she decided to ask Effie's advice. So when they had finished all their chores and were about to go up to bed, Ellie broached the subject. "So, what do you think? Should I tell him do you think?" Effie pondered for a moment then said," Yes dear. I think you should. There is nothing better for a relationship than total honesty. If you intend to take up with him again when he comes back, then I think you must. If he doesn't like it, better to get it over with now, for both your sakes."

So. After sleeping on it, Ellie decided that she would take the bull by the horns. The next time she had a quiet hour to herself she wrote...

> Dear Sid,
>
> It has been wonderful receiving your let-
> ters over the past few month and it seems
> that we are getting very fond of each other,
> which is lovely. But, I feel that before you
> get any more ideas about me there is some-
> thing I must tell you. I want to be totally
> honest with you, so here goes. I have a
> baby daughter called May. She is two and

a half and I'm not married. My home is in the Channel Islands where I lived since I was born in Guernsey. When I was fifteen I went to work as a scullery maid in the Manor House. I was very friendly with Clifford, the boot boy and we were always in trouble, running off to climb trees or swim in the river and such like. We loved each other very much. At least, we were only young kids so I suppose it wasn't really love, but, well we did things, you know and I got pregnant. I don't think we knew what we were doing really. Anyway, Father Peter and my parents decided it was best to send me away. His sister is a nun at St. Peters here in Plymouth and they run this place where girls who get themselves into trouble can stay quietly away from gossip and such like. Then have their babies and give them up for adoption before going home again. Well, my Dad was so angry he said I was never to go back. My parents are Catholics you see, so Mum said it would be wrong for me to have my baby adopted and that she would bring her up for me. So that's what I did. I came over to Plymouth, had my baby, then my Mum and father Peter came over and took her back with them to Gernsey. That was nearly three years ago now. I've been working here in the pub with Effie ever since and I haven't been with any other blokes, honest. I'm sorry if this letter upsets you but I had to tell you now, in case you don't want to see me any more. I will understand if you stop writing, but I hope you don't. love Ellie. (your girl)

An agonizing three weeks went by before she heard from Sid again. She had almost accepted the fact that he did not want her any more and that there would be no more letters. But suddenly, to her delight, one morning Effie called her telling her she had some post. Three letters came at once. The first two had been delayed somehow and were obviously written before he got her particular letter. She slipped into a quiet corner, opened the third, and read …

My dear Ellie,

I am sorry if I have taken a while to reply to your letter but, well, my first thought when I read it was great anger. I was real mad at you for what you'd done. I got so mad I went out and got drunk and punched my P.O. in the face. So I was put in the brig and I lost my new stripes I told you I got in my earlier letter. Anyhow, sitting in the brig I had time to think like. I read your letter over and over and first I want to say, thank you for being honest with me. That means a lot I can tell you. Then I started thinking how young you was when you did it and how probably that Clifford didn't know what he was doing except enjoying himself. You aren't the first and you won't be the last to get caught I mean. If you mean that about how you haven't done it since then I reckon that's all right with me.

We'll talk about it when I come home which should be in a couple of months now. I shall have a few weeks leave before we do a two years stint to the far east. Anyway, till then, let's not mention it again. I'm sorry I got angry with you at first but I'm alright now.

Lots and lots of love and kisses from your own Sidney.

After reading it twice, Ellie sat there with tears streaming down her face. Effie found her sitting there and sat down beside her, putting her arm around her, she said,"Never mind, love. There's plenty of other fish in the sea." But Ellie looked up and through her tears, smiled, "No Effie, you don't understand. It's alright. He doesn't want to break it off. It's OK. You can read it, here." Effie took the letter and read it, then sighed and she too had tears in her eyes as she said, "Well, bless his heart. I knew he was a good 'un. But, oh dear, fancy getting locked up for hitting his P.O.!" "Yes" replied Ellie." He's told me he's got an awful temper and if he drinks he doesn't care who he hits." "Well, he'd better watch out he doesn't try to hit you dear, or he'll have me to deal with."

1937

Life at Mayon might have seemed quiet and lonely for a four year old only child but each day brought it's moments of interest. On waking, one of the first sounds was Mister Pellow leading his cart horse down from the field at the top of the road, to his stables and vegetable store; where everything was being made ready for the days business. Mr Pellow and his two sons had a small holding behind Penlee Road next to the slate quarry. He owned some fields there where he grew potatoes and cauliflower and the other field was for pasture for the horse. Mr Pellow would ply his wares around the streets of Stoke until early evening when he would return to the stables, unharness the horse and lead him up the street to turn him out in his field. Sometimes, if Pammy timed it so that she was standing outside her house, old Mr Pellow would lift her on the horse's back and let her ride up to the gate.

There were other traders who broke the quiet of Mayon with their calls of "Milko!" or "Saalt!" The Milkman would arrive every morning with his pony and trap which held two large milk churns, on the outside of which hung several different sized measuring ladels like large metal beakers with long handles that curved at the tops so that they could be hung on the side of the churns. Charlotte, on hearing his call would go out with a large pitcher and buy the milk for the family, It was lovely farm milk, fresh every morning and if you were lucky he would have some thick Devonshire clotted cream which his wife had made.

He was not the only caller, for once a month the cry of "Saalt!" rang out. Another pony and trap but this time with a flat bed on which was carried a large sack containing a huge block of salt. He would cut off a chunk, weigh it and place it in Charlotte's stone salt jar.

The Baker's van called three times a week and if she was good Pammy was allowed to choose a fancy cake for her tea.

But the tradesman that Pammy looked forward to see-ing most was the man with a cart that rattled and tinkled as it came down the street with all the many different sizes of pots and pans. He had no need to shout, for the rattling sounds of his wares could be heard long before he turned the corner at the top of the road. He was half gypsy so he said, and his wife would walk behind him with her basket of home made wooden pegs.

Now and again a knife grinder would come round calling out "Knives to grind! Any knives to grind!" and Charlotte would take out her carving knives to him and Pammy would watch as the sparks flew off his fast moving stone wheel.

Then there was Mister Harvey the coalman. He was always dirty with coal dust but when he smiled his teeth looked so white within his grissly grimy face. He would heft a large sack on to his back and carry it round the side to the coal bunker and heave the coal in with a great grunt. Pammy loved to help whenever these jolly tradesmen came by and they always passed the time of day with a special friendly word for herself.

The old man who lived at number four was called Mole. Old man Mole as everyone called him had been retired from the Dockyard after an accident at the age of forty and had not worked since, just living on his pension. He was happy enough tending his allotment at the top of the road in the corner of one of Pellow's fields. But for Pammy, one of her delights was when he would sit out on his doorstep and carve things out of bits of wood. One of the things he made was a dancing doll. He had made a sort of paddle which he held between his knees and the doll had a handle in the middle of it's back which the old man held as he stood the doll on the paddle. Then, as he bounced the paddle with his fist in a rhythmic way the dolls legs would jerk in a kind of dance as old Man Mole hummed a jolly tune. He was always in demand when the children gathered outside to play.

So life was never boring for this small child for she enjoyed helping about the house with her own small broom and duster, and whenever the call of "Coal!" or "Saalt!" rang out she was the first to run to the door with a whoop of delight.

One of the things the family loved to do together was roller skating. At West Hoe near Millbay docks was a roller skating rink combined with a boxing ring, which was set, raised in the centre so that skaters would traverse clockwise around it. When Pammy was four her parents took her along with them. She was much too small to use any of the hired skates so Jimmy, the man in the booth offered to make a pair for her. The following week when they arrived, there was Jimmy with a big smile on his face. "Now then young lady, if you will kindly step into my office I think I may have something for you." Sure enough, there on the shelf was a very small pair of roller skates. Pammy whooped with joy. "They are adjustable so will last her until she's old enough to use our proper ones." He added. Jack thanked him and offered to pay for them but Jimmy wouldn't hear of it. "My pleasure, I'm sure." He grinned as he helped Pammy attach them to her shoes.

Then, holding her parents hands she began to slowly skate along. In no time at all she got the hang of it, but it was tiring for her little legs so after a bit, Phyllis told her to sit down and have a rest while they had a turn with the faster skaters. The music played as the crowd skated to the tune as they circled the boxing ring. After a couple of circuits Jack glanced across to where they had left Pammy, but she was nowhere to be seen. "Now where has that little monkey gone?" he moaned to Phyllis. The next thing they heard was some laughing and a commotion. They spotted Pammy skating away happily amongst the grownups, circling the boxing ring the wrong way! Dodging in and out the legs of the oncoming traffic enjoying herself. Jack and Phyllis quickly reached her and brought her to the side and gave her a very important lesson on the difference between clockwise and anti-clockwise, which she never forgot much to everyone's amusement. She was delighted when Jimmy told her she could take the skates home with her and she gave him a big hug. For days afterwards all Pammy wanted to do was skate up and down the pavement and would have skated everywhere they went if she had been allowed.

Charlotte thought the funniest sight was Pammy skating and pushing her dolls pram at the same time.

Phyllis decided it was time to start teaching Pammy how to play the piano. After all they had this gorgeous baby grand which Henry had given them. Mabel had taught Pammy her letters at an early age so she thought the time was right.

Pammy took to it very well, she had a good ear and knew at once if she was playing a wrong note. She never needed to be pressed to practice, indeed she enjoyed music so much that there were times when she had to be told to stop.

GUERNSEY

Far away in Guernsey, May lived a very quiet life. When she was six she was sent to the convent dayschool and proved to be a good scholar learning to read very quickly. Once she discovered the pleasure of reading she spent as much time as she could sitting out on the cliffs with a book or on rainy days, curled up on the window seat in her room with which ever book was her latest favourite. She had learned very early to keep out of her grandfather's way. He clearly did not approve of his wife's decision to bring up the child. But as long as he did not see too much of her he made no fuss about it.

Her grandmother loved her very much and talked often to her about Ellie. She was delighted with the photograph that Ellie had sent and had it framed for May to keep on her bedside locker. May did not understand why her Mother was not with them and got no satifactory answers if she asked. But as long as she could walk the cliffs and read, she was content enough for the present.

When Sid's ship came into port a couple of months later, they were so thrilled to be together again. He said if he had any parents he'd have taken her to meet them but they were both dead now. He had a sister though, who lived at Plymstock, on the outskirts of Plymouth; that's where he stayed whenever he was on leave. So, the following Sunday he took her there to meet his sister Lucy and her husband

Fred Price and their two children Margaret aged eight and Jonathan aged six. They had lunch and stayed to tea, then caught the bus back into town and went for an evening stroll on the Hoe.

They talked for hours about the letter and how they felt about each other. Then Sid said, "How about we get engaged? Then when I come back in two years we can get married. What do you say Ellie love?" Ellie didn't know what to say at first but she knew that the idea of marrying Sid made her feel very happy. It's a long time to wait, I know," he said, "but that's the way it is when you're a sailor. I can't take you with me!" She laughed and they began to make plans. Then he said," Just a minute, young lady, you haven't told me you'll marry me yet!" She looked at him squarely and said," It all depends, Sid, how you really feel about my daughter May. Yes, I think I do want to marry you. But you see, my dream is to have my baby girl with me. Do you think you could take both of us?" "Adopt her as mine, you mean?" replied Sid. "Yes, that's what I'd like. In fact Sid, that's the only way it has to be if you want me to marry you." She declared.

"Well, that's asking a lot, my girl. Some other blokes kid an'all. But I suppose it it's the only way I can have the girl I love, then that's how it will be!"

The next day they went out and he bought her a lovely little ring.

They were hardly apart during his leave. Effie gave Ellie all the time off she wanted. Then when it was time for him to go back to sea, they promised to be faithful to each other and always be honest.

"You'll tell me if you fall for another bloke won't you Ellie? Only I know how often that happens when we sailors are away for so long, and there's nothing worse than finding out that it's been going on behind a fella's back. Some nosy busy body will write and rat on you and that's a horrible way to find out. I couldn't bear it. I think I'd kill somebody if that happened to me. So, you will be honest Ellie?"

"Of course I will silly. And I won't look at another man while you're away., but I can go to pictures with some old friends sometimes can't i?"

"Of course you can love. I don't want you to turn into one of them nuns of yours!"

And so the couple parted and the two years began to go slowly by.

Ellie saw a lot of Cathy during the first year; Sheamus and Mick had both joined the Merchant Navy but Patrick and Sean were still working in the Dockyard. Patrick made up a foursome with Cathy and Sean quite often, going to pictures or walking on the Hoe after Mass.

He told Ellie that she'd better tell Sid she was quite safe with him. He was a born bachelor and a Mummy's boy and intended staying at home to look after Bridie. He didn't think he was the type to ever get married, he said. Seeing as Sid had claimed the only girl he fancied, he would be content to treat her as though she were his sister. In fact, she soon got used to his brotherly ways and enjoyed his 'no strings' company. It would have been a long two years without it.

Cathy was so happy being married. Sean had been promoted to an electrical fitter and was earning enough to keep a wife.

1938

When Pammy was five she began school at Stoke Dameral Infants The Infants were set in the same block as the Juniors but separated by a fence. There was a large building for the toddlers at the top of the playground in a big room where the little ones had afternoon naps on fold away metal beds with little blankets. That Christmas Pammy had been given a huge dolls house by a cousin who had grown too old for it. It was beautiful but Phyllis thought it was much too large to keep at Mayon. So they agreed to give it to the infants, that way Pammy could still play with it and share it with her new friends. The Teacher was delighted to have it. At the other end of the playground in the main building was a large hall, where the children had prayers. It had a huge cupboard which opened out into a shop with shelves and boxes of pretend goods. It had a set of scales and a till and cardboard money so that the children took turns to be customers or shopkeepers and played at going shopping. It was a brilliant way to teach them to count money and weights and measures as they played. This was Pammy's favourite lesson.

Grandad Baker's old Mother lived in a little terraced house in the middle of Stoke village in Tavistock Road., just around the corner from Stoke Dameral School. Once or twice a week Mother would meet Pammy from school then they would walk up to visit Great Grandma Baker. She seemed extremely old to Pammy in her long black dress and black shawl with her white hair piled up in a bun on top of her head. The front room seemed dark behind thick lace curtains but the room held many fascinating trinkets and photographs that fascinated Pammy. She loved to hear her tell stories about her younger days especially the story of how she was nearly buried alive in India. She had gone into a faint and the Indian women thought she was dead and started to prepare her for burial when she opened her eyes and sat up they all ran away in fright. Pammy loved the pictures of Grampa when he was a little boy in knee length trousers and matching jacket and strange boots. But the treasure in this room was the musical box. Great Grandma wouldn't let her open it every time but now and then she would say that she might, and play a tune. It was a very large ornate box with a glass top which when opened revealed a large metal disc sitting on a pin beside a roller covered in spikes. Pammy would be allowed to wind the handle not turning it too much before Great Grandma would start the machine playing. It was a sound like no other. The tinkling bells and the slowly turning disc enthralled the child as she watched the cylinder with it's little spikes turn slowly making this amazing music. There was never a second tune for Great Grandma knew that the magic of the moment should be savoured and left to enjoy again another day.

Then it was time for their cup of tea. The cups were unlike any Pammy had seen before. They were delicate and square shaped rather than round and the sides were fluted so that when you drank from them you could feel it's shape with your mouth. And the biscuits too were different though always the same. Mother said they were called water biscuits. They were hard and plain but with a little butter on them were quite delicious.

Sometimes, after saying goodbye to Great Grand Ma, they would go to the shop a few doors up where they sold tobacco and sweets. The shop had an distinctive aroma of the many brands of tobacco but the rows of jars of sweets were what attracted the child most. But then there was the shop keeper's parrot. When anyone stepped over the threshold they set the bell above the door jangling., the old parrot would yell out "Shop!" several times until it's owner appeared to serve the customer. It was said that the parrot had a sense of humour because it sometimes would shout "Shop" when there was nobody there and when the shop keeper came and found it empty the parrot would laugh and laugh.

Pammy was allowed to buy a small scoop of her favourite sweets, jelly babies, and on occasion they would buy some very special chocolates sold individually for Mabel and Charlotte. Mabel just adored the ones with the violets on the top.

1938

Ellie had lived life in her own small world and took little notice of the world outside. But regular visits to the cinema and Pathe news reels brought the wider world closer.

Everyone had seen the sad processions of old King George's funeral at the beginning of nineteen thirty six and the controvasy over Edward the eight wishing to marry Mrs Simpson. There wasn't a household in the land which hadn't listened to his broadcast of abdication in December, followed quickly by the grand coronation of King George sixth. The whole of Plymouth was decorated with flags.

But Patrick was very concerned about the news films showing the growing menace of Nazi Germany and Hitler's troops marching into the Rhineland.

Ellie worried about the dangers that a war might bring. Lots of men in the pub brought this topic up regularly. She was, in a way, glad that Sid's ship was far away from these troubles at present, but who knew where these things would lead?

"Politics and war! Politics and war! That's all they talk about these days." Moaned Effie. Some said that Churchill was right and that we should put Hitler in his place. Others talked of the Prime Minister's promise of appeasement.

Suddenly she got the news that Sid would be coming home soon now. In their letters they agreed to get married

quickly and quietly, then before Sid had to join his new
ship, they would send for May.

Effie said they could have the whole of the top floor
of the pub. She said that if Sid was to be away again then
what was the point of Ellie living in a flat by herself when
she could stay put and have Effie to help her look after May
That way Ellie could go on working as well, then they could
save up for a house.

All this was agreed to; it just needed Sid to come home.
Ellie felt as though she would die waiting. The weeks
crawled by until finally it was just a matter of days.

When it happened it was a surprise. Ellie looked up
from drawing a pint and there he was. They froze, staring at
each other across the saloon bar. Ellie was the first to move;
she dashed out from behind the bar and rushed into his
arms to the sound of cheering from the customers.

They slipped away upstairs and used Effie's sittingroom
to share their first private moments. Ellie thought that after
two years he would be a bit of a stranger, but no such thing.
It was as though they had never been parted. Sid was a little
heavier and quite sun-tanned whilst he thought Ellie even
more beautiful than he had last seen her.

During the next two days they never stopped talking.
They decided that they would get married at the first opportunity which proved to be in three weeks on a Friday
afternoon in the pouring rain. Even though it was a civil
ceremony and not at St. Peters it was the happiest day of
their lives. After just one days honeymoon in a hotel down
by the Barbican, they worked on their new little home upstairs on the third floor. Just as Effie had promised. Sid only
had one more weeks leave, then he was due to join his new
ship Royal Oak based at Scapa Flow in Scotland.

The day before he left they had a letter from her Mother
saying that a family called Clark were leaving the Islands

to live in Plymouth and they would bring May over with them. Sid was disappointed that he would not be there to meet her but was sure that he would be getting some leave now that he was on a ship nearer home, and anyway it was probably better if Ellie and May were on their own at first. After all, May was only young.

The little room that had been Ellie's for so long was decorated prettily and made for her little daughter. Then Sid was off on the train to Scotland. Leaving his bride, knowing that it would only be a matter of weeks before they would be together again.

It proved to be quite some time however, before the Clarks were ready to come. The next letter from her Mother told Ellie that they would be arriving with May at four o'clock on November the first. Just before May's eight birthday.

Ellie could hardly believe that it was eight whole years since she had given birth in Bridie's house. So much had happened since. She wondered what had happened to May in that time. They would have so much to learn about each other.

The meeting on the quayside was not what Ellie had expected. There were several groups like the Clarks with an unusual number of children. They quickly explained to Ellie that several families were very worried there was going to be a war and wanted to get the children safely away before it happened. Many expected the Channel Islands, being near to France, would be occupied by the Germans.

However, when May stood before her Mother, quiet and solemn and not a little afraid, Ellie forgot these other people's troubles and knelt down in front of May. They looked into each other's eyes and smiled a silent 'hello'. Ellie took her hand and took up Mays suitcase as they turned to say 'goodbye' and thank you' to the Clarks, exchanging pieces of paper with addresses on them promising to keep in touch.

Finally they walked away hand in hand towards the Octagon together. May forgot her shyness for a moment in the astonishment of the size of everything in this enormous city. Ellie could see the wonderment in her eyes and was taken back to her own arrival and the feelings she had had when she first came here.

Ellie was delighted when they saw a dray, so that she could show the horses to May. It broke the tension and suddenly May was a wide eyed little girl full of endless questions. It was only a short walk to the Red Dog Pub and Effie had been watching out for them. "Welcome! Welcome! Tea's all ready upstairs with some very special fancy cakes!" She ushered them up the stairs to Ellie's newly decorated living room at the top of the house. Not long after tea Ellie could see that May was very tired so she took her along to her new room and tucked her up in bed.

To celebrate May's birthday a couple of days later, Ellie and Effie took her on the Pier where she had some rides on a carousel and a round-a-bout. They listened to the band before having a special tea in the café with lots of ice cream.

May was a very quiet child and very polite. She spoke perfect English with a charming French accent. Her Grandmother had always insisted she speak English and had certainly done a good job looking after her in her formative years, and she spoke of her fondly; however, when asked about her grandfather she had little to say. Clearly the stern rigid man of Ellie's memory had not changed.

Perhaps his intimidating presence was the reason for May's quiet shyness.

Arrangements were made for May to attend the primary school connected with St Peters. One or two of the nuns taught there and of course, Sister Josephine was particularly interested in keeping an eye on her welfare at the school. May did not make friends easily but loved to read and was quite content to be alone with a good story book.

The day before Sid's next leave, Ellie sat down and explained to May that she was going to have a Daddy. The child was not sure how to deal with this new situation but Ellie wisely kept it simple and hoped that events would take care of themselves.

On the Friday just after May returned from school and was just finishing a glass of milk, she heard a door bang and a man's voice calling her Mother. The next moment she saw Ellie and Sid in an embrace. Her first feelings were of jealousy, though at seven, she was not to be aware of that.

Then Ellie led Sid over to May and introduced them. "May, this is my husband and your new daddy. I told you about him. Do you like his uniform?" May looked at him carefully and then nodded, though she hadn't seen such strange clothes before. Sid was very careful not to frighten her and asked her if she liked her new bedroom. "I hope you do like it because I chose that wallpaper with the teddy bears on it, and I put it up myself. Do you like teddy bears?" May nodded again but still had no words for this tall man in the funny clothes. "Let me open my kit bag and see what's inside, shall i?" He led her over to his enormous bag and slowly loosened the rope. May watched, fascinated, as a brown parcel was lifted out. Sid gave it to her and asked her if she would like to open it. May laid it on the floor and carefully opened it up. Her large brown eyes were huge as she lifted up a golden coloured teddy bear, exactly like the ones on her wallpaper. Without saying a word she held her new bear in her arms and walked into her own room with it. A few moments later she ran back and put her arms around one of Sid's legs and hugged it saying very politely, "Thank you very much." Then she was gone again. Ellie and Sid smiled at each other and Sid winked. "I think we are going to get along together just fine."

May loved her teddy bear and would not be separated from it for a minute.

Sid only had a weekend pass this time but he was pleased to tell his new family that he would be home for Christmas.

During the weeks leading up to Christmas Ellie was so excited to be doing her flat up with festive decorations. The next Saturday she and May went into town to the market and bought a lovely little Christmas tree and some tinsel and decorations. May could not stop smiling. She was still a very quiet child but was slowly coming out of her shell. She had settled down in her new school quite well and proved to be very good at English with a good standard of reading. Effie noticed that the child was looking rosier and less nervous than when she arrived. Ellie was pleased too, that she and her daughter were beginning to get used to each other. May was now starting to get used to calling her 'Mother' more freely, which gave Ellie so much pleasure. She was only sorry that she had had to miss her earlier years, but that couldn't be helped. At least they were making up for lost time.

The day before Christmas Eve, Sid came home for his leave. May was shy with him at first but he won her over when he offered to tell her a bed time story. Their little festive celebrations went off well, and May was thrilled with her presents of books and toys. But the best present of all were the papers which came just in time to be displayed on the mantelpiece. The adoption papers naming Sidney officially becoming May's father. She was now May Louise Evans.

Sid gave Ellie a locket and she gave him a cigarette case. Ellie cooked a chicken dinner in her little kitchenette in the corner of the living room and Effie and her husband joined them bringing a bottle of wine, a box of chocolates and a Christmas pudding. There was just time to see the New Year in before Sid was off again on the train to Scotland. Ellie treasured her little locket which had Sid's and May's pictures in it.

1939

For Ellie and her daughter 1939 was a year of settling down in their new life together. But for the country it was a time of great political tension.

All eyes were upon Europe. Hitler had already seized Austria. Next he cast his hungry eyes on the republic of Czechoslovakia. The Czechs were allied with France and Russia. Britain too might be aroused if he attacked them. The republic's backers however, were not prepared for war. Then on September the first, Hitler invaded Poland.

With the threat of war' Sid's leaves were infrequent, much to his family's disappointment. Then on that very day, he was home on a weekend pass, with millions of others on Sunday September the third they sat around their radio as Chamberlain announced that Briton was now at war.

Sid caught the next train back to Scotland. Ellie and May both went to North Road Station to see him off. Sid and Ellie clung to one another as though it was for the last time...and it was.

Just a few weeks later a 'U' boat crept into Scapa Flow and sank H.M.S. Royal Oak with the loss of 39 hands. Ellie would never be the same woman again.

The evening it was announced over the radio., Effie and her customers were gathered around the set as they did most evenings. Ellie had just finished clearing up her flat after putting May to sleep, when she heard it on her set.

From the bar they heard the terrible scream from upstairs. Effie rushed out of the bar and up the stairs. When she got up there she found May standing in her nightdress clutching her teddy bear in the doorway of their living room staring at her Mother who was on her knees clasping a cushion to her chest and moaning and wailing as she rocked herself to and fro.

Effie coaxed May back to bed, then hurried over to wrap her arms around Ellie. The wailing had subsided to a whimper as she continued to rock back and forth. "Oh, my God, Ellie, my dear. I'm here." Whispered Effie with tears streaming down her face. Ellie rocked herself into a state of oblivion where she neither heard nor saw anything. She was only aware that her world had come to an end.

Effie tried to persuade her to sit in a chair but she could not move her. Although Ellie was not a drinker like herself, Effie's next solution to the problem was a drink. She hurried downstairs and fetched a couple of glasses and a bottle of her best Brandy. Then climbed the stairs as quickly as she could. She first poured herself a quick one to steady her own nerves then filled a glass for Ellie.

At first she could not get Ellie to drink, then after gentle persistence Ellie took a sip. She coughed as the strong liquid hit her throat then, as the warmth seeped into her cold body, accepted more. She still continued to kneel, clutching the cushion and rocking, but the moaning only quietened down a little. It was a terrifying sound, so tragic and desperate, it really frightened Effie. Her husband had just come over from the Palace Theatre and persuaded the regulars to let him close up. They drifted quietly away with their caps in their hands showing respect for the terrible loss this young woman was suffering so soon after her marriage.

Effie stayed with Ellie all night, then in the morning she sent her husband to fetch Sister Josephine. Cathy arrived first and was appalled and shocked to see her dear friend still rocking and moaning. She could coax no words from her but tried to let her know she was there. In a way it was fortunate that Cathy had just given up work because she was expecting a baby in six weeks time; so she and Effie agreed that she should take May home with her for the time being. As Cathy was helping May pack a few things she tried to explain to the child why her Mother was 'poorly'. Sister Josephine arrived. She immediately knelt down beside Ellie, took her hands in hers and began to pray.

Nothing seemed to penetrate through to the stricken girl except the odd sips of Brandy which Effie gave her every now and then. After praying, Sister Josephine said that she would go and fetch Doctor Joseph, he would know what to do. A while later when the Doctor came he gave her an injection which he said would put her to sleep. So Effie and Sister Josephine managed to put her to bed as May left with Cathy.

As the morning wore on Effie said that she must open up the pub so Sister Josephine remained sitting by the bed slowly whispering her beads.

Ellie slept for two days but when she awoke and remembered, she began to cry again. When she saw Sister Josephine praying she became hysterical and shouted for her to go away. She said she felt that God had turned against her and wanted none of Him. Praying would not bring Sid back. It was some time before Effie could get Ellie to eat anything. She just shut herself away upstairs, giving no thought for anyone; not even her child. The only thing that helped her was drink. Effie was afraid that she would become too dependant upon it. Then the official telegram came. It set her right back to shutting herself away with a bottle of whisky keening half the night. Over night she was taken ill so Doctor Joseph rushed her off to hospital where Ellie had a miscarriage. No one, not even she, knew that she was pregnant but the shock had made her lose the baby. She was depressed for some time. Then, suddenly Ellie came out of it. She came down to the bar and without saying anything began to serve the customers.

She had smartened herself up somewhat, but her face was totally blank. After they closed in the afternoon Ellie asked Effie to get Cathy to bring May home. "Are you sure you can manage, my dear?" she asked. "I have to, I have nothing to live for for myself, but I must think of May." Ellie answered. Effie wisely decided that at least this was a start and having the child around might cheer her up. The next day, after school, Cathy brought May home. The child was very quiet and had obvious misgivings of how it would be living with her Mother again. But, to give her credit, Ellie tried her best to make life as normal as possible for the child. But the joy had gone out of her life. She worked in the bar and was polite to the customers though she seldom smiled much but they understood.

One thing did change though; previously, if anyone offered to buy her a drink she would make herself a weak shandy but now she always took whisky. Effie noticed, but as it did not seem to effect her in any way she let it pass without comment.

So Britian was at war. Everyone was rushing around preparing for the worst. Collecting gas masks, building shelters, stocking up on tinned food before the inevitable rationing. May's school reinforced the cellar as did Effie in the pub. After clearing up, Effie's husband built a strong partition wall to make it more secure. When kitted out with chairs and a table, a primus stove and a paraffin lamp it was made quite cosy. May went to school each day with her square cardboard box slung over one shoulder which held her gas mask, and her schoolbag over the other. Ellie just kept on working without showing much interest in all the goings on. She did help Effie make the blackout curtains and stuck brown paper strips on the windows, but inside she didn't care if she lived or died.

Prior to the time in 1939 when war seemed imminent, Jack had been preparing for a very special holiday for the three of them. He was planning to take them to the Channel Island of Guernsey where he had been corresponding, for some time, with one of his French customers. And they had invited him to come and stay at any time at their boarding house adjacent to their iron monger's shop. But Jack had, for some time been concerned about the political climate.

On September 3rd 1939, that fateful Sunday morning, they were all packed and ready to go as the voice on Mabel's radio announced that the Prime Minister was to make a statement. Pammy was sitting on the third stair, dressed and ready to go and her Mother and Father stood by their suitcases waiting for the taxi. They listened to the announcement in shocked silence, then Jack said, "I'm sorry my darlings, but I don't think we should go, do you?" "You're quite right, of course. It wouldn't be safe, would it?" answered Phyllis.." Aren't we going Mummy?" asked Pammy, confused. "No my darling. The gentleman on the radio said there's going to be a nasty war and we must all stay here where it's safe, for now anyway." Smiled her mother reassuringly. "We'll go as soon as we can another time, don't worry. I'm sorry." Jack said to his wife, "I'll tell you what I'll do. I'll use the money we would have spent on a nice fur coat I've always been promising you, and you can have a new party frock, Pammy, what do you say?" They laughed as they took off their coats as the taxi man was being sent away by Mabel. "That's right, make the best of it, don't let old Hitler dampen your spirits!" she said, "and put the kettle on." Added Charlotte, who was always one of those women who was convinced that nothing was as bad but a good cup of tea wouldn't cure.

At school the children were all drilled on how to use a gas mask and told they must carry them at all times; and how to march in an orderly fashion down to the shelters which were hurriedly being carved into the hillside on Underhill Road next to the school. When finished it was a laberinth of passages lined with wooden benches where they sat in rows until told to march back to their classrooms again. Everyone got used to hearing the air raid sirens which were constantly practicing so everyone would recognize the rising and falling wail of the alarm and the steady note of the all clear. All this practice seemed to be pointless to the children as nothing actually seemed to be happening.

At Mayon, the back garden lawn was dug up and in the far corner they dug a deep hole for the Anderson shelter to be sunk and covered with rockery. The rest would be planted with vegetables. The shelter had a thick heavy door made out of old railway sleepers with four steps down to the inside. Sets of bunks were built on two sides and a cupboard and a small table on the third side for holding the kettle, food and drinks. It had a primus stove and Jack had even put in electricity, but there were candles and a lamp just in case.

To begin with, it was a great place to play, the serious use was yet to come. The family at number one, were called Ross. George had just joined the regular air force and was therefore away a lot. His wife Lilian, and her son Terry, two years older than Pammy, lived with his Granny. Terry pretended he didn't like girls but actually he and Pammy were good friends. Pammy was very fond of Auntie Lil, as she called his mother. She was, of course, not a real aunt but as Lil ahd no daughters of her own, she loved to have

Pammy popping in and out. Terry used to tease Pammy a lot and pretend to throw her out when she knocked at the door much to the horror of his gran whom he called Ide, her name being Ida actually. She loved making elderberry wine and when their Anderson shelter was sunk into their front garden her priority was to store the wine in it under the bunks.

Because Terry's father was away such a lot he was very willful and got his own way a great deal of the time. But Lil was a very placid person and never seemed to get ruffled by his moods. It used to wind Ida up which made him do more devilment, like popping paper bags behind her chair when she was having a nap.

A few months after war was declared Pammy heard Mabel and Charlotte having a huge row. "It's no use you arguing with me Charlotte, you are going and that's that!" declared Mabel not prepared to have her decision changed. "But I don't want to go, Mabel. I've always been here to look after you, and how will Phyllis get on without me?" Charlotte was in tears by this time. Pammy could hear her sobbing as she sat listening on the stairs, playing. "You'll be safer in Gunnislake with Harriet. Anyway I shall be away all day at school so I won't be here with you when the air raids do start, will I?" continued Mabel. "As for Phyllis, she's not ill anymore, she's quite capable of managing on her own. I don't want to have to worry about you when I'm at work do I?" "No dear, but" tried Charlotte, once again, "It's no use, you're going as soon as I can get Jack to take you. I'll be able to come and visit you at weekends whenever I can. I can get a bus to Tavistock and change to the one for Gunnislake with no problems." There was a long pause as Charlotte realized that Mabel was not going to let her stay. "Very well then. If I must, I must. But only if you promise to look after yourself properly, and have regular meals with

Phil and Jack." conceded Charlotte reluctantly., not letting Mabel have her way without at least some conditions on her part. Pammy was relieved to hear them kiss and make up.

This seemed to be a time for decisions. Jack had been doing some thinking about his boat. He came home from work with a very serious expression on his face. "You look very solemn darling, is something the matter?" asked Phyllis. "Well, I think there's something we need to talk over." He answered. "As you know, fuel is rationed now and we won't be able to get any for 'Pickles' and I doubt we'll even be allowed to use her". "Of course, I hadn't thought. No more picnics on the beach for a while I suppose eigh?" Phyllis said sadly. "That's right, so, I hate to say it but I think we should sell her. "They looked at each other gloomily. "As it happens, that chap where we were going to stay in Guernesey asked me if I'd like to sell it to him. He made a good offer. He's coming over next week and would like to take her back with him. What do you think?" Phyllis smiled and said, "I suppose if we must, it's better that you let her go to someone you know than a complete stranger isn't it?" "You're right there my love. So, shall I telephone him and accept his offer? It was a very generous one." Jack took a deep breath and waited for Phyllis to have the final word. After all the boat was named after her. "Alright" she said, "I shall miss her terribly but perhaps we'll have another boat when the war is over." They said no more about it. The next morning Jack rang Guernsey and agreed the deal.

Another decision Jack had to make was whether to join up. He had always fancied being a pilot, so without telling Phyllis he went to the Royal Air Forsce recruiting office to enquire. They gave him a preliminary medical and told him that his eye sight was not good enough for him to be a pilot. As he was coming out he met a friend from school days who told him he had just signed up with the Marine

Police. "the job is to guard the gates of the Dockyard. It's an important job and as it's shift work you can keep your own job, part time too." "That's not a bad idea." Said Jack. "I'll think about it. "They had also told him at the recruiting office that he was too old at 32 to serve, so this might be just the ticket. He went home and discussed it with Phyllis who agreed that the Dockyard Police would be a very worthwhile job for him, and the next day, his bosses agreed that he could work his hours as he wished. They certainly didn't want to loose him to the services altogether. So this is what he did. A few days later he had signed on and been issued with his uniform and was sent off for six weeks training.

The Sunday after he returned they all got into the car and drove Charlotte to stay with Harriet in Gunnislake. There were quite a few tears as they set out but it was a beautiful day and they settled down to a pleasant drive across the moors. Number one Sims Terrace was the first in a row of semi detached two up two down cottages on the side of a steep hill overlooking the Tamar valley on the Cornish side. A quaint house with a front door entering straight into the living room. Ir had a large kitchen range on the party wall, a huge table in the centre surrounded by six chairs and a tall dresser on the back wall. A door led through to the scullery where all the washing and food preparation was done. From this room a steep flight of wooden stairs led up to the two bedrooms. The front bedroom was for Mother and Father, when he was not at sea. Charlotte would share this bed with Harriet and Bill would sleep downstairs in a truckle bed. The back bedroom had a double bed which the two girls Joan and Doreen usually shared. There was a small single bed which Charlotte would use if Fred came home. Father was a full time seaman, so he was away a lot. Each room had a wardrobe and a washstand. Of course the house had no bathroom, just an outside privey; a stone shed with a wooden seat with a round hole in it, set over a stream. All washing was done in the scullery.

They were welcomed at the gate and taken in for a hearty tea. The children had a jolly time running around outside until it was time to leave. Charlotte began to cry as they put their coats on. "Now then Char, "Mabel said gently, "I'll come and visit you as much as I can; I'll be able to catch the bus and stay over. You'll see. You'll be much safer here." She gave her a kiss. Charlotte clung to her and said, "Remember you promised, you'll look after yourself properly, and eat right." They clung to eachother for a moment more. They had never been apart since they were children so it was hard. The engine started up and before Charlotte could say more, they were gone, waving out of the windows until they turned the corner.

After a few months of piano lessons with Mrs Withers at her music school in Tavistock place, her teacher told Pammy that she was doing so well she was going to enter her for a first grade examination. Phyllis was delighted that her daughter was ready and agreed. Pammy learnt the set pieces and practiced hard at the sight reading which was the part her teacher said she was best at. A few weeks later the time for the exam came round. On the day, Pammy had a new dress of dark red velvet and a new pair of shiny patent leather shoes. Mabel said she looked very smart as she waved her off. The examination was to take place in the Atheneum in the centre of town. This was an imposing Greek styled building with enormous elegant Corinthian columns set at the top of a short flight of steps. Inside the large double doors the rooms appeared gigantic to little Pammy as they wandered through to a smaller inner room where they were to sit and wait. Of course she was nervous but not nearly as nervous as her Mother. After about ten minutes a young boy just a little older than Pammy came out of a door across the room. Then a lady appeared and beckoned to Pammy to come forward. She was a very pleasant person and tried to put Pammy at her ease, as they entered the large examination room, leaving Phyllis to wait in agony.

To her left was a piano not unlike her own but bigger. She was told to come forward and speak to the three judges who sat at a large table at the far side of the room. They asked her a few theory questions then told her to sit at the piano and play her test pieces. Pammy took a deep breath and remembered her aunt Mabel's advice. "Just take your time and pretend you are playing to your Aunties." With this thought in her mind she played as best she could When she was done the lady brought her a short piece of music which she had never seen before and told to study it for a moment then when she was ready, to play it.

The little melody floated confidently across the room and the three examiners nodded and smiled. After she had finished playing they thanked her for coming and said that she had done well, especially with the sight reading as her teacher had predicted. They did not have to wait too long for the result which was a good high mark, much to everyone's delight. It was to be the beginning of a big love affair with music.

1940

As time went by Ellie would occasionally be pressed by a customer to go out with them but she became experienced at repelling their advances. Then one quiet Sunday morning, Fred Parker came into the bar. He sat in the corner and called Effie in a familiar way. "Hello Effie, my old love, how's life been treating you then?" he said with a deep soft sensuous voice. "Well! If it isn't my long lost lover, Fred Parker, in the flesh!" she squealed and came out from behind the bar to give him a big hug. They exchanged small talk about their families and so forth for a moment then Effie offered him a drink on the house. "The usual will it be?" and as he smiled and nodded she called, "Ellie love, bring me over two double brandys will you dear? The best bottle at the back." Ellie studied the stranger as she poured out the drinks. He was about thirty five, tall, well built but not fat, with smooth brown hair and a broad grin showing a row of good teeth with a gold filling at the side. He was dressed in an expensive looking suit.

"And who is this delectable creature then?" he asked as she approached with the glasses. "This is Ellie Evans. She's been with me a few years now, haven't you darling?" "Yes" replied Ellie, "Almost nine years now." "Then it's time you left and came to work for me!" Fred winked at her appraising her all over quite blatantly. "Oi! You keep your hands and eyes off of my Ellie! She's too good for trade to loose, she is!" declared Effie. "Anyway, she's part of the family now, aren't you dear?" Ellie nodded. "She's a quiet little thing isn't she?" asked Fred. "Too quiet for your place, Fred. Your girls are hard cases, game for anything." Responded Effie. "Of course they are and I pay them well for it., as you well know, and they make more on the side if they want." Stated Fred proudly.

"You mean, when YOU want!" laughed Effie. They nudged each other and laughed. Ellie saw customers coming in so she went back behind the bar to serve whilst Effie and Fred had a long chat and a few more doubles before it was time to close up for the afternoon.

After they locked the doors, Fred remained and when Effie's husband came down from his nap they sat drinking into the afternoon. Ellie slipped upstairs after finishing up washing the glasses and wiping down the bar. That evening as they were preparing to open up again, Effie said, "Fred wants you to go and work at his place." "Where's his place then?" asked Ellie casually. "That night club up behind the Palace Theatre. You know, upstairs just past the stage door." "But I like working here. Why would I want to work in a nightclub 'til the early hours of the morning? They don't open 'til ten p.m. It would be awful tiring." Ellie said. "Yes, but for awful good money!" replied Effie. "Are you trying to get rid of me or something?" Ellie spoke quite sharply and began to get annoyed with the whole conversation. Change was the last thing she wanted. "Of course not love!" answered Effie trying to pasify Ellie. "It's just that, well, Fred owns this pub not me, you see. I only manage it and I don't like to cross him. He's the sort of man that gets what he wants when he wants it." "Well, he's not getting me! So there! I can't help it if you feel you have to please him, but I don't. I'm stopping here with you. You've been good to me and May and I've got a lovely flat upstairs."

"Well, alright, I'll tell him, but he won't like it. He doesn't like the word 'no' doesn't Fred Parker."

"Why haven't I seen him in here before then?" asked Ellie. "He's been away. He's been in Dublin for the last six years opening up a casino. He set his younger brother Albert up there to manage it for him. Fred got married to an Irish girl there but he said she died last month so he decided to come home." "Who's been looking after this place then?" was her next question. "Marty Bridges. You know Marty. Him with the red hair that comes in and plays with the darts team on Thursday nights." "Oh, yes. I know who you mean. He's the one who smokes cigars all the time." "That's him. He's had a free hand while Fred's been away. I hope he's done a good job of it or Fred'll have his guts for garters."

A couple of days later, just as they were closing up for lunchtime, Fred came in and ordered a double brandy and bought one for Effie.

"And what will you have Ellie, my dear?" he invited. "Just a small whisky, thank you." She answered and poured herself one, putting it on the side. When he and Effie had drunk each other's health he said, "Well then, Effie, have you asked Ellie if she'll come and work for me then?"

"I have asked her, Fred, as you said, but, well, she says she's happy here and doesn't want to leave." She sounded worried at having to tell him that, but he smiled good naturedly and said, "Well Ellie, I'll pay you more than double what you're getting here, you know." He leered at her directly. "Thank you, Mister Edwards, but I've got a little girl to look after and I'm not keen on such late hours, besides, I like living here with Mrs Stone."

"I see, well, I'm sure we could arrange for you to keep your little flat, couldn't we Eff? And do call me Fred, please." "Oh, yes. I'm sure we could if that's what Ellie wants." Stammered Effie.

"But I don't want, Mister Edwards, thank you. I'll keep the job I've got." And she turned back to serve two sailors their last pints before closing. Much to Effie's relief they heard no more about it until a few weeks later, when Fred came in and invited Ellie out to lunch. "That's if Eff can spare you for the rest of the morning. How would you like to have a slap up lunch at the Continental Hotel?" he coaxed with a broad grin. "What for?" she replied bluntly. "Ellie!" exclaimed Effie. "What a rude girl you are! Of course I can spare her Fred. Ellie, how can you pass up a posh lunch at the Conte? Especially with rationing just around the corner. Who knows when you'll be able to again? Now don't be a silly and get changed and go and enjoy yourself. I'll look after May when she comes in." Ellie could see that Effie was sending her a silent message to go with Fred. She was obviously in fear of him, so she said "Well, alright, but only if he promises not to try and talk me into going to work for him again." Fred laughed, "I promise. Look, the truth is I have a table booked to have lunch with a business college and he can't make it and I hate eating alone. So I thought you might like to join me." Ellie hadn't heard that line before and had to admit it was very flattering and hoped she would know how to behave in such a posh place. But she didn't have to persuade herself for long so she went upstairs to put on a clean dress.

The Continental Hotel stood on a corner not far from Millbay Docks. It was considered one of the best hotels in the city and was determined to maintain it's standards in spite of impending shortages. The style and elegance was as impressive inside as it was out, It succeeded in cheering Ellie up for the first time in many months. Fred treated her with gentlemanly charm and turned a blind eye whenever she stumbled over the correct spoon or knife. Ellie relaxed and with some crafty persuasion began to talk of her home in Guernsey colouring it somewhat to make it sound as though she actually lived in that Manor house instead of working there. Of course she did not mention her 'problem' but let Fred to believe that May was the daughter of her late husband.

Fred took her out several times after that; then one evening when they were strolling along the Hoe after a meal at the Lockyer Hotel, he took her arm and told her how much her company meant to him. "You cannot believe how lonely I have been since my wife died." Then when he saw the pain in her face he continued," Oh, but how stupid of me! How could I be so unfeeling! Of course you know. You must be lonely too. Forgive me."

"It's alright Fred. I know you didn't mean to be thoughtless." Ellie replied quietly.

"But it was thoughtless, you're right. But what I meant to say was that being with someone like you who knows all too well how painful being with other people can sometimes be. But with you, I feel, well, I feel that we can relax in each other's company knowing there are no demands being made on either of us." He sounded so sincere, but there was a corner of his mouth which curled up slightly and would have warned Ellie had she seen it in the darkness, but there were no street lights or uncovered windows now to give him away. And when he took her back to the side door of the pub he kissed her gently on the cheek and wished her 'goodnight'.

Ellie was captivated by his charm. He really seemed to like her company and want to see a lot of her. Naturally she was flattered. He was the first man who ever took her out without getting suggestive or trying it on, except Patrick, of course. She felt guilty and at the next opportunity talked to

Effie about her growing pleasure in Fred's company. Ellie was surprised that Effie did not show more enthusiasm.

After all he was her friend.

"Don't you think I should be seeing so much of him?" she asked.

"Oh, I don't mean anything like that dear, it's just that, well, he's a different sort of a man from what you're used to. No, it's just that I've known Fred for a long time and there's another side to him from the 'nice guy' you've seen." Effie stopped talking, not sure whether she should say any more. "What do you mean Effie? Tell me." Ellie frowned waiting.

Effie decided to be frank and taking a deep breath, began.

"He mixes with some shady customers and isn't always on the right side of the law, if you know what I mean. And like I told you before, he likes his own way. Just be careful, that's all I'm saying."

The next time he took her out for an evening, he asked her if she would like to come and visit his club on the way home. Her curiosity got the better of her and she agreed. It was a little after ten o'clock so the club had only just opened. The entrance was up a flight of stairs with the walls all painted black with pictures of scantily clad girls decorating them. At the top they entered through a pair of padded double doors guarded by two heavy weight men in evening dress which strained across their broad shoulders. They both touched their forelocks in a feudal fashion as Fred appeared and muttered "Boss" as they passed. They were in a very large room heavily draped with dark red velvet curtains in which were gaming tables spread around; a semi-circular bar filled a corner bristling with coloured lights. Soft music played in the background. A few members of Fred's staff were preparing for the evening, distributing packs of cards and stacking chips.

In the opposite corner behind a cublicle with a set of bars in front sat a man counting money. They strolled through towards a door at the back marked private which opened into Fred's office. The room was quite large and smartly carpeted in dark blue with a huge desk in the centre and blue velvet curtains drawn across the windows. In the corner was a door standing ajar, through which Ellie could see the beginnings of a staircase. The phone rang and Fred answered it. He put his hand over the mouthpiece and said to Ellie," Would you like to go up and see where I live while I deal with this call?" he invited with a coaxing smile. "It's quieter up there and not so smokey and we can talk. I'd like to show you the pictures of my new casino in Dublin. My brother has just sent me…" he was abruptly drawn back into his phone call so Ellie nodded and turned towards the door. She climbed the stairs to the floor above.

Here, it was a very different world. Nothing brash or flashy about this flat. It was smartly furnished and decorated in subtle shades of green. The curtains were made of expensive fabric as were the two large settees set in front of an elegant fireplace. All the ornaments were clearly antiques. Through a door into a kitchen; everything was clean and uncluttered with a glass cabinet full of cut glasses. Just a kettle and a coffee pot stood on the stove. The rest tidily out of sight. The door at the far side of the flat, Ellie guessed must lead to the bathroom and bedroom but her courage would not allow her to investigate. She sat on the settee slowly taking everything in. Clearly Fred Edwards was a wealthy man. How he made all his money seemed to have been suggested by Effie, that it was not all by legal means.

Plymouth being a naval town, she, of course, knew many boats had traded with France for hundreds of years, for contraband such as Brandy and the like; sometimes a Matelot would come into Effie's pub and offer her a couple of bottles of Cognac cheap.

Shortly. Fred came into the room and apologized for leaving her so long. He indicated around the flat.

"Do you like my humble home then, Ellie?" he asked her, careful to sound casual.

"It's very nice Fred, and as you said, lovely and quiet." She spoke with a tremour in her voice letting her nervousness show. "You've got some nice things." She added. He smiled, pleased with her approval. "Let me give you some coffee, then I'll show you those photos I was telling you about." He crossed to the stove and lit the burner under the coffee pot after checking it was charged; then he took down two cups and saucers from a side cupboard, also a jug of milk.

"Now then, while that's on, where did I put those photos? Ah, here they are." he said, crossing to the sideboard where a brown paper package rested. He brought it over to the coffee table in front of the sofa where Ellie sat. For the next few minutes they browsed through the snapshots of a building from lots of angles then some interiors. "Very nice." She said, not very enthusiastically, because they just looked like pictures of a building and meant nothing to her.

While drinking their coffee he told her how he intended to build himself a grand house in Dublin soon. "Mark my words Ellie, it's an expanding city. I may even invest in building an hotel there in a few years time, we'll see."

He glanced at the mantle clock and declared it was high time he took her home. As they rose from the sofa he stepped in front of her and placed his hands on her shoulders, then he moved them up to her cheeks, held her face for a moment then he gently kissed her. "You're so easy to talk to Ellie. We get on well together don't we?" Ellie was flustered from the warmth of his kiss and murmured, "I suppose we do."

"It's Sunday tomorrow Ellie, let me take you and May for a drive in the country and we'll have lunch somewhere, how's that?" he spoke like a school boy asking for a treat that she hadn't the heart to say no. "That would be lovely so long as Effie doesn't mind", "Oh, I'm sure she won't mind, I'll see to that don't you worry."

He took her back downstairs and out into the street, across the road to the pub, in through the corner door just as Effie was calling "Time!" As the pub cleared Fred told her that he would like to take Ellie and May out to the country for a lunch the next day to which Effie agreed was a lovely idea. With a quick squeeze of Ellie's hand, he was gone.

"My goodness," said Effie, as she bolted the doors, "He's really got it bad for you, hasn't he?" "What ever do you mean? He's taking us for a drive, that's all." Ellie did not like the idea that a relationship with Fred might be in the offing. "Oh yes, well, I've known Fred Edwards for a long time and he don't take girls out like other chaps do. Employ them, yes. Take the odd one out when he needs a partner, yes. But you, my dear, he's positively smitten." "Don't be daft Effie, you'll be telling me next he's going to ask me to marry him.!" She joked as she helped with the clearing up. "And I wouldn't be surprised at that neither. I think he's been lonely since his Irish wife died and he's really enjoying your company, there's no denying that."

Ellie went up to bed with mixed feelings. Was she ready for another relationship? The pain of loosing Sid was still with her especially when she was alone at night. Would it be disloyal to him?

Fred picked May and Ellie up at Twelve o'clock the

next day and they drove out on to Dartmoor. As they drove along they talked about petrol rationing and the fact that people would not be allowed to travel more than fifteen miles from home for the duration of the war. As they approached Yelverton they saw preparations going on for an airfield; although small, the roads within the cordoned off area from the Rock were being widened into runways with dugouts and shelters. They drove on in glorious sunshine and tried to forget the war as they approached Princetown. As they were getting near they could see an imposing set of buildings behind a huge wall, all built of local grey granite. "What is that over there?" Ellie asked. "That, my dear, is Dartmoor prison." He replied." Some of my best friends have lived there some time or another. "he laughed." Who knows, maybe I'll be popping in for a visit one of these days!" Ellie was not sure what he meant but felt quite disturbed; then they left it behind and turned away towards a charming pub beside a river with two bridges across it. One an old clapper bridge and the new one which they drove over to the charming Two Bridges Hotel. Where they were to have lunch.

As always with Fred, where they went the lunch was simple but perfect. He made it his business to be especially attentive to May who blushed and smiled a lot. When they were in the lounge having their coffee May went outside to explore the clapper bridge and the riverside, leaving Fred to pay attention to Ellie. They had a brandy and he lit a cigar. When they were sitting relaxed and watching May out of the window, Ellie was so pleased to see her daughter enjoying herself, throwing stones into the water and trying to catch a small Dartmoor pony which kept following her but dodging away if she tried to stroke him. Even after Effie's words about Fred the previous night, she was still taken by surprise when he took out a little square box and opened it, revealing a diamond ring. He gathered Ellie's hand in his and looked into her eyes. "Ellie my dear, I know I'm a lot older than you and I've been married before but I can honestly say that I have never been happier than in your company, and I think your daughter is delightful. Do you think you could see your way to marrying me?"

Ellie did not know quite how this made her feel; only that she did not really like saying no. "Oh, Fred, I don't know what to say. I'd like to think about it before I answer. You see there's things you don't know about me, just as there's a lots of things, I'm sure, I don't yet know about you. Will you give me some more time, please?" "At least you're not saying no, that's a good sign." He laughed as he put the ring away in his pocket. "I quite understand my dear, and I won't rush you. But I promise you you'll not get away from me easily." She was not sure how he meant that. Again she remembered what Effie had said about Fred being a man who always got his own way.

They drove across the moor to Buckfastleigh and back to town through Plympton. May slept in the back after all that fresh air. She thanked him politely without prompting as she alighted from his car. He promised to do it again soon.

Ellie confided in Effie that evening and was not really surprised at her less than enthusiastic reaction.

All she said though was "Be sure before you say yes won't you? He's a very different prospect for you." Effie lay in bed that night very worried. She had to admit that she was somewhat afraid of Fred Edwards. He could easily turn her out of the pub if she made him angry. She had known him for many years, long before he rose to owning the Black Rose night club. He started out as a market trader like his father before him, but soon found ways of wheeling and dealing, getting a reputation for acquiring anything a prospective customer required, especially if they weren't too fussy how he went about it. He didn't care who he stepped on in his persuit of wealth.

The tales that had been whispered around over the years had often found their way into Effie's pub. In those days the pub had belonged to an elderly couple and Effie was their barmaid. But Fred made them an offer they couldn't refuse and he bought them out and put Effie in as manager. Knowing that she would be in his debt should the need arise. How he became the owner of the Black Rose night club had always been a closely guarded secret, but before it became Fred's, it was a small card club with a bar and a few slot machines. Effie believed that he won it gambling and probably cheating, but no one really knew. The man he got it from went away very suddenly at any rate, no one knew where. It was soon obvious that a lot of money was spent on it and two months later it opened with a private party for all the local people who mattered; tradesmen and councillors as well as friends.

All his croupiers were men. He would never let women handle money. He always said it was putting too much temptation in their way. Besides, Fred also believed that there were more important uses for women. He had eight very attractive girls working at the club, mainly to keep the customers drinking and to encourage them to gamble

But Effie also knew that they were expected to do more than this; if their boss required them to. In other words, for special clients he had rooms upstairs where they could privately entertain the young lady of their choice. Fred was not a pimp, Oh no. He was much too careful and selective than that. There was much more to gain from accommodating a 'friend' for an hour or two's pleasure. It put them in his power. The hold he could have over certain gentlemen was more in Fred's line.

There was a cleverly disguised door to a staircase leading to these rooms above; decorated to appear as private sittingrooms with large settee beds; all very tasteful which the police had so far never found. Effie was worried that Ellie was going to get drawn into this seamy side of Fred's life, but was also afraid to warn her about it. Then suddenly, a couple of days later, out of the blue, Marty Bridges came into the pub and told them that Fred had unexpectedly returned to Ireland on business. His brother had sent for him he said, also that his wife was anxious for him to come home.

Effie exclaimed, "His wife? But he told us his wife was dead!" At this moment Effie was glad that Ellie was upstairs putting May to bed. "Oh, that's typical of Fred," replied Marty, "He'll say anything to suit his purposes, he will. The greatest lie teller of all time, he is. It wouldn't surprise me if he's been nicked again or at least on the run. The last deal with, well I can't say really, but, it went wrong and he let a bloke down, so it may even be he's running from a disappointed customer. At any rate I don't think we are going to see much of Mister Fred Edwards for a long time to come. I guess it's up to me to hold the fort once again." He laughed. It was a pattern that Marty was used to. An absent boss every now and then.

Effie chose the time to tell Ellie carefully. She decided to tell Ellie everything she knew. She told her that in her opinion she had had a narrow escape. Effie was sorry she hadn't told her everything before but when she explained her position Ellie said she understood. "Let's hope he stays in Ireland for a long time, if that's where he is."

Ellie was off men for some time. But she didn't have much time to worry about it because suddenly Plymouth was plunged into the Blitz.

Things settled in to a routine. Jack at his post on eight hour shifts at the gates of the Dockyard in Fore street, and when not doing this he worked part time in the warehouse in the Octagon. Phyllis had not worked since her illness but felt that it would soon be time to think about a job now Pammy was at school. Then five days before her birthday the Blitz began. The papers said that the night of March 20th 1941 during four hours, a series of attacks from about 100 German bombers dropped 20,000 incendiary bombs and 1,000 explosive bombs, killing hundreds of people and turning the city into a wasteland. It lit up the night sky with fires and searchlights and the terrible noise of gunfire and screeching falling bombs. The next day it continued. Their beloved Pier was destroyed and the Octagon was hit destroying Jack's place of work. During a lull in the raids the next morning they drove there to see if there was anything they could save. It was a mad jumble or rubble, bricks, chairs and pots and pans. Pammy stood on the pavement and called to her mother," Look Mummy, there's a little black dolly under daddy's chair, can I rescue her?" "I'll get her for you darling, don't you come any nearer, it's not safe. Both Jack and Phyllis had sensibly brought their helmets with them. Phyllis climbed carefully over the wreckage and picked up the doll. There was another slightly larger one there too. Jack's office had had a large display of their stock of dolls on some shelves. She also found two soft toys dressed in sailors costumes, they were Laurel and Hardy dolls. Dusting them off she brought them over to Pammy. "Oh thank you Mummy. We've saved them haven't we! Now don't be afraid, I'm going to take you home and clean you up and you can live with me." She took great pride next day in telling all her school friends how they had rescued these poor dolls.

The main priority for Jack and his bosses was to find

somewhere for Hodge and Sons to carry on trading. As it happened, half way down Penlee Road, next to Pellow's yard there was an old yard and livery stables. They had not been in use for some time but Jack thought it would be ideal for the company to use as temporary premises at least until the war was over. It was actually remarkable how much stock was recovered and the quick acquisition of the stables was a God send.

Meanwhile Jack and Phyllis had been very busy during the raids as Air Raid Wardens. When these raids began they still came as a shock, even though everyone had been prepared, they could not have imagined the scale of it all. The sirens were wailing for real this time. Most of these raids were at night. Mabel and Pammy were rushed off into the shelter and Jack and Phyllis would don their helmets and sally forth to put out any incendiary bombs with sandbags or water. In the beginning, many houses near the Dockyard were bombed. Phyllis's father had invested in property there and lost seven houses in one night.

That same week, a bomb hit St. Bartholemews Church next to Somerset Place school. The bomb also demolished the baby's classroom at the top of the playground. Next morning the children stared at the wreckage before going into the main building which was unharmed. The infant's classroom was gone and so was Pammy's doll's house. She wasn't sure whom she was more angry with, Hitler, for sending the bomb, or her Mother for giving it to the school. As she said, "If you hadn't given it away I'd still have my lovely dollies house.!"

Directly across the road from the Church lived Frank and Elsie Cochran and their young son Frankie. The blast from the bomb took out all their windows and knocked down their chimney. The front door was blasted off it's hinges. They were lucky they weren't in their beds for the plaster ceiling in the bedroom came down too. Frank and Elsie had been childhood friends of both Jack and Phyllis so when they were to be temporarily homeless whilst repairs were done, they offered them beds at Mayon.

Now, the problem with that was Elsie. She was one of those women who opened their mouth when they awoke and hardly closed it until they slept again. Frank rarely got a word in edgewise. It was Elsie's habit to drop in on Phyllis of an afternoon for a cup of tea and a gossip or perhaps it was more of a monologue. She knew everybody's business and was not slow in passing it on. Not maliciously, it has to be said, she just couldn't help herself. How to stop the flow was the problem. "Don't you think it's time you went home to get Frank's tea?" rarely worked. She was often still in full flow when Jack returned from work. It very often had to be as obvious as, "Well I'm sorry to chuck you out Elsie but I really must get Jack's meal on the table, Cheerio." And see her to the door before she could start up again.

So when Phyllis told Jack that the Cockrans would be moving in whilst their house was put in order, he blanched in dismay. "Where are we going to put them?" he asked nervously. "Well", said Phyllis, "I thought they'd have our room and we'll use the put you up in the front room and we'll put Frankie in Pammy's room and she'll have to come in with us on the camp bed." "How are you going to stand her yapping?" he wailed. "It's alright for you Jack, you'll be out to work all day, I'll have her here with me all day long!" "You're braver than me my love." He said. And so the next day the Cochran family moved in. Elsie never stopped wittering on about the bomb and the fright they had had and how the cat had run off and the mess of the house.

After three days Phyllis's patience was wearing thin. In bed that night she said," Oh, Jack! I don't know how much more I can stand, I really do feel sorry for her, I mean, it was a frightful scare and she's worried about her cat and young Frankie keeps complaining because he hasn't got the right school books. Then you went out this evening with Frank and left me to it some more!" "I'm sorry love, but I felt sorry for him too. He has to listen to it every day. I don't know how he does it, so I took him up to the A.R.P. club house for a game of darts."

"Well, how long did he say it's going to be before the work on their house is done?"

"Well, it should be habitable by the end of the week but the work won't be finished for another two."

"I just hope my temper holds together, that's all." Phyllis said this with little faith in her will power.

The next day, after sharing the kitchen and the ironing board and trying to listen to the news on the radio against Elsie's non stop flow, Phyllis could feel the moment getting nearer when she would explode. The last straw came when Elsie said for the umpteenth time, "it's alright for you Phyllis, your house didn't get bombed did it? It's not fair, why should it have been our house, that's what I can't understand! It's not fair!" Then it happened. "For God's sake Elsie, SHUT UP!" Silence. Elsie did shut up. She stared at Phyllis for a moment then quietly left the room and went into the bedroom where she closed the door. Some two hours later both Frank and Jack came home from work and the silence which met them was truly palpable. They came through to the kitchen where Phyllis confessed and apologized to Frank. "I'm afraid I've upset Elsie; she's in the bedroom, she won't talk to me." "Lucky you" muttered Jack. "I'm afraid I just flipped and told her to shut up! I'm really sorry Frank." "Don't you worry old love." He said. "somebody was bound to say it sooner or later. It won't do her any harm. Anyway, I'm delighted to tell you that our house will be habitable again the day after tomorrow, so we'll be going back." "Oh, dear Frank, you're a darling; you ought to be mad at me but you're not. Go and tell Elsie I'm sorry would you?" she asked. "Certainly not!" replied Frank. "I'm sure it will do her good to be told once in a while. I often wish I'd done it years ago!"

Elsie spoke hardly a word until they were leaving on the Friday, when she thanked them both for their kindness. Off they went back to their patched up house and everything returned to normal. Within a week Elsie was back for her weekly cup of tea and a gossip as though it had never happened. "Talk about water off a duck's back" commented Jack when he came home to find her in full flow as strongly as ever. Phyllis was glad of the excuse though that she would be starting work the next week. Jack's secretary had joined up in the Wrens so Phyllis was going to take her place for the duration. So Elsie would have to find someone else to share her chats with, at least for the time being.

They all got quite used to broken nights with two, sometimes three in a night. One morning at breakfast Pammy said to her daddy, "Fancy us having no air raids last night Daddy." "No air raids?" replied Jack. "You're getting so used to them that you didn't wake up when I carried you down to the shelter and put you back to bed afterwards. No air raids indeed! I did that three times young lady!" They laughed about it often. As everyone did laugh about the strange adventures people were having in the crazy world of the Blitz. If it didn't involve actually getting killed folks managed to see the funny side of most things. Like one night, in the middle of a particularly heavy run of air raids, Jack and Phyllis went out as usual as soon as the sirens sounded with their tin hats on and in whatever they had been wearing before. Phyllis was often caught wearing her fur coat. There was no time to change clothes. On this night they grabbed their stirrup pump and shovel ready to extinguish any incendiary bombs that might fall in their area. Stores of water were always standing by wherever they could be placed. Sometimes it was necessary to cover such a bomb with soil or sand. They had been trained in the most efficient way to carry this out. So, picture the scene; a dark night illuminated only by searchlights and gun fire from the nearby gun implacement in the park., Phyllis, in her fur coat and tin hat, trying to bury an offending incendiary with the correct rhythmic movement, but adding her own extra ones; One-dig shovel in ground, two: push up glasses, three: push up helmet from eyes, four: lift soil, Five: soil on bomb. This training called for three movements but Phyllis being so little, her hat was too big and it would push her glasses down her nose., hence five movements instead of three much to Jack's amusement. Another night, in the darkness, Phyllis could hear Jack calling for a bucket of water. She rushed off to the horse trough at the top of the field where there was always a bucket, filled it and set off to find Jack. She kept calling and he kept answering but she was having trouble locating him, slopping the water from the bucket as she struggled along. Finally when she at last found him with her now less than half full bucket of water, he said, "Where the hell have you been? I've put it out with soil now!" and promptly tipped out the rest of the water much to Phyllis's disgust.

Biddie had died just before the War began so the family had another airdale called Rex. Like many dogs it seemed as though he had a sixth sense whenever as air raid was due and where ever he was, he would be back inside his kennel well before the siren had stopped.

After a particularly tiring night with several raids and no chance of any sleep, the all clear finally went just before dawn. The intrepid wardens returned home to Mayon exhausted and very surprised to hear peels of laughter coming from the shelter. Pammy and Mabel had been playing a mime game, guessing what the other was doing. Mabel had been pretending to apply lipstick and Pammy shouted out "Lipsticking!" the word struck them both as funny and they laughed so much that they didn't hear the all clear!

The whole family were very lucky. No one was killed or injured. Though they certainly had a couple of close calls. Jack was returning from the A.R.P. wardens clubhouse down Park Street and had reached the T junction near the bottom of Penlee Road, when a bomb fell in the garden on the other side of the twelve foot high wall opposite. As Jack threw himself to the ground and covered his head with his arm the bomb blew the wall apart. The hail of stones showered down all around him. When the noise died down he stood up. There, in the centre of the road where he had been laying was the clear shape of his body surrounded by huge stones. Some of them quite near where his head had been. It was a tale often told of his good fortune.

The only enemy aircraft to be shot down and actually crash within the city happened at the top of Penlee Road only two hundred yards from Number Three Mayon Cottages. Phyllis was coming down the stairs with Pammy on the way to the shelter when they heard the horrendous noise of the plane diving. Instinctively, Phyllis knew she had not time to reach the shelter so she pushed Pammy into the corner of the front bedroom and threw herself on top of her, holding her close to the wall. They listened as the plane roared up the street at chimney pot level. At the top of the road it banked and crashed into the front garden of the big house at the end, where it burst into flames. Fortunately it had dropped all it's bombs so did not explode. When Phyllis stood up she saw that Pammy was crying. "It's alright darling, it's all over, you're quite safe, don't cry." Pammy replied, "I'm not scared now Mummy, but I'm crying because you pushed me down on one of my roller skates and it's been sticking into my bottom, and it hurt!"

They both laughed as Phyllis hurried her out to the shelter where she left her with Mabel., grabbing her helmet she hurried up the road to see if she would be needed. She was the first warden to appear on the scene but many of the public were coming out to see the sight. It was up to her to keep the crowd back from danger until the police and soldiers arrived.

It was certainly a spectacular sight to see. Two German airmen came down with the plane. The pilot had not got out in time and his body could be seen still sitting up in his cockpit completely burned. The other had parachuted too late and had got caught in a tree a few yards away. Falling to the ground but leaving a leg hanging in the branches. He died very quickly afterwards and was taken away by an ambulance but it was very strange to witness how some people reacted. This was the closest most of them had come to the enemy and seeing the blood and skin tissue of the German at the foot of the tree, they paraded past, stopping to stare and some of them spat on it. An impulsive reaction to all the horrors these bombers had inflicted on their beloved city.

After a break of just a few weeks, the company moved in to the stables in Penlee Road, and were soon able to start trading again. Mr Hodge had recently died so it was re-named Harris and Company Limited after the new managing Director. Jack had his own office and because it was so near to home it was easy for Phyllis to keep his office ticking over when ever he was on duty as policeman on the Dockyard gates.

Gate duty could be very dangerous indeed for the Dockyards were a main target. One bomb just missed the gates and hit the pub on the corner. The oil tanks across the river at Torpoint were hit several times lighting up the sky for miles around. Charlotte said that they used to stand outside the cottage at Gunnislake and watch the sky all lit up during the raids.

Along with garden railings which were carted off to the munitions factories to make shells, lawns were vanishing everywhere. Like many people Grandpa Baker helped Jack plant the back garden with potatoes. Everyone did their bit to provide food for their families. Ration books allowed only the bare essentials. Then Jack had a stroke of luck. The big houses in Penlee Gardens opposite Mayon, behind the high wall, had enormous back gardens and the owner of number eleven told Jack he could use it as an allotment. He himself was away and the house was being used for billeting Wrens. They, of course as service personel had special rations; much better than the general public and their food waste bins were a great source of food for the chickens and geese that Jack kept there. The big house at the top of the road where the German plane had crashed had a large reserve water tank in it's back garden surrounded by a wilderness of grass, ideal for the herd of geese to graze during the day. Pammy thought it great fun to help her Father shepherd them back and forth to their pens each evening. It was quite a spectacle.

1941

The continuous bombings and the need to keep ones family safe was everyone's priority. Union Street, being not far from the docks had several hits on it's buildings but their pub, The Red Dog, and the Palace Theatre opposite stood firm. Each night when the sirens went off everyone in the pub rushed down into the cellar and shut themselves in behind the strong extra door Effie's husband Bill had put up. Some nights there were so many raids they spent the whole night down there; but they had everything they needed so put up with it. Anything was better than being caught outside at these times. Even falling shrapnel could be a danger.

As time went on Ellie occasionally went out with some-one but her experience with Fred as well as the constant pain of loosing her husband made her very depressed. She would often return to her room and seek out the bottle for comfort and would cry herself to sleep until the next time the sirens would rend the night once again. As her depres-sion deepened, her temper sometimes turned to bouts of violence. If her bottle was found empty she would throw it across the room where it would smash noisily, frightening May if she was nearby. As the drink took hold, she became less steady handed and would often drop a glass or a cup which would anger her enough to throw more at it.

Ellie abandoned all her friends, even Cathy. She could not bare to watch her friend who was so happy in her marriage now, with two lovely children. May would often slip away there, especially if her Mother brought a man up to the flat. This was something she began to do more and more as her drinking increased. Effie tried to help her but Ellie was in no mood to take advice. She behaved herself reasonably well when she was working although she still was drinking more even in her working hours. One evening when May was eleven, she came back from Cathy's and accidentally walked in on Ellie and a soldier, half drunk, groping one another on the settee. As May gasped loudly, Ellie sat up and yelled at her, "Get out! Get out! You spying little sneak!" She threw an empty bottle across the room as May dodged back and ran down the passage to her room. The soldier grabbed his clothes and straightened his uniform quickly before running down the stairs and out of the building, slamming the door behind him, leaving Ellie sobbing and swearing. The yelling brought Effie to the stairs as the man rushed by her. She hurried upstairs to find May cringing behind a chair as her Mother could be heard throwing things, anything she could grab, and at that moment her hand closed over the handle of the carving knife. She burst into May's room and began to brandish the knife at her." It's all your fault! If I hadn't had you none of this would have happened!" She threw the knife and it stuck into the woodwork of the fireplace. Effie stepped forward and slapped Ellie across the face. "Stop it! Do you hear me? Ellie, for God's sake! You'll kill your child, or yourself!" she said as she shook her. May ran to Effie who pushed her out the door and sent her downstairs to her husband who was standing on the lower landing. "Aunty wil come in a minute darling, go down with Uncle Bill." But she did not go all the way down but lingered to listen. By then Ellie had gone back into her sittingroom sobbing and looking for a bottle that might not be empty. When she found one and started to drink Effie tried to take it away from her, "Don't you dare!" growled Ellie. Effie sighed and sat down on the settee beside her. "Oh, Ellie, my love, what are you doing to yourself? You can't go on like this, you really can't. I know how you feel but…." "Oh, no you don't!" interrupted Ellie. "How can you know how I feel? I can't stand any more! I lost my husband and my little baby! Even Fred didn't really want me! Nothing ever goes right. Now I just know damn Hitler is going to take away everything else!" She sank down and sobbed piteously.

"Oh, my God, Ellie. Don't! Don't!" Effie did not know what to do to help her except to hold her in her arms. After a while Ellie fell asleep on the sofa. Effie covered her over with a blanket and then crept downstairs to May.

Something had to be done, that was clear. The child could not stay in the house with Ellie in her condition. Effie sat down and wrote a note to Cathy, then sent May round there with a few of her things, then she sent her husband to fetch Doctor Joseph. When he came she took him up to her own sittingroom and explained the situation. He listened and said "Well, I'll examine her later, but it seems to me she needs to go into a sanitarium for some treatment. What do you think about that?" "That sounds like the best thing, Doctor. But what about May? She's supposed to leave Junior school and go to the High School next term. Bless her, she did very well in her eleven plus exams. She's such a bright child, always reading, you know?" "Yes, well, she won't be able to live here if her Mother does go away. I'm sure you have a lot on your hands running this pub Mrs Evans will be away a long time I'm afraid. Have you talked to Sister Josephine about it?"

"No, but I will later this afternoon" said Effie, feeling much better having the Doctor's sensible support.

When they had finished talking Doctor Joseph went

upstairs and woke Ellie and gave her an examination and then they talked over some coffee Ellie managed to make. At first Ellie was troublesome but soon after the alcohol wore off a little she conceded that she did need help and agreed to go right away to the sanitorium for rest and treatment. The Doctor went off to make arrangements telling them to be prepared for a car to collect Ellie later in the day. Effie helped her pack. They didn't say much but Effie assured her that May would be well taken care of. Ironically, May was not uppermost in Ellie's mind.

In an hour the car came and took Ellie to the Crownhill Sanitorium where they made her comfortable. Back in the pub Effie had a long discussion with Sister Josephine on what would be the best way forward for May.

The most important thing was, where could she live as well as where would she go to school?

St'Peter's had it's own private High School but with no boarding facilities., but only one road away, in North Road was St'Dunstan's Abbey. Also a private school and with boarders. Though it was closed to boarders for the duration of the war. It was not a catholic school but very high Protestant. Not that this was a concern. The nuns of both establishments often worked closely together. Sister Josephine took it upon herself to arrange an interview with the Mother Superior as soon as possible. This she did two days later and they agreed that May's circumstances warranted some bending of the rules. It was agreed to, that before term started May could move into her lovely little room above the enclosed garden used for silent meditation by the sisters. There were lay teachers who came daily as well as the nuns who also taught.

When she had settled in May felt the tranquility and calm that pervaded the old buildings especially the beautiful chapel and for the first time in ages felt at peace.

Meanwhile her Mother began the long process of drying out. Although the depression became worse. They tried sleep treatment which proved to be only a temporary success. This continued for many months. Then after a while they began to think she was improving and allowed her to go out for short walks in the fresh air.

But one day, in poor weather she went out and did not return. She had walked up onto the moors and got lost in the fog and rain. When they found her she was suffering from Hypothermia and developed Pneumonia from which she never recovered.

Ellie Evans died on March 17th 1942.

1942

One morning at breakfast, Jack had an amazing tale to tell the family.

"I came off duty at 2.a.m." he began, "and started to cycle up Fore Street when I saw thousands of rats crossing the road." After the family had all reacted in various ways he continued; "Naturally I got off and climbed out of the way and stood up on top of a wall and watched. A bomb had hit a water main in last night's raid, also the sewer must have been hit, so all these rats were suddenly homeless. They waited for the quietest time just before dawn, then set off all together to cross Devonport in search of another sewer to live in, in peace. Probably down in the creek that comes out under Ha'penny bridge., that would be the nearest I should think. I have never seen a sight like it before and I doubt I ever shall again. There really were thousands." Being females, the rest of the family could have done without being told about it at all and everyone hoped that it wouldn't give Pammy nightmares. Actually what she said was, "Was the Pied Piper anywhere around Daddy?" which made everyone laugh.

It seemed to be the week for rats because on Friday night Jack and young Terry Ross from number one and the dog Rex of course, decided to go rat hunting. They had been causing concern around the dustbins and nibbling at the sacks of potatoes in Pellows yard. Halfway down Penlee Road just beyond Harris's warehouse, where Jack worked,

143

was a large gate which led to an old disused stone quarry that stretched along the back of the old stables and behind Pellow's potato fields. Because it was no longer in use the council had decided to take it over and fill it in; they would then reclaim the land for building prefabs, the temporary bungalows to re-house those people who were bombed out of their homes. Unfortunately the refuse attracted the rats. Not that anyone had seen rats coming into their gardens but Jack thought that rat hunting now and then would help to keep the numbers down as well as provide some sport.

Terry's Gran was appalled at the idea and tried to persuade his Mother to stop him. But Lil said that he would be fine as long as he was with Jack. Sometimes Terry's school chum, Stan, from Park Street would join them and off they would set with lanterns and cudgels at the ready, complete with Rex who couldn't wait for the chase to start.

Phyllis didn't object but insisted that Jack have a bath as soon as he got in, which was just as well as they stank of rubbish., and on no account ever to bring any dead rats home! Lil agreed!

The long spells of bad raids were beginning to tell on everyone. Jack was holding down two jobs and working as chief warden. He was a sergeant now in the Marine Police so he had more responsibilies both there and at the office; the staff had depleted through the call up of more men so the warehouse was short staffed. He was also in charge of ordering stock. Though Phyllis was a God send. She was always one step ahead of him and kept everything running like clockwork, so that he only had to talk about a problem and she would get it sorted out. But they both worried a lot about Pammy. Were they being selfish keeping her with them? She was nine now and in the Junior school. So many of her class mates had been evacuated or sent away to relatives outside the city. The bombing had been very bad and although Penlee Road houses had not been hit, perhaps they had been too complacent about their daughter's safety. Maybe it was time to send her to Gunnislake with Charlotte. They talked about it that evening after their meal whilst Pammy was doing her homework with Mabel. When they told Mabel how they felt she said, "Well, you know I'm here with her, but you must worry about her when the raids are on. I know I would if Charlotte were here."

When they told Pammy she said "Oh, Mummy, I don't want to go!" "Now, now, darling, don't make a fuss". Phyllis soothed her daughter with a cuddle. "It wouldn't be for long and you know very well these raids are making life very hard". "I know, but Aunty Mabel looks after me.!" She persisted. Jack looked up and said the clincher, "Not when she goes to visit Charlotte she can't. No, let's not argue about it any more. I've decided. We are going to take you to Gunnislake tomorrow. It's Sunday and we can set out early and make a real day of it. I killed a couple of rabbits yesterday, we can take them with us and Aunty Harriet can make us one of her delicious rabbit pies." "There's plenty of vegetables in her garden but I think we ought to take some, and some of our eggs." "They won't be expecting us will they? That's a good idea." added Mabel.

So the next morning they got up at six thirty after what had been, thankfully, a raid free night, soon packed Pammy's things in the boot of the car and were off to drive across the moors to Tavistock and to Gunnislake. Over the old bridge across the Tamar and up the hill into the village.

As they turned into the lane by the house, Bill was kicking his football against the wall and Doreen was helping her Mother dig up some potatoes. "You'd better dig a few more, I've got some hungry beggers here." Shouted Jack as he got out of his car. They welcomed them warmly, especially

Charlotte who cried as she hadn't seen Pammy for a long time. "Oh, my lovely darling! How I've missed you! Come and give your old Charley Barley a kiss!" They cuddled and kissed one another and Pammy said, "You can cuddle me lots now'cos Daddy says I've got to stay. The bombing is getting worse you know!" "Will it be alright Aunt Harriet?" asked Jack. "I should have written and asked you first, but we only decided last night. We can take her home if it's not." "Bless you, of course she can stay. Charlotte is sleeping in with me and Pammy can sleep in the little camp bed. That's no trouble." "Another bloomin' girl in the house! I'm going to move into the privy!" said Bill. They all shrieked with laughter. "Oh good," said young Joan, "I've been dying to bung you down the toilet for years!"

The rabbit pie was a great success and there was indeed plenty of vegetables. The children had a great time playing with Bill's trolley on the hill, until suddenly the grownups heard a scream and shouting. They rushed outside to find both Pammy and Bill hurtling down the hill on the trolly much too fast and ending up at the bottom of the hill in the river.

They weren't hurt but they were very wet and had to be taken indoors and cleaned up, warmed by the fire and dressed in clean clothes. "What a great start!" exclaimed Jack. "Are you sure it's safe to leave her?" he laughed. "Oh, don't you worry. Bill isn't usually that stupid." said his Mother. "Oh, I didn't mean him," said Jack, "I meant my bundle of mischief!" "Dad! It wasn't my fault the brake handle broke!" shouted Pammy.

When it was time for Mabel, Jack and Phyllis to leave, there were lots of tears, but they promised to try and visit every Sunday if Jack wasn't on duty. It would be a lot easier for Mabel now, as several of her journeys had been very difficult. Twice she had caught the bus to Tavistock only to find that the connecting bus had already gone and she had walked the five miles to Gunnislake in the dark. Traveling with Jack in his car would be a luxury. Though the shortage of petrol may make it difficult for them to come every weekend.

Pammy soon settled into village life. She went to the junior school with Joan and Bill although in a lower class. Being an only child she enjoyed living with her cousins. It was difficult at first learning to share things like toys and books and even clothes sometimes, especiallyl socks. Noone could work out why, until one day they found out. She used to come home from school a different way sometimes where she paddled through a stream carrying her shoes and socks round her kneck tied together with the socks stuffed into the shoes. Sometimes a sock would fall out. Doreen found one there when she was on her paper round.

Every Wednesday evening the village hall was transformed into a cinema. Everyone would go along and watch the latest Pathe news reels along with Laurel and Hardy and Roy Rogers films. Sometimes Mr Wills, the projectionist, managed to get some cartoons. The news reels were a bit out of date but better than nothing, for the residents were virtually cut off from late night visits to Tavistock as the buses were even less frequent than before fuel rationing made economies necessary and if a bus wasn't likely to be full, it was taken off.

After the picture show was over the family would troop out to the chip shop and have two pennys worth of chips and a bottle of ginger beer, a great treat.

Some evenings they would stop and watch the night sky over Plymouth. They could hear the guns and see the searchlights flickering across the sky like fireflies catching the silver barrage balloons in their beams. Pammy said, "It looks pretty from here but it's very scary down there, I can tell you!" On nights like those she would say her prayers for her parents extra hard.

Many of her new school chums would gather round her at playtime and listen to her graffic tales of the Blitz. The most popular story she had to repeat many times was of the night when the German plane came down, "only inches above our heads!" she would explain dramatically.

That Christmas of 1942, the whole family came together briefly, in number one Sims Terrace. Jack Phyllis and Mabel were not able to stay overnight as there was no room. Uncle Bill was home on leave so the little house was crowded. The table heaved with good food in spite of rationing. Things had been especially saved. Jack killed the largest goose and brought it the week before. Of course they had no spices or dried fruit to make a Christmas pudding but they had apples so Harriet had made lots of apple dumplings. Everyone had more than enough to eat.

Jack and Phyllis gave Pammy a toy magic lantern show with slides of Snow White and the Seven Dwarfs and some Mickey Mouse as well. That evening they blacked out the back room and hung a sheet up on the side of the stairs. The little room was crowded when they all squeezed in to see their own little picture show. Pammy stood in the doorway and collected pennies for their tickets to come in and Joan had a torch to show them to their seats, while Bill pretended to sell icecreams in the intervals

It was a jolly day and a welcome break for Jack and Phyllis from the pressures of the Blitz. "Look for us next Sunday darling." Said her Mother as they kissed goodbye. "I'll be waiting for you on the old stone bridge. Doreen says I can walk along the river path and meet you there." "That's wonderful. It will be about eleven o'clock, I expect. Now be good and help your Aunties clear up after we've gone." But Harriet and Charlotte would have none of it. "No helpers needed!" they both declared. "We can get it done quicker on our own. Off to bed with you. Uncle Bill will read you a story from one of your new books, won't you?" she asked him. "Only if they get to bed quick, or I might fall asleep before you're ready." He teased. The children all dashed up the wooden stairs rushing to be the first in bed.

After six months of being away from Mayon, Pammy began to grow homesick. She went off her food and that worried Harriet. It was so unlike her, she was a child with a good healthy appetite and for her to refuse a meal must surely be a serious sign that something was wrong. Charlotte took her to the village surgery to see the Doctor and he confirmed that physically she was fine but that the signs were definitely that of home sickness. Only one cure, to send her home.

The following Sunday Pammy met her parents and Mabel at the bridge as usual as she climbed into the car she burst into tears, as her Mother cuddled her. When they got to the house Harriet explained the problem.

"Well," said Jack, "It's not quite so bad now; Jerry seems to be running out of bombs. If you think it's best we'll take her home. What do you think Phil?" "I won't deny I miss her terribly. It would be wonderful to have her back home again." So without delay they told Pammy that she could go and pack and come home that very day. No child ever tidied up her things and packed so fast! She was smiling again, and ate her dinner properly for the first time in days. Charlotte was the only sad one. She wanted to come home too but Mabel was not so accommodating. "No Charlotte, not yet. It won't be long now, besides Harriet needs you more than I do. She hasn't been too well lately." Charlotte knew better than to argue with Mabel, once she had made up her mind. She wanted to be sure that the Blitz was really over.

They had been very lucky. The house had only suffered minor damage. A couple of windows and a chimney pot, although two of the big houses in Penlee Gardens had been hit by incendiaries. Mabel's school in Devonport had not been so fortunate and temporary classrooms had been erected in the school yard, though nothing ever stopped Mabel from attending. She never missed a day, even if she had to walk the two miles to school, nothing would have prevented her from being there for her children.

On returning home that summer, Pammy began to take up her favourite pastimes once again. Life with three cousins had been great fun, but as an only child she had always enjoyed her solitary hobbies of drawing and making things. She was very artistic, a talent she had inherited from Grandfather Henry. He had made the most beautiful model yacht when he was at sea between the two world wars and when fully rigged stood over four foot high. Jack had sailed it behind the 'Pickles' many times in Plymouth sound. Henry had also done some lovely etchings of the Royal Chapel at Windsor as well as several water colour paintings.

Pammy was never happier than when she was doodling or making something out of nothing. Once when she was in bed poorly, she had a shoe box and some bits and scraps and made her own tiny dolls house. The first Christmas after returning from Gunnislake she persuaded her father to give her some plain tooth mugs from the warehouse and she painted them with Disney characters for her cousins for presents. On returning to school she discovered that her chums were going to put on a concert in the empty top floor of her friend's house to raise money to buy wool for their Mothers who were knitting socks for soldiers. They persuaded Pammy to join them and she agreed to learn a song called Animal Crackers. It was a Shirley Temple number. Her Father helped her practice but when the day came to do it at the concert. She was overcome with stage fright and ran home in terror.

Having been away from town for six months when the Blitz was at it's worst, seeing the city in ruins was a great shock. Lots had been bombed before she went of course, but to see vast areas of the centre bulldozed to make it safe was distressing. The old pier was gone; her lovely skating rink and many of the beautiful shops and civic buildings that used to stand so proudly in the city centre were just rubble. Shortly after her parents had taken her to Gunnislake, Grandfather Baker had retired from his job as Devonport Park keeper and taken his wife to live in Plympton where it was safer. One weekend they went there to visit them. Of course Pammy hadn't seen her grandmother for some time and was shocked to see how frail she looked. Phyllis explained that Granny had been very ill that year with her lungs and it had taken all her strength to get better. They were delighted to see each other and talked until Mother said she mustn't tire her Grandmother too much. So they left after tea.

One Friday evening a couple of weeks later, Phyllis and Jack received a telegram from her Father to say that her Mother was seriously ill and to come at once. They left Pammy in Mabel's care and drove off to Plympton.

The Doctor was there with Herbert as they came in. "I'm afraid that your Mother is suffering from severe stomach pains and due to her weak lungs after the bout of pneumonia she had a few months ago any medication I might give her would kill her." Phyllis was horrified. "Is there nothing you can do Doctor?" "I'm afraid not my dear. You must face the fact that your Mother is dying. I will be back in the morning."

Phyllis and Jack rushed up the stairs as Herbert let the Doctor out the front door. Mary Ellen lay in the large double bed. "We can't let her just die Jack!" exclaimed Phyllis. "That Doctor's a fool!" Herbert returned to the room and told them how she had been. "As you know, your Mother doesn't eat much but lately her food has been choking up her stomach and giving her a lot of pain. The Doctor says she'll be gone by morning and there's nothing we can do. He has left me some sleeping powder for her to sleep away." "Nonsense Father! We've got to do something. We can't let her suffer like this! If she's constipated we can deal with that." "But the Doctor said it would kill her my dear!" Herbert was distraught and slumped into a armchair and began to sob. "Jack, take Father downstairs and set him to make some tea. Then go and find a chemist and buy some laxatives. I'm not going to sit here and watch my Mother die!" As Jack took Herbert downstairs Phyllis prepared herself for a long night. She turned out the linen closet and set out sheets and towels and fetched a bucket and soap. When Jack returned with the medication Phyllis prepared a double dose. "For God sakes Phil! You'll kill her!" "Don't be a fool Jack, if you believe the Doctor she's dead already! There's only one way to deal with this. Now you go down and look after Dad and keep plenty of water on the boil." Jack left her to it in the full knowledge that when Phyllis was determined nothing or no one would dare interfere.

It was a long night. About half an hour after Phyllis had given her Mother the strong dose of laxative thing certainly got moving. We will not go into the sordid details but suffice to say that Phyllis did not get much rest as she constantly washed and changed her Mother and tried to keep her comfortable, making her drink lots of water. At about four o'clock things slowed down and Mary Ellen seemed to be resting more easily. Phyllis dropped into a chair and fell asleep exhausted. Well, at least her Mother hadn't died. The morning would show whether she had killed or cured her.

At eight o'clock the door bell rang. It was the Doctor returning. He did not even climb the stairs but went into the sitting room where Jack and Herbert had spent the night. He opened his Gladstone bag and took out his death certificate pad and his pen, preparing to write, as Phyllis entered the room. "You can put that away Doctor, Mother is going to live, no thanks to you!" She then explained what she had done. "But you might have killed her!" he said, very shocked that anyone should disobey his instructions. "But you told me she'd be dead by this morning and she isn't, is she!" said Phyllis triumphantly. "You'd better come upstairs and see for yourself." He followed her up the stairs into the bedroom and stopped in his tracks. There was Mary Ellen resting against her pillows sipping a cup of tea. "Well young lady, I can only say you have done a miracle. Nothing less."

"No Doctor, not a miracle," said Jack, " It's just that Phyllis is a stubborn woman. She wasn't going to let her Mother die without a fight." "And I won!" laughed Phyllis.

Mrs Withers Music Academy was in a large three story house in Stoke village. The owner was a widow and she had turned every room in her house, except the top floor where she lived, into a classroom. She had five pianos one for each room. The best piano, a baby grand, was in the frontroom where she herself taught; the second room had a good quality upright which was where Mrs Williams came in to teach four afternoons a week. In the back diningroom was another upright where pupils were sent to practice and out in the wash house was an old upright where naughty children were sent to do extra practice.

There was another piano upstairs where Mrs Withers taught very special students, mainly adults during the evenings. On Saturday mornings children came for one hours theory class.

Pammy did not like Mrs Withers and much preferred her lessons with Mrs Williams as she was much kinder. Mrs Withers had been known to wrap pupils over the knuckles with a ruler if they did not keep time or play too many wrong notes. After Pammy had been back to her lessons for a while, Phyllis thought it would be nice to take up lessons again herself and so she arranged to have one lesson a week at the same time as Pammy. So Pammy got used to having a lesson in the back room whilst her Mother had hers in the front room with Mrs Withers. Therefore she was naturally quite horrified one afternoon to overhear her Mother being wrapped over the knuckles as if she were a naughty child. As they both left to go home Pammy noticed the tears in her Mother's eyes. "Did she hurt you Mummy?" Pammy asked taking her Mother's hand and looking at the red marks that the ruler had left. "Yes dear it does hurt and if she does it again I may be in danger of breaking it over her head." Which is exactly what happened the following week. So Pammy and her Mother left the music Academy for good. Shortly afterward one of the last bombs to fall on Stoke fell on the Music Academy and killed Mrs Withers in her bed.

Mrs Williams made it known that she would give lessons in people's houses at an hourly rate and thereafter began to call at Mayon every Wednesday afternoon at four o'clock to teach Pammy, then Phyllis. These lessons were much more enjoyable than those run by the deceased Mrs Withers. Mrs Williams never felt it necessary to wrap any of her pupils knuckles. In fact she had a charming and encouraging nature which led Pammy to absolutely love all her lessons. As an only child Pammy treated the baby grand almost like a beloved member of the family. It was never a chore for her to practice and so she progressed very well with her grades very much to everyone's delight. In fact Mother and daughter often learnt to play duets together.

1943

Not so her schooling unfortunately. Mabel had always helped her with her reading and writing which was of a good standard, but poor Pammy could not get on with Arithmatic at all. The system of chanting tables was the only thing that saved her from complete disaster. These, she could trot out to order like all of her class mates, but when it came to actually working out sums, she came to grief more often than not. Her parents were very concerned that she might not do well when it came the time for her to sit the eleven plus. She liked to read but truth to tell, Pammy would rather draw or make things than do sums.

The bombing raids were not so frequent now but certainly not over. Just when everyone thought things were quietening down St. Augustines Church was destroyed.

The Americans were in the war with us by this time and for some, it was their first taste of war when their ships sailed into Plymouth Sound. One group were surprised to see Jack and his Marine Police collegues were armed. Of course the Americans were used to carrying guns at home and a large Texan bragged of his prowess with his six gun and challenged any one of Jack's men to a contest. Little knowing that there was a Bisley champion amongst Jack's friends. They soon stopped their bragging when they lost the contest but they took it in a friendly spirit and rewarded Jack and his friends with tins of fruit; something which had not been seen in Plymouth shops for a very long time.

That Christmas there was a great shortage of decorations in the shops. Factories had other more important work to do than make such things and imports were down to zero. Pammy read in a magazine how to make coloured streamers with crepe paper and shearing elastic on a sewing machine and went into production! She threw herself into the enterprise, running up stretch streamers at a great rate on Mother's sewing machine. Father had a new secretary now and Mother was offered a job managing a hardware and general shop in Union Street, which belonged to a friend who was opening another shop in Peverell. So Pammy bought the crepe paper wholesale from her Father's warehouse then sold the streamers in Mother's shop.

The decorations went like hot cakes and Pammy earned enough money to buy all her family Christmas presents. It gave her a thrill to be so independent.

During the spring a shop keeper from Looe complained to Jack that it was impossible to buy decorated tourist items any more because many of those who used to produce these items were off fighting in the war, or working in munitions factories. Only plain jugs and trays were available. This gave Jack an idea that Pammy might like. "How about painting a few jugs and trays for this chap? Do you think you could do it? He'll pay you of course." "Oh Dad! What a good idea! I'll give it a try." So Jack brought home some black bakelite trays and some brown earthenware jugs which she set about decorating with seagulls and flowers and 'a gift from Looe' written on them. The shopkeeper was thrilled and paid her handsomely. He would have ordered a lot more but Jack did not want Pammy to get too involved, her schooling had to come first, but he did not want to stifle her sense of enterprise. Just doing enough to let her earn some pocket money and some in the bank. Phyllis warned Jack not to let this interfere with her homework; "I know she loves painting and making things but I am worried about her lessons, they mustn't be neglected." "Alright, I'll keep it down," said Jack, "but don't stop her. She's so happy. Besides, she's darn good at it!"

One Sunday they drove up to Totnes to visit Phyllis's sister Winnie and her family. They were all delighted to see each other and whilst the grown ups chatted over a pot of tea the children went up to their huge attic playroom to play John's favourite game of dressing up. He was very hung up on the idea of going into the priesthood one day and loved playing at being a bishop. So they all dressed up. Pammy being the eldest was the arch bishop who would perform the ceremony, Mary who was eight was the Queen, with Susan aged five carrying the train. After they had exhausted that game they went downstairs to turn out their Mother's sewing box to find some buttons to play with. While they were doing this they dropped a needle. They all went down on their knees to find it. Mary found it all right, with her leg. The needle broke and a part of it went into her leg. She screamed and in no time Jack was whisking her off to the local hospital. Poor Pammy being the eldest got the blame. Her Mother said she should have known not to let anyone kneel down to look for the needle. However, Mary soon returned with the piece removed and a bandaged leg to show off. After they all had tea Jack and his family drove home. Pammy was never to forget that incident and was always careful to keep needles safely in her pincushion.

The war was hotting up all over Europe. At home the factories were working very hard to provide the tools for the job.

Grandma and Grandpa Baker came back from their rented house in Plympton when it was damaged by an unexploded bomb which had been buried for several months in the garden opposite, went off. Fortunately it did not kill anyone but did quite a lot of damage to the houses. They bought a terraced house in Peverell across the park from Mayon. It was approaching the time of their golden wedding anniversary and Phyllis and her sister were determined to give them both a memorable day. Fortunately Cecil, their brother who was in the navy, was home on leave, so the whole family including Cecil's wife Renie their eight year old daughter Jean, and thirteen year old son Eric came to tea bearing gifts. The six grandchildren brought a joint gift in with great ceremony. It was a beautiful padded golden coloured eiderdown. Grandma cried with pleasure and had it wrapped around her knees all through tea. A couple of days before, Jack had arranged for a photograph of all their children and grandchildren to be taken in the garden at Mayon. It was beautifully framed and was given pride of place on the wall. It was a very happy day. The following afternoon Jack took them both for a drive out on to Dartmoor so that Mary Ellen could see her old home at Dartmeet once again, and visit the church where they had got married. It was to be the last time, as her health rapidly deteriorated during the following months.

1944

After another Christmas at Gunnislake Charlotte was getting restless. She thought it was time to come home. There was no excuse any more; the Blitz was over and the air raids infrequent. She, like Pammy was getting homesick. So the next time Mabel came to visit she decided to confront her.

"Mabel, I want to come back home. I miss everyone, especially you dear. It's not the same here. The children are getting older and this house is very small with three growing children in it. Of course I love Harriet and have enjoyed her company but I think it's safe now, don't you?"

Mabel could not resist Charlotte's pleading. She was outwardly a hardfaced person but underneath she had a warm heart and had to admit, nothing would please her more than to have things return to normal again. "The war is by no means over yet but I'm sure it's safe for you to come home. I'll arrange for Jack to come up next weekend, will that suit you?" she asked with a smile. Charlotte said nothing but hugged Mabel tightly with tears in her eyes.

The following weekend they came in Jack's car. They had a jolly day with Harriet and her children then when tea was over they said their 'goodbyes' and after loading up Charlotte's suitcase were on their way. When they stopped at three Mayon in the gloaming, Charlotte sat in the car for a moment looking at the house. "I'm home" she whispered, then got out of the car and went indoors straight to the kitchen where she put on the kettle for Mabel's cocoa as though she had never been away.

Pammy ran about the house cheering, for she loved her two aunts dearly. All was right with her world again and as Phyllis put the excited and happy child to bed she heard her prayers thanking God they were all back together again.

The eleven plus examination time was drawing even closer. Miss Morell, Pammy's teacher, took the children through several dummy runs in order to prepare them. The nearer the time came though the more nervous Pammy got. The results of her dummy runs had not been good. She knew that her Arithmatic was poor, and try as she might with her homework, it did not get any better. Mabel tried to encourage her to rely on the tables and to take her time so that she could check each step.

All the hard work was in vain, however, for whilst her English was good, she failed to get enough marks to pull her through. "Well," said her dad, "I'm sure you tried your best darling, don't cry. It's not the end of the world." "It is!" she wailed. "All my friends will be going to high school without me!" "Nonsense dear!" said Phyllis, "You are not the only one who failed. Anyway, I've been thinking." When she said that, Jack knew that Phyllis had a plan which would save the day. "What have you been plotting my dear?" he asked with a smile. "Well, if we can't put her into the high school, what about a private school? You may not be cut out to be clever so perhaps we can make you more ladylike." "Fat chance!" Jack laughed. He rolled about on the floor with Pammy when she jumped upon him in disgust. When he sat up for breath he said, "No, seriously Phyl, what school had you in mind?" "I was thinking of St.Dunstan's Abbey. Your cousin Joan Causley goes there and she loves it. And it's not far away." "But surely that's a boarding school isn't it?" asked Jack. "They don't take boarders now because of the war but I hear good things about the staff, and the nuns are charming so Joan's Mother says." "Aren't they Catholics?" asked Charlotte. "No, though they are high church and celebrate saints days and so forth but I don't think that is important, do you Jack?" "What do you think about the fees though?"

"Well, we're both working full time and I'm sure it won't be a hardship. Shall we find out some more, what do you think Pammy?"

"Anything's better than going to a bloomin' secondary modern!" was her opinion, so they were all agreed.

The following week Phyllis wrote for an appointment to meet with the Sister Superior. On the Wednesday afternoon, Jack Phyllis and Pammy went along to North Road. The School nestled into the hillside sloping down to Victoria park. A high wall ran all along the main road. At the East end set into the wall was a very large pair of oak double doors, covered in bolts and huge hinges., it had a small door set into it with a closed grilled small window. By the side of the door hung a metal bar which was the bell pull. Jack rang it solemnly and they waited. A few moments later the small door opened and a nun, who smiled warmly, invited them inside. "Good afternoon, Mister and Mrs Holemans? "She enquired." I am Sister Jessie. Mother Superior is expecting you, do come this way." They slipped through the small door into a covered courtyard which led through on the left into the secretary's office. The secretary was not a nun but a bright middle aged person with an efficient air. "Do sit down won't you? Sister Superior will be along in just a moment." They sat down in the neat office, lined with books and filing cabinets. Trophies and long school photographs hung on the walls. "There are some school brochures on that table if you would like to look at them." She smiled and slipped a new sheet of paper into her typewriter leaving them to peruse the booklets. They only had a few minutes in which to look at the pictures of classrooms, building and gardens before the other door opened and the secretary immediately stopped typing and stood up as an elderly nun with a slight stoop entered, supported by her walking stick.

"May I introduce Mister and Mrs Holemans to you reverend Mother, and this is their daughter Pamela."

Pammy got the sudden premonition that her days as Pammy were coming to an abrupt end. They exchanged 'how do you dos' and the Sister superior gave her name as sister Mary Gerda and led them across the passage into her sanctum.

It was a delightful room with a large window overlooking a tranquil garden with a myrtle tree growing at it's centre surrounded by colourful flower beds. The garden was flanked by the high walls of the school buildings. They spent some time discussing the curriculum and other formalities. Sister Mary Gerda was gentle and friendly to Pammy. She was very interested to hear that she was very artistic and during the conversation it transpired that Jack knew the Art teacher.

Miss Wright whose father was an ironmonger and a customer of Harris and Co. After about half an hour of talking about the school, they were given a guided tour. Of course it was in the school holidays so they did not expect to see any pupils. Passing out through the French windows into the garden with the myrtle tree. Mother Superior explained, "This tree is very special to us. It first came from Jerusalem and is said to have been blessed by Our Lord and whenever any of our old girls get married, she has a sprig of our myrtle in her bouquet. Perhaps you will have a sprig one day my dear" she said warmly, patting Pammy gently on her head.

A young girl of about fourteen was sitting reading on a bench at the far side of the garden. Jack asked, "Excuse me for asking, but I thought you had no boarders because of the war." "That is correct," answered the sister, "May is an orphan from the Channel Islands and we were asked to take care of her. She is a studious child and content with her books."

The girl did not look up and they moved on to the school buildings. Most of them were within the old stone walls with granite left exposed in the glass corridors that linked them. There were also one or two wooden extra rooms in the grounds between the tennis courts and a large hut used for gym and assembley. Returning towards the garden they travelled along a cobbled enclosed cloister which led to the refectory. A high ceiling room with beams and a huge old fireplace. Beyond which were the kitchens. Returning to the cloister they climbed a set of steps which led to another oak door not unlike the front entrance but smaller. Through this door was the convent proper with a beautiful chapel with statues of the Virgin Mary and a stained glass window with Jesus on the cross. At the rear of the chapel stood a small organ with pipes going up to the roof. They returned through the chapel door and down another corridor past the nuns cells and found themselves at the end, back where they had started in Sister Mary Gerda's office. They sat down once again to conclude the arrangements for Pammy's commencement in September and received the list for her uniform and other necessary items. This done they made their polite farewells and left the way they had come.

Coupons had to be stringently gathered to provide Pammy with everything on the list. The complete uniform needed a blazer, jumper, tunic, three sports skirts, tie, hat and navy blue mac with navy blue underwear and black shoes. At this time it was a struggle to find enough coupons to buy everything at once but the whole family pooled what coupons they had to get the job done.

Dingles had been one of the largest stores in the centre of Plymouth to be destroyed in the Blitz and were managing to continue business using a large Edwardian house in the Mannamead area of town for their clothing department. It took several visits there, to eventually gather all her uniform together.

Also with these clothes were the school badges which had to be carefully sewn on the hat and blazer. Everything also had to have name tags sewn on securely on absolutely everything. Mabel presented her with a brand new school bag and pencil case and Charlotte made her a shoe bag with her name embroidered on it. Then when all was ready Charlotte and Mabel were treated to a fashion Parade. They clapped and cheered declaring that she really looked grown up and ready for her new life at St' Dunstan's Abbey.

"Please everyone, would you call me Pamela or Pam instead of Pammy now? It won't do at all at school and besides it will make me feel more grown up." A tear appeared in Charlotte's eye as she nodded in agreement. Her baby was growing up but whether she liked it or not, at home she would still be Pammy to her aunts.

SEPTEMBER 1944

The day dawned for Pam to start school at St. Dunstans Abbey. She rose early and dressed very carefully in her new uniform and shiny new shoes. Her hair was tied back in the regulation two bunches with navy blue ribbons. Aunt Charlotte made sure that she had a clean hanky in her pocket and gave her her packed lunch wrapped up in a brown paper bag with an apple placed carefully in her new school bag. Nothing was left to chance, she was checked over by her Mother as they got into the car. On this first day she was driven there on Phil's way to work at the shop in Union Street. Pam was given some money to catch the number fifteen bus home from Wyndham Square to Penlee.

As they drove down the road Jack waved as they passed his office. Pam felt like a shop manakin sitting there dressed in what the best dressed school girl should be wearing this season, though she didn't much like the hat with it's old fashioned brim. How long would she look this crisp and clean Phil wondered.

It was only a short distance to the school, down Molesworth road to the park at the bottom and up the hill the other side where they turned into North Road. As they turned the corner they could see other girls at the school entrance. Not the one they had gone through before but at the nearest end of the building there was a double door which stood open where Sister Jessie, the nun who welcomed them on the interview day, stood directing them inside. Pam jumped out of the car after giving her Mum a quick kiss and joined the line of clones. They were directed downstairs to a large cloakroom where prefects allotted each girl a peg and a shoe locker for sports gear, Pam was just settled as the bell rang. This was the call to assembly. They were marched, or rather walked, no running allowed, in a silent, no talking allowed either, convoy down to the main hut where the new girls were placed at the front. Although different shapes and sizes they all virtually looked alike. Whispering could be heard as the older pupils sized them up, perhaps for possible hockey players or tall ones for netball teams. "They won't get much joy out of me for sports" thought Pam aware of her plump short body's limitations in that regard. As she stood looking around, she thought she saw the girl in the garden.

The nuns all filed in and faced them from the stage, then last of all came the Sister Superior who conducted prayers which ended in a hymn. "And now it is my pleasure to place the new girls into their houses." Said Sister Mary Gerda. Sister Jessie stepped forward with an armful of coloured girdles whilst another read from a list. Green girdles were for Wantage, Red for Downton, Purple for Pusey and yellow for Sellon. Each stood still while Sister Superior placed their girdles in their hands. They did not put them on until everyone had received one. Then as the school applauded they all were helped to remove their black ones and tie the new ones through the loops at the waist of the tunics and tie them in the correct knot. Pam was so proud as she tied her new red girdle on hoping that she would not dishonour it too much. They were told that they could gain points for their houses with good behaviour and progress in the lessons but that if they received more than ten demerits in a month their girdle would be taken away and they would have to wear the black one in disgrace until they redeemed themselves. This sounded very serious and indeed so it was.

Assembly over, they were led back to their classrooms; Pam was placed in 1A which was situated directly above the south entrance, with a large set of windows looking out over Victoria park and far up the hill the other side. Pam thought she could almost see the roof of their house. It was a very busy morning with lots of information to absorb. Timetables for lessons were distributed before break time. It was a relief to pause and look about at the other girls as they went out into the playground. The girl Pam had been sitting next to in class was called Wendy Church. She lived across town at Manamead and they took to each other immediately. She was warm and friendly and had the most beautiful thick pair of plaits. Pam's hair was too short and too fine to make plaits at all but she would have loved to have had some. She also made another friend called Myra Vosper whom she discovered lived quite near to Penlee so they agreed to travel home together at the end of the day.

The break was soon over and on returning to their classroom continued to collect even more information and were given books which they had to sign for. They were school property and if they lost them they would be expected to pay for new ones. At lunchtime, their minds quite fuzzy after taking in so much information that they were grateful just to sit on a bench in the sun by the side of the netball court where they ate their sandwiches and chatted. Some girls went into the refectory for school lunch bit it was an unnecessary expense, Mother thought, as the family always ate together in the early evenings, besides those pupils were obliged to give some of their precious food coupons to the school. The afternoon was equally frantic. Apparently most of her classmates had already been at the school for a year in

1B so they were ahead of Pam in French. As she had never learnt any at all she was told that she and five others would have extra French to help them catch up.

At the end of the afternoon Myra and Pam collected their things and staggered along to the bus stop under the weight of all their new books.

When the number 15 arrived they climbed aboard dropping into the nearest seats, exhausted, speaking little as the bus chugged up Molesworth Road. At the corner where the bus turned into The Elms they got off and parted company, Myra crossing to continue on to her house and Pam to walk up Penlee Road sighing with the weight of her ten ton school bag. Actually it was not much heavier than when she set out but she was tired so it felt more. Aunt Charlotte was waiting at the door and welcomed her home. Mabel arrived shortly afterwards and they all had a nice cup of tea. They knew better than to bother her with questions about her day but waited until she would share it with all the family at supper. Although she was tired she had enjoyed her first day. She was proud to be wearing her red girdle and had made two good friends. It was the beginning of a new life.

The Saint Dunstan's Abbey nuns, though protestants, were very high church and unlike most C of E parishes revered the saints. On many saints days throughout the year the school would abandon the first two lessons of the day, to everyone's delight, and walk in crocodile fashion along to the church which was just one street away. There, Father Howard would hold a communion service, and those girls who were confirmed participated. It was quite different from the services at Stoke Damerel Church where Pam's family often attended evensong. Most of the service was chanted in Latin and incense perfumed the air. Most of the hymns were familiar and she soon got used to the very different style of worship. During this first term the parents of new pupils were contacted offering their daughters the opportunity to be confirmed in the school Chapel. Pam's parents would, no doubt, have considered confirmation for her at some time or other so they thought this was a great idea for Pam to do so with some of her friends in such beautidul surroundings as the Abbey's Chapel. The family discussed it with her and it was agreed. So the dozen girls who were to be confirmed began classes once a week to prepare. The service was to be held during the Christmas holidays just after New Year's Day. They would spend the weekend staying in the convent rooms near the chapel.

During the classes they were asked to consider adopting the practice of taking confession. Pam's parents did not want her to as they felt that whilst St. Dunstan's was very high church, confession was one step too far towards catholicism.

When the Christmas and New Year celebrations were over Pam's parents drove her to the Abbey and dropped her off with her suitcase, promising to see her at the service. The jolly dozen gathered in the refectory over tea and cakes before they were shown to their rooms. Then they met in the chapel where Sister Superior gave out the itinerary for the weekend, beginning with a very special treat. One that only pupils who were about to be confirmed were allowed to share, which was to be shown the secret passage that ran beneath the chapel.

With great excitement they were led down the winding stairs at the back, down into a dark corridor which was only lit through the glass tiles set into the courtyard pavement above. It seemed to come to a dead end, but at the touch of a hidden button a large cupboard swung aside revealing a dark passage. They all moved into it excitedly following the Sister who carried a torch. They walked a few yards silently, then stopped and waited as Sister Superior pulled a heavy lever which made a creaking noise as a panel in the wall in front of them slid aside and to their amazement they stepped through the back of the big fireplace into the refectory, where supper was set out ready for them. They all cheered with delight and promised very seriously never to reveal the secret. They enjoyed their meal and as they chattered they laughed at the number of pupils who eat there every day without ever knowing of the secret behind the fireplace.

After supper they were sent off to their rooms to read and get an early night

Saturday was spent in the final classes and the rehearsal for the service the following day. Father Howard came and talked to them. It was not all work however; they had time to walk in the gardens and some played a game of netball. They were all very excited and anxious that they would look smart in their newly pressed uniforms and white veils. Prayers and another early night brought the day to an end.

On the Sunday morning they did not have any breakfast as it was the custom not to eat before communion. At nine thirty they were all dressed and ready as their parents arrived. When they were all seated the girls were marched in to sit in the front row. Pam caught a glimpse of Jack and Phyl who smiled and gave her a tiny wave. Then it all began with a hymn and then an address by Father Howard. It was a very moving service in such beautiful surroundings they could not help feeling privileged and close to God as each girl came forward to be blessed. They stood and repeated their pledges as their Godparents had done at their Baptisms. Then the moment came for everyone to take communion, the girls including their parents. And finally a joyous hymn. It made them feel strangely grown up.

The service over the parents surged forward to

congratulate them then they were all led down the steps
to the refectory where a magnificent breakfast had been
prepared for them all. They were all very hungry and very
excited but were glad to be going home at last.

Now that they were confirmed it meant that on Saints
Days they must not have any breakfast before taking communion at the school service. Sometimes one of them would
be chosen to be acolytes and help Father Howard, carrying
the plate and generally helping him in the service. Only the
older girls actually used the incense burner as it was quite
an art to swing it correctly. The bonus however, was that on
returning to school, instead of going out to play, they were
treated to a breakfast in the refectory with porridge and
delicious dripping on toast or chunky bread.

The Spring term brought little or no improvement in
Pam's grasp of French. Sister Jessie suggested that she might
benefit from some individual help from a senior pupil during some of her prep periods. Her parents readily agreed
that this would be a good idea, and so it was arranged.
Pam was to meet May Evans on Wednesdays and Fridays
at 2.30pm each week for half an hour. May was the quiet
girl Pam and her parents had first seen in the nun's garden.
The orphaned girl; the solitary boarder. Pam had seen her
about the school of course at different times. After all she
was a prefect in the fifth form. May was very pleasant and
explained that her family were from the Channel Islands
which was why she was very good at French. May asked
her why she thought she was not getting on learning it.
And she explained that their teacher was a French lady with
an accent which poor Pam could not tune into. "I have to
keep on whispering to my neighbour, 'what did she say?
But you haven't got an accent, why is that if you come from
there?" she asked. "I probably did have when I was little
but I have been here so long now I have lost it, except when

I speak the language then it comes back, you'll see." May explained. "Well. When you do, please don't go as fast as Madamoiselle!" They both laughed and got off to a good start. So, May took her time and soon Pam progressed forward but only very slowly and not really very well. After a while as they got used to eachother May began to tell her how the nuns had taken her in when she was orphaned. She did not explain how and Pam assumed that they had been killed by an air raid. May said "I am so happy living here with the nuns. I enjoy the peace and quiet and perhaps I might become a nun myself one day."

May did not seem to have many friends as Pam noticed in break times she could often be seen quietly reading alone somewhere about the grounds. As time went on Pam certainly benefited from her help although May could be quite strict at times and did not hesitate to punish Pam with extra work if she did not do her homework very well. When Pam told her parents about May they felt rather sorry for her and thought Pam might like to invite her home for tea one weekend. When she asked May at their next lesson she said that Pam's parents would have to write to the Mother Superior for permission as she was in their care. She was apparently never allowed out on her own, which they thought rather strange.

In the time May had lived in the convent she had grown plump through lack of exercise due mainly to her dislike of all sports. Naturally she had to join in during her lessons but this dislike for P.E and team games helped to form a small bond between the two girls for pudgy Pammy was not really built for sport either. May also wore her hair in a thick long plait down her back which was something else Pam always admired and no matter how she tried could not coax her hair to grow long enough or thick enough to achieve this longed for effect.

Phyl did write and shortly after she had a reply which thanked her and accepted on May's behalf for a Sunday during half term. Jack took the car and, with Pam, went to the convent to fetch her.

When they returned home, May was introduced to everyone. She was polite but very shy, and would not be drawn into talking about her family but chattered about school and the convent. After tea she was taken back to St. Dunstans; the family naturally discussed this unusually quiet girl. What had they learnt. She was almost fifteen, three years older than Pam, and was rather plain and stockily built which Phyl said would probably wear off as she got older. Aunt Charlotte was very quiet, however. When asked her opinion of Pam's new friend she hesitated, then replied, "I may be wrong but there's something about her I don't trust. She's too polite and too simpering to be genuinely sweet and innocent. I'm sorry if you don't agree but I think she's trouble." None of the family could see why Charlotte would feel that way but nothing they said in May's defence would sway her. She said it was a gut instinct which she could not shake off. "Just be careful, that's all I'm saying." She said closing the subject. Mabel was inclined to feel as her sister did but had no real reason to substantiate it.

During the next term Pam's confidence grew. There were some lessons she absolutely loved. Writing was one. In this lesson the quality of their penmanship was the most important thing. The girls were given cards with poetry or quotations written on them in beautiful copper plate letters. The object, to achieve the same high standard as the originals. Pam always excelled, getting nines and tens. Sister Jessie often sighed," If only you could do your work as well as you write it!" Then, of course, Art classes, where she was in her element. Miss Wright was a 'spiffing' teacher, the in word for such a great person, so we are told. She was young and enjoyed encouraging those with some talent. She certainly recognized this in Pamela. The time in her classes were never long enough.

Pam's sports teacher was Sister Eileen Mary. She was an amazon of a woman, tall and muscular. She always wore sandles and when teaching hockey on the pitch down in the park, would gather up the bottom of her habit at the back, bring it through her legs and tuck it into her girdle. As she dashed off down the pitch after the ball with her veil flowing out behind like a sail, she moved at great speed shouting instructions as she went. She soon discovered that Pam's short plump body was not built for running and placed her in goal. Her friends said that it was the best place for her as she filled up the hole!

She was pretty useless in the gym too, as poor Sister Eileen Mary learnt to her cost. One particular morning Pam had been driving the poor woman to despair. The school hut had all the equipment for good gymnasts; pride of place was taken by Pegasus, the trusty wooden pummel horse, with it's accompanying spring board. The class would line up along the length of the hut, then, as they came to their turn, would come up on their toes, balanced and poised for the word, then on the command" Go!" would break into a sprint, hitting maximum velocity as they reached the springboard which would lift them high in the air so that they barely brushed the handles of the horse as they splayed their legs, then landed lightly on the mat beyond, springing up and away to make room for the next agile young thing. But, when it was Pam's turn, she would break into a forward stumble, gaining little speed as she approached the springboard and on reaching it, gave a pathetic bounce and ran chest first, into the back of the horse coming to an abrupt halt, much to the amusement of her class mates. She was the class buffoon. Oh, not that she minded the laughter. She knew her own limitations., but Sister Eileen Mary did not. She was not going to admit failure. After everyone had completed another successful round she called the class to rest, then brought Pam forward.

"Now you know you can do this if you try." Sister Eileen Mary smiled encouragingly. "Just try and run a little harder then when you reach the springboard, let it lift you up. I am here to catch you, so as you come up in the air, aim with your heels, forward, here Towards me." She patted her stomach to show Pam the target area. "Now try again and remember, bounce hard and aim forwards with your heels." Pam took her place at the end of the hut, accompanied by cheers of encouragement from her class mates. She took three deep breaths, gathered her body up to it's limited height, paused, then dashed down the runway gathering speed like an optimistic beach donkey, hitting that springboard with a frightening crash. She amazed herself as she rose into the air! She remembered to bring her heels forward to aim for the target, and hit it! Square on! Her left heel contacted with Sister Eileen Mary's abdomen and it sent her gasping to the floor whilst Pam sat astride the horse like a knight without his armour.

The class fell silent. An occasional giggle came from the corner of the hut as two girls rushed forward to help the sister to her feet. All waited for her words. She gulped in some air and shakily said, "Well done Pamela. You, at least, got on to the horse this time which is more than you have done before." She paused to gather her composure then added, "But I think in future you will join me as a catcher." The whole class applauded and fell about laughing. They had all seen the funny side, including Sister Eileen Mary, and it earned Pam the nickname of "Bullseye" for the rest of the term at least.

MAY 7TH 1945

On this date peace came to Europe, prompting massive parties in Plymouth and across the country. City celebrations began with a service of thanksgiving in the shell of the bombed-out St. Andrew's Church, but shortly a huge crowd gathered on the Hoe and the party started. On the Barbican there were more celebrations with open-air dancing on the Mayflower steps. Jack, Phil and Pam joined the excited crowds, cheering and waving union jacks. There were street parties where people pooled their rations for the refreshments. They joined in the nearest one in Park Street where everyone laughed and sang for joy. Flags and bunting went up, and effigies of Hitler were thrown onto the bonfires. Now life could begin again and the work which had already begun on the rebirth of the city could proceed in ernest. A model of the new city centre was on display in the guildhall where everyone could see the new open plan of the modern Plymouth that would rise from the ashes.

On May 9th the Channel Islands were liberated.

During the months that followed, families were finding it possible to return to their homes in the Channel Islands. May received a letter from Father Peter to say that she would be able to come home to her Grandmother for the summer holidays and that she would travel with a family named Bonnette who had been living in Plympton. He supplied the address so that arrangements could be made.

The fare would be paid by him from a fund especially set up for children like herself.

Her first reactions were of horror. She did not want to go back there. It had been six years since she was last in Guernsey and was sure that she had nothing in common with her Grandmother anymore. thank goodness, she thought, that her Grandfather was dead. He had been imprisoned early on during the occupation and had developed a heart condition which, with pneumonia, led him to become very ill and die in 1942. Her memories of him were all bad. He had been mean tempered and could often be violent, especially after drinking and would not have his daughter Eloise mentioned in the house. He tried to ignore May as much as possible as she was growing up which suited her better than having him vent his temper on her as he did all too often on his poor wife.

She expressed her wish not to go back, but Sister Mary Gerda persuaded her that for her Grandmother's sake she should go. Besides, school holidays was always difficult for them to look after her, it would be a relief for them, though they did not say so of course. So when the arrangements were finally complete May packed and on the day, set off for the docks to meet the Bonnettes who were a very pleasant couple with two young children. They were looking forward to being reunited with all of their family on Jersey where they had previously run a small hotel. It had been taken over and occupied by the Germans of course, so it would need a thorough refurbishment before they could start the business once again. They took good care of May on the journey, chatting excitedly most of the time which May found extremely boring and was thankful when they parted company.

On arrival at Guernsey harbour Father Peter and her grandmother were standing there waiting almost as if they had never moved from the spot all those years ago when her Mother had been sent away. There were shy hugs and kisses and exclamations of "My, how you've grown!" and such like as they moved off towards the cottage. May hardly recognized her grandmother, she had aged greatly in those six years from the rigours of the war and the loss of her husband. Father Peter left them together and promised to return another day. They had tea together and then May went to her old room. It still had the same old curtains and faded bedspread. It all looked very tawdry and disgusting to May and she wished she had never come, and yet, Grandmother was her only living relative now, except for the aunt who had worked at the Manor house. That too, now in a sorry state Grandmother had said, after the Germans had stripped it bare and taken anything of value when they left.

Her aunt was retired now and lived next door where they could keep an eye out for eachother.

Over the next few weeks May wandered around the island enjoying the solitude but dreading the occasions when Grandmother insisted on showing her off to her friends as the clever daughter of her poor dear Elouise. May soon got tired of answering questions about her Mother and found herself telling various lies to keep them all happy. She told them what they wanted to hear which was certainly a long way from the truth. How could she tell them that her Mother had almost lost her mind and chased her around with a carving knife.

Once the novelty of her return wore off, her Grandmother's friends drifted away leaving them in peace which suited May very well. They had become very irritating and she had had to be very careful with her stories that she did not slip up and alter any of it. Except for Father Peter. For some reason she was aware that he knew all about her Mother and the circumstances of her death better even than her Grandmother. She suspected that his sister had kept him well informed during the growing up but advised keeping the details from anyone including Grandmother. May respected that and felt she could trust him. On one occasion they met as she was walking along her favourite cliff path. He had been visiting a dying member of his congregation and was on his way home. They stopped and sat on a bench together looking out to sea. He sensed that she needed to talk.

"Father, forgive me if I am asking you to break a confidence, but I feel that you are the only one I can ask." began May. "I will answer if I can child." Suspecting that which she was about to ask.

"Well, can you tell me please, who my Father was? And why did they send Mother away?" Father Peter paused for a moment, then began," I can answer you May, only because your Father is now dead. He died during the occupation. Like many young men left here, they tried to resist and some were captured, locked up or shot. Your father was shot whilst trying to escape."

"but who was he, Father?"

:His name was Clifford Moret. When he was a young boy he worked at the Manor House as a gardener's assistant and boot boy. Your Mother went to work there too as a scullery, maid. She was a wild restless thing and hated scrubbing and the other menial jobs and was constantly in trouble for running off to explore the beach and the woods," he paused for a moment before continuing.".as did Clifford. They became close friends running loose like two wild innocent animals, along these cliffs and rocks escaping from the boredom of work. They were two free spirits who swam and played with no care of where life would lead them. Your Grandfather was so angry when he found that Eloise was pregnant. He refused to keep her in his house.

Your Grandmother just wanted to hide the scandal and turned to me for help. My sister, whom you know is Sister Josephine, took charge of the situation and your Mother was sent to Plymouth. The rest you probably know."

"But why was I not adopted?" asked May. She had always resented the fact that she had got stuck with her Mother instead of perhaps being brought up in a happy home somewhere.

"Your Grandmother decided that she would rather bring you up herself, here, rather than lose you, her only Grand-daughter to strangers."

"How dared she interfere!" exclaimed May, much to Father Peter's surprise. "She had no right to do that No right!"

"But weren't you happy here with your Grandmother at the beginning?"

"Happy? No! Grandfather saw to that. He terrified me. I was afraid to cry or laugh or make any noise when he was around. Oh, Grandmother was kind but she was afraid of him too. I know only too well even though I was young at the time. But I remember how she tried to protect me from him. I think she hated him as much as I did. I'm glad he's dead Father. I don't think I could have come back if he had still been alive. He tried to rob me of any love I might have had when they took me away from my Mother. I shall never forgive them for that."

Her outburst came as a great shock to Father Peter and he felt guilty for his part in it all.

"Then you must blame me also for it was I who per-suaded your Grandmother to send for you when you were born."

May sat for some time in silence then said, "I shall go back to Plymouth tomorrow, please. There is nothing here for me."

She stood up and walked away leaving Father Peter feeling very disturbed. What had they done to this poor child? Had they done the wrong thing in saving her from adoption? Was their alternative worse? She seemed to be a soul in search of love. Love which had been held back at every stage of her life so far. He could only pray that she would find it in time.

The next day as she had said she would, she said good-bye to her Grandmother and caught the boat back to Plymouth. She could not wait to return to the peace and quiet of the convent school, where she could shut out the world most of the time.

Perhaps she would see more of Pamela's family where everyone seemed so happy. She was a very lucky child. It wasn't fair.

It had been difficult for most children to settle down to school work during that summer term. There had been such excitement celebrating the end of the war that the mundane life of lessons seemed a great anti climax. The sisters were wise enough to allow for this and the general atmosphere was kept light and they were not punished for their high spirits and excitable pranks than they might otherwise have been. The end of the summer term however brought them down to earth as last minute revision took over. It was the end of Pam's first year and she did not have much hope of doing very well in the exams in any of her subjects; so when the final results were recorded in her school report, she carried it home to her parents with some trepidation.

Some of it was indeed, predictably poor, especially the Maths and French but Sister Jessie kindly wrote that it was not for the want of trying. Pam was very grateful to her for that. In other subjects she had acceptable reviews, but of course, as expected, her best came from the lovely Miss Wright who gave her a glowing report for Art and

Needlework and said that she had artistic talent. However, the general report, written by Sister Mary Gerda was not so good . The inevitable, 'could do better' rather said it all.

Jack and Phyl were pretty good about it but agreed that she had better work harder during next year. That summer was idyllic. The weather was good and Pam had some newly made friends to spend it with She and Myra had had new roller skates the previous Christmas and spent lots of time on them in the park, when they were not climbing trees or going swimming. The pool on the Hoe had suffered some bomb damage but the girls were often taken to Bovisand or went to Mount Wise.

Now that the war was over Jack left the Marine Police and returned to his job as sales manager for Harris and Company full time.

It was nice that it was only 100 yards from Mayon so Pammy was able to pop her head into his office as she returned home most afternoons. On one particular afternoon, her father called her in to meet someone. He was the traveler for a company who made toothpaste and shampoo. He told Pam that they were about to launch a new product called Luster cream and needed someone who could set up displays at dance venues where they would be giving away samples.

"Your Father tells me that you are very artistic and would be just the person I need. How would you like to earn a few pounds setting up six displays?" Of course she agreed and thoroughly enjoyed the experience. Naturally her Father came with her and provided the crepe paper and dummy boxes of Lustre cream to create the displays. The salesman was more than pleased with the result so once again Pam had managed to earn some money towards Christmas presents.

They saw nothing of May during the holidays but when

the Autumn term started in September it was suggested that they take up the extra French lessons where they left off. Now that Pam was in form two there wasn't quite so much free time to fit these extra French lessons in so Phyllis suggested that May could come to the house every other Saturday. This arrangement went smoothly enough for a few weeks but as half term approached May suggested they ought to take advantage of it and meet daily. Pam certainly didn't like the idea of spending the whole of her half term holidays sitting indoors studying when she could be out having fun with her friends. She persuaded her parents to decline the offer. May was not pleased. In fact she rather surprised Pam with her reaction.

"Well, I don't know what your parents are thinking of!" she said quite sharply. "I am doing my best to get you to reach what is actually a pathetic level in French, and they stupidly reject me! don't they know that if you don't improve you may well be kept down from form Three next year? You wouldn't like that would you! Your dear little friends would be moving on without you wouldn't they!"

She was really angry and when Pam tried to answer she just stormed off leaving her standing in the middle of the playground with her mouth open. It was a side of May that Pam had not seen before and when she returned home that day and told Charlotte what happened she said "Well, I wouldn't tell your Mum and Dad about that if I were you. They may change their minds to please her, which I think is exactly what she wants. You are doing your best and I don't think you should miss your half term break just so 'madam' can come here every day." "Are you sure it will be alright not a tell them?" Pam asked, because she never lied to them and shared almost everything. "You aren't telling lies darling, just saving your parents from a difficult situation. May is probably teaching you well enough but she can be a bit of a kill joy. You are only young once my sweetheart. You enjoy your half term."

May spent her fifteenth birthday alone except for the sisters who made her a cake. Which made May even more bitter towards Pam. During the extra French at school prep time the following week May was much more dominating than she had previously been; though Pam noticed May was very sweet to her in the house on those Saturdays when her parents were around, especially at tea which she now stayed for each time before being returned to the convent. Charlotte noticed and tutted to herself quietly. This was a devious young woman to be watched, she decided.

On the last French lesson in December May let slip that she would not be going home to Guernsey to her Grandmother for the festivities but would be going to an old friend of her Mother's which was difficult as they had only a small cottage with nowhere for her to sleep. So she would have to return to the convent each night. Pam was sure that her Mother was about to invite her to spend it with them when Charlotte said, "It sounds as though her cottage will be nearly as full as we will be here. Pammy's cousins and their Mother will be spending Christmas here with us. It will be great fun but packed to the rafthers, won't it Phyllis?" Common sense prevailed and Mother said, "yes, I'd forgotten what a noisy bunch they are." Pam quickly added, "Yes, it's going to be great! We are going to have to sleep two to a bed! What fun!" May's face clouded over for a moment but she quickly covered it up and smiled," I'm sure I am going to have a lovely time too. The children at Aunt Cathy's are very fond of me." That look had not gone un-noticed by both Mabel and Charlotte and when they were in their own room that night they both agreed that May would take some watching.

That Christmas was great fun. The house certainly was

full with cousins Mary John and Susan and their Mother, Winnie, Phyl's sister. Winnies's husband was still not home yet after being in a Japanese prison camp for two years. The war with Japan was now over so they were sure he would be home again soon.

Pam was excited when she had a grown up bicycle for Christmas. The house seemed to be drowning in wrapping paper that morning. Grandpa and Grandma Baker came for Christmas dinner. And when Uncle Cecil and Aunt Irene came with their daughter Jean for tea, Grandma said, "How lovely to have so many of our Grandchildren all together! Goodness Phyllis where are you putting us all?" Indeed the house was full with joy and happiness." We're going to have tea in relays!" laughed John. Everyone laughed at the thought of queueing up for sandwiches and buns.

Other relatives came on Boxing day when they all went to the Pantomime at the Palace Theatre in Union Street to see Tommy Trinder in "Jack and the beanstalk"

1946

On returning to school Pam was delighted to find that Myra also had a new bicycle for Christmas so they agreed to cycle to school together every day except if it rained then they would catch the bus. On January 9th it was Pam's thirteenth birthday and her Mother said that she could have a party. She invited her two cousins Mary and Jean, the twins Joan and Betty her aunts, Myra and Wendy, Dotty and Pat from school. Although rationing made food difficult to obtain, Charlotte and Mother put on a great spread. Charlotte even made a lovely sponge birthday cake with eggs from dad's chickens. Mum wanted to invite May but Charlotte managed to persuade her that she was too old and as she was a school prefect now it would probably inhibit Pam's other school friends. It was held on a Saturday which would normally have been Pam's French lesson so Mum let Pam cancel it for this one occasion. May was not amused. In fact she was quite scathing. "I hardly think celebrating being thirteen is a good enough reason to neglect your abysmal education, however I will give you extra homework so you can do it on Sunday. I shall expect to receive it first thing on Monday morning." Then she stormed off flicking her long pigtail behind her.

Once everyone had settled down to the reality of the war being over, they were struck by an urge to start anew. Old damaged furniture and belongings were thrown out or burnt along with anything else that was a reminder of the disasters which the war left in it's wake.

Our family was no exception. Father decided to build a huge bonfire in the back garden and have a clear out. The first thing to go was the oil painting which hung in the stairwell. It was very large, at least eight foot by six and was a charming picture set in a children's nursery, with a pretty blonde ringleted girl in a pale blue and white be-ribboned dress, sitting on a dappled rocking horse. She wore ribbons in her hair and at her feet sat her little brother playing with his toys. A spaniel lay in the corner with a ball. Goodness knows how old it was or if it was painted by anyone of importance, but Pam had always liked it and was sorry when her father decided to assign it to the bonfire, along with some old rickety chairs, and an old bed from his attic bedroom where he slept as a boy.

Then he decided to do something about Mabel and Charlotte's bed. They slept together in their parent's old four poster. It was made of mahogany and had heavy draped curtains which were permanently tied back. He proclaimed it unhealthy and far too big for the room, the drapes making it too dark. But when he suggested they let him butn it they were very upset.

"This is the bed in which my Mother was born!" declared Mabel. "And indeed we all were born in it. We couldn't possibly get rid of it!" Charlotte fiercely agreed. "But it can't even be comfortable!" Jack responded. "It's just an old feather tie which must be long over due for replacement. You can have a proper mattress which will be much nicer." He coaxed. "No Jack, you're not going to get rid of our bed but perhaps a mattress would be softer, Charlotte." Said Mabel, trying to compromise. Charlotte wasn't entirely convinced and was about to agree when Jack dropped the bombshell. "What I was thinking was, the drapes are very old and dirty and the four posts do get in the way, why not let me saw them off at the headboard, then it will make it much lighter in here?" Poor Charlotte nearly fainted. Saw off the posts? And throw away the drapes? She was too shocked to speak. Mabel could see Jack's point, but didn't want to upset Charlotte. Jack knew them well enough not to rush them and with the parting remark, "It will be so much easier for me to decorate your room with some nice new wallpaper," and left them to think it over. The following day they reluctantly agreed.

"Do you really mean to saw the top off Jack?" asked Phyllis later. "Of course I do." He replied adamantly. "It must be full of dust and germs, it's got to go."

And the next weekend Jack took Mabel and Charlotte up to visit Harriet at Gunnislake for a couple of days while, on the Sunday morning Jack ascended the stairs and Phyllis watched as he pulled down the drapes and carried them down to the bonfire. He was right, they were heavy with years of dust and made them cough. Next came the feather tie, all lumpy and grey with age. Then he sawed through the four mahogany posts; they came down like masts from the Spanish armada; and he cut them up into small pieces and burnt them too. Suddenly the room looked twice it's size. Phyllis had already bought some rolls of wall paper, and after she and Pammy had given the room a good scrub they began to peel off the ancient floral print that revealed itself from behind the wardrobe as having been quite pretty once. That done they spent a couple of days painting and wall papering and generally freshening the old room up. Next, Jack went out and bought a new mattress. Phyllis made the bed and put back everything ready for the sister's return. On the Wednesday he fetched them home and they were delighted at the bright new room. They had to admit that the mattress was very comfortable but Charlotte was never really happy about it and was often seen shaking her head sadly at the descecreation of her Mother's pride and joy.

Once Jack had passed this major hurdle there was no stopping him. He persuaded his aunts to spring clean their cupboards and throw onto the bonfire an old trunk full of musty teaching books, a kaleidoscope with strips of pictures which Pam remembered being enthralled by when she was very young.

Everyone was doing it, clearing out the old and worn and replacing it with new 'utility' furniture. The post war word!

The whole house then got the treatment that spring. No longer would they tolerate an outside toilet. Going out through the kitchen door and up the yard in all weathers would not do. The back of the house was single storied; from the front passage one turned right in a small porch into the diningroom with a black leaded grate and oven. This would be replaced by a modern tiled fireplace. Through, towards the back, next came the small kitchen which had a little flight of stairs up to the tiny attic room where Jack had slept as a boy. These stairs were taken away and the room above consigned to storage with a trap door. New fitted cupboards were installed and the door into the garden was closed off and a window put in it's place. But the major work was done on the last and largest part, namely the wash house. Previously this was accessed from the garden through a stable door. it contained a round copper boiler set in brick with a fire hole under it. And finally at the end of the property was the outside loo.

Jack gutted the wash house, removing the boiler and installing a lining to the roof. The rest of the wash house was transformed into a kitchen with a rayburn solid fuel cooker as well as an electric one and a new sink and draining board under the new window. The best bit was the interior door through to the loo. Finally a door was knocked through from the old wash house into the little kitchen which now became a breakfast room. In time Jack intended to build a modern bathroom at the side of the main house with access from the back porch.

Last but not least the air raid shelter was demolished and the garden restored to it's former glory, replacing the lawn and rockery borders. Grandpa Baker so enjoyed planting it up with what would be a dazzling display of flowers that summer. To see them dancing extravagantly in the breeze instead of cabbages made everyone feel that the war was finally over at last.

Jack still had the use of the garden across the road as the house would not be re-occupied by it's owner fro some time. So there were still plenty of fresh vegetables grown there and the chickens and geese provided meat and eggs.

The rabbit hutches still occupied the back shed although Jack had long term plans to turn it into a car garage one day. They belonged to the Fur and Feather Fanciers Association and kept their rabbits for competition now more than for food, although one of the family's favourite meals would remain rabbit pie. Pam had some guinea pigs which she showed in these competitions and her favourite boar, . Bengie, won quite a lot of rosettes and she bred some good ones from him. The only drawback with keeping so many rabbits and guinea pigs was that every time they went out in their car at the weekends they had to fill some sacks with dandelions and grass to feed them on.

SEPTEMBER 1946

Pam was now in form three. During the autumn term a most bizarre event happened. Two of her classmates who lived in Torpoint were often the centre of a group prone to giggling about boys. The main reason for this was because there was a naval base for young artificers close to their village and when the girls crossed the river Tamar on the ferry these 'Tiffies' as they were called might be seen to flirt with them. Two other girls lived in the pub next to the ferry on the Plymouth side and these lads sometimes frequented their parent's establishment. These four seemed to have more contact with the opposite sex than most of the others, though it was all very innocent and only at the giggling stage, certainly not up to dating. However, when boys were the topic of conversation you may be sure that these four were at it's centre.

On this particular occasion, at morning breaktime a bunch of girls were gathered around these four seated in a gazebo where the topic of how babies were made seemed to be the subject of the whispered conversation. Pam and two of her friends were passing and stopped at the outer edge of the group to try and catch what the giggling was all about. There was so much whispered laughter that they could catch no more than the gist of it. At that moment May happened to come by and on hearing the subject matter slipped away and reported it to the first nun she came upon. The sister quickly pounced upon the group grabbling

191

the first three she could which happened to be Pam, and her two friends. They were waltz off immediately to the Sister Superior's office. She was very angry and chastised them for such disgusting a lewd conversation, and demanded to know who else were present at the gathering. Of course the girls kept silent.

"Very well." said Sister Mary Gerda, "You will be put on detention. I am disgusted with you all. I am sure you would not like your parents to know about this would you?"

They all mumbled a quiet "No Sister." "Very well then, I will not inform them, this time. You are dismissed."

When they returned to their classmates they were thanked for not giving any of them away Naturally Pam was very surprised and dismayed when on the following Saturday morning her Mother came up to her room and said that she had had this letter from school describing the incident and threatening the possibility of expulsion. The letter also stated that if the parents wished, she would give them special tuition on the facts of life. Pam told her Mother exactly what had happened, and that she and her friends had done nothing wrong. "We got called in because we were on the outskirts of the group. We couldn't even hear anything! Anyway, they were only giggling. But they never even asked us what happened. Sister Superior just took the word of Sister Brigit!" Mother laughed. She could see the funny side of it until Pam said, "You know what Mum? She as good as told us she wouldn't say anything to our parents about it and now she's written to you threatening to expel us!" Then Phil was angry. Pam began to cry and her Mother hugged her and said "Now don't get upset, I'll go and have a talk with Sister Superior and put it right."

Over the weekend she contacted the other two girl's mothers and they were agreed that they should all go together. On the Tuesday following they had an appointment.

Pam thought she would love to have been there because she knew that her mother would be like a mother bear if her cub was threatened. That evening Phyl told the family all about it.

"The other two mums let me do the talking so, I explained to the sister that our daughters had done nothing that they would need to be ashamed of, merely to have been observed to be on the edge of a group of girls having a perfectly normal and harmless chatter about boys. If the conversation developed to the subject of babies, then what could be wrong with that? I told her I thought it much more unhealthy to deceive them by writing to their parents after being told that this would not happen. And then in the letter to talk of possible expulsion over such a trivial matter. We also told her that if there was any teaching on the subject to be done we would do it ourselves in our own good time. I added that I was proud of my daughter that she did not tell on her friends as she had been asked to do. Indeed we left her with no doubt that we thought the whole incident nothing more than a storm in a teacup., if not highly amusing. The other two mums said the same so I think we can safely say that you will hear no more about it my dear." Phyl gave Pam a hug as everyone laughed and praised Phyl for a good job done.

The following week when Phyl told May about it, she was shocked that Phyl had gone up against the Sister Superior in such a way and suggested that the girls had lied. But Phyl only laughed and declared that she knew her own child well enough to know if she had lied or not.

Later when May and Pam were studying, she brought the subject up. "By the way, I heard how you lied to your Mother about the disgusting talk about sex. You should be ashamed of yourself. Your poor Mother doesn't realize what a deceitful daughter she's got!"

"That's not true!" Pam shouted. "I haven't lied about anything! We were just in the playground trying to see what all the giggling was about! We didn't even hear anything. We were just picked on because we were on the edge."

"Oh, yes. And who were these wicked other girls then?" May asked slyly.

"I'm not going to tell you. I'm not a snitch and anyway, if I told you, you'd tell one of the sisters, so I'm not saying any more." As she stormed out of the door Mabel was outside and she gave her a wink, which made her feel much better.

One day Jack came home from work quite excited. The London based Trade Fair at Earl's Court was starting up again and his board of directors had agreed that he should go. This meant a four day trip to London to look at all the new products coming on to the market now that businesses were rapidly trying to return to normal. When the day arrived he set off for the station promising to bring back some presents.

He certainly enjoyed the Fair, meeting other reps from different companies, some large, some small. Seeing all the stands advertising all manner of things from kitchen gadgets to beauty products, all on display for the first time since the war ended. Everyone there was in an optimistic mood about the future of trade. He made many useful contacts and brought away bags of samples, brochures and leaflets. He also made time to do a little shopping just before he left.

When he returned he told them all about the excitement and the buzz of the fair. Then he produced their presents.

He had bought Phyllis a beautiful Jaguer linen scarf with a design on it of Trafalgar Square; Phyl was delighted and wore it for the rest of the day. He bought home for Pam a new kind of stretch hair band which had so many colours in it, it sparkled.

Then Jack told them about his last visit to a Lyons Corner House., a shop and a restaurant where they had an amazing delicatessen counter where you could buy little cartons of various salads like Russian salad and Waldorf salad, and other tempting foods. Then out of his bag he produced six containers which, when opened held an assortment of these tasty salad mixtures the like of which they had never seen or tasted. But to cap it all he produced a round box which held a confection called "Wonder Cake", Lalyers of sponge in different colours sandwiched together with ice cream and jelly. Such a mixture of delicious flovours that held them all spellbound until every mouthful was gone. Nobody minded that it had melted a bit on the journey. "Now I can believe that the war is really over." Said Phyllis with a sigh. They had eaten a most delicious supper that they would never forget.

The company was very pleased with his report and were delighted to browse through the many leaflets, brochures and samples that he had brought back with him. They felt sure that this could certainly be an annual trip for him.

Jack told the family that if all went well, he would try and take them with him on one of these trips if he could.

That night in bed he told Phyllis about London.

"Poor old London. Like Plymouth, it was in a sorry state but the activity of rebuilding was evident everywhere, just like us here. Clearing the rubble and starting again. Theatres are beginning to light up the London sky telling everyone that it would take more than old Hitler to spoil the sites and sounds of good old London."

1947

That winter was very servere. One February morning as the children sat in their classroom, about ten thirty it began to snow. Within half an hour it was laying. The Sisters conferred and decided that those girls who lived farthest away should leave for home immediately. Lessons continued until lunch time when it was declared that this was obviously going to be serious so everyone was sent home. Myra and Pam left their bicycles in the shed and set off for the bus stop in Wyndham Square where they stood waiting for their number fifteen bus. Opposite them was the bus stop for the people going in to town, and standing there was a man with bushy eyebrows and a mustache. As they stood waiting they watched him as the snow built up on his facial hair. It was quite fascinating to watch his face slowly disappear behind the gathering snow. They could not stop giggling and were relieved when their bus arrived. They climbed aboard and sat in the warm seats.

The journey up Molesworth Hill was hazardous. The tyres of the bus could hardly get a grip and had to make several attempts to climb, as the hill got steeper and the snow got thicker. At last it reached the turning to the Elms, much to the conductor's relief. He said that this certainly would be the last bus to make it for a day or two. Pam and Myra parted company and agreed that they would meet the next morning and if the snow eased they would build a snow man. There would., certainly be no school for the next few days. All the children loved it of course, and had great times tobogganing down the fields on tea trays and anything else they could find.

The following months Pam saw very little of May as this was the year for her to take her School Certicate exams, and Sister Mary Gerda suggested that she should use all her time for revision and postpone teaching for the time being.. So in June, all the upper fifth were ready. The rest of the school were told to keep away from the hut where the examinations would take place. The sisters felt sure that May would do well, as indeed she did.

But the excellent results brought with them a problem.

She would be leaving the convent to persue a career.

The following Saturday May returned to Mayon to help Pam prepare for her end of term French tests. When they were finished, whilst Pam went out to play May went to ask Phyllis's advice. First she explained how she would not be able to stay at St Dunstan's Abbey after the end of the summer term. "Should I look for a flat do you think?" she asked. "Though I'm not sure how I would pay the rent until I'm working." "What do you want to do?" Phyl asked her. "Well, I'd rather like to train as a nurse. The trouble is a student nurse doesn't get paid much to begin with. Perhaps I'd be better off getting a shop assistant's job and study at night or something. But that would take me so much longer and I so want to be a nurse." She took out her handkerchief and dabbed her eyes, peeking out from under her lashes to see what Phyllis would do. "I thought there were student nurses quarters near the hospital or something?" she answered, searching her memory for any knowledge she might have of the like. "Oh, Sister enquired about that but she hasn't been able to arrange anything at all." said May quickly knowing that this was entirely untrue.

"Well, if you can't get student accommodation just yet,

I don't see why you couldn't come and stay here with us until you get settled. I'll talk to my husband about it this evening." May threw her arms around Phyllis's neck and cried. "Oh, thank you! You are so kind! I'll work hard I promise and I wont be any trouble." "Woah! I haven't asked him yet! Let's wait and see, shall we?"

Charlotte was in the kitchen preparing tea and over-heard the conversation and she told Mabel about it later when they were in their room. "She can wind Phyllis round her little finger, that girl. She was crying, but there wasn't a tear in sight. She knows they'll take her in, then Lord help us. You should have seen the triumphant smirk on her face behind Phyllis's back when she hugged her, and again the one she gave me as she passed me at the front door. I don't trust that young woman any further than I could throw her!" They both agreed that they would keep a sharp eye out to see that no harm came to their precious Pammy.

So Jack and Phyl talked about having May to live at Mayon. They felt sorry for her not having any family to turn to and agreed that the least they could do was to offer the girl a roof over her head until she could get a student room, just temporarily. It would probably mean that they would have to support her as she certainly had no income of her own. They finally agreed to do it as long as Pam was agreeable to sharing a room with May.

Pam thought about it and decided that as May was older than her and she was having a great time with her own friends she couldn't see that it would make much dif-ference to her life, especially as now she wouldn't be teach-ing her French any more.

Of course this would mean some changes about the hosue in the way of bedrooms and such. Up until now Pam had been using the box room, it was big enough for her, but with May moving in, they would need to share a bedroom. The other upstairs frontroom had been Mabel and Charlotte's living room, but they hardly ever used it because they liked to use their bedroom more as a bedsit; so it was agreed that this large room would be ideal as a double bedroom for the two girls and the box room became a little diningroom for the aunts, where they could boil their kettle for their tea and eat there when they were not down with the family, which from now on seemed to be their preferred choice. They never really took to May and certainly decided to keep themselves more to themselves, at least as far as she was concerned.

May was to move in after the end of the summer holidays. The Sisters gave her their blessing and were grateful to Jack and Phyllis for taking on the responsibility for taking care of May. Rationing and clothing coupons were still in use so kitting May out with a nurses uniform and some other new clothes made for some sacrifices amongst the family. The nuns did what they could of course but once May had her interview at the hospital where she would start in September, her link with the Abbey ended. When the shared bedroom had been freshly wall papered and a new single bed installed, a desk was set up on May's side of the room where she would study. Pam's side, nearest the window which had a lovely view over the high wall of the back garden of number eleven Penlee gardens and down over the town where Pam could see the spire of St Peter's cathedral and beyond, out to sea with the east end of the breakwater and Statton heights clearly in view, provided her with a nice spot for a table on which to do her homework.

May said that the matron was putting her on the waiting list for student accommodation and that when a flat became available she would move out and be no more trouble to them. Another lie. The last two weeks of the summer holidays, Pam was away to guide camp. She had joined the girl guides that spring with Myra and had been looking forward to going away camping on Dartmoor. So she was not involved in all the complicated arrangements preparing the family home for the newest arrival.

When summer was over Pam returned to school, in form four and May began her first year as a student nurse. She had a long list of all the books she would need. She would come home loaded with paperwork which seemed to need her attention into the small hours. This made it very difficult for Pam to get to sleep as May would insist on keeping all the lights on. She told Pam, when she complained that she should not be so selfish and told her not to take her petty grumbles to her mother. Eventually Pam got used to going to sleep with the lights on. Like most young people she soon adapted without too much trouble. The two girls seldom met except at meals and as May said she was now far too busy to help with her French. As far as she was concerned, Pam's chances of ever being any good at it was very remote anyway. Pam tended to agree with her but struggled on, sharing her homework with her cousin Mary who was now also attending St. Dunstans since her family all returned from Totnes. She was in the form below but shared Pam's forlorn attempts at grasping the grammer of the French language. At least they suffered together.

As the autumn moved on, May was clearly not enjoying her studies. Hygiene, Anatomy etc. seemed to consist of pages and pages of homework which only succeeded in making her extremely crotchety. She wasn't prepared for the amount of it. She stayed up late nights trying to memoirse the names of muscles and veins and bones. Endless lists which simply had to be learnt and of course, be tested. She would scream with frustration and despair when tests had to be retaken or essays re-written before they came up to the standard that the Sister tutor required of her students.

Mabel remarked to Charlotte, "She thought it was going to be all caps and Florence Nightingale flitting around the wards. To achieve anything, whether it's nursing or teaching, at the beginning there is a lot to learn and there are no short cuts, I should know, you simply have to grit your teeth and buckle down to some hard work, which is something this young lady doesn't like."

May proved to be a very difficult person to share a room with. Whenever her frustration with her studies got the better of her she would try to take it out on Pam, who soon got wise enough to keep out of her way. When Mother wasn't around May would throw things and yell, saving the sad tearful eyes of pitiful distress for Phyllis, who tried to help her by hearing her recite endless lists. Poor May certainly did have a lot of studying to do and Pam had to sympathise with her but May didn't make it any easier for herself getting into such dreadful moods.

During this time Phyllis was very distracted with worry over her Mother's health. Her chest was very delicate and her laboured breathing was proving to be a great strain on her heart. Many nights Phyl would be away from home staying the night with her parents so that her father could get a nights rest. May complained that she needed Phyllis at home to help her, especially, as she said, there was nothing they could do if the old lady was dying. Charlotte was disgusted with her callousness but said that it didn't surprise her as we were all getting to know that there was only one person important to May, and that was May herself. Everyone, that is except Jack and Phyl. Fortunately for May, Phyl didn't hear any of this and was away for almost two weeks as her Mother slowly slipped away. After her funeral, her father went to stay with his son for a while.

When Christmas arrived it was a quiet affair. No-one felt like hanging up any decorations or even cooking, but

Phyllis said that they must try and cheer up as Grandma would not have wanted them to be miserable at Christmas time. So they decorated a tree and hung up a few things and tried their best, but they were all glad when it was new year and Christmas could be forgotten.

1948

January 9th was Pam's fifteenth birthday.

She had half a dozen school friends round for tea. They were in the middle of a noisy game of blind man's buff when the door burst open and May came screaming in. She forgot that Phyllis was at home. "You noisy little brats! I'm trying to study for an exam upstairs! You're a pathetic bunch of inconsiderate infants! Either shut up or go somewhere else!" She rushed out of the door and up the stairs slamming her door behind her. The girls stood staring at each other wondering what to do. Having heard the uproar from the kitchen, Phyllis came in demanding to know what was wrong. Mabel came up behind her and saved the girls the trouble of explaining. "I'm afraid the girls are disturbing May's studies. I think it would be a good idea if you suggested to her that she wait until tomorrow or at least until the party is over before attempting to do her work. The girls are having a lovely time, aren't you girls? Let's play pass the parcel shall we?"

Dear old aunt Mabel soon got them playing and laughing again much to May's disappointment. She had hoped to bring it to an abrupt end. Phyl climbed the stairs to speak to May about her outburst and found May sobbing on her bed. "I'm so sorry!" she wailed." I didn't mean it! I have such a headache." Of course she got the sympathy she was seeking and vowed to be more careful in future not to let her temper show in front of Phyl.

Shortly afterwards the girls had a great tea then Mabel took the eight of them to the Palace Theatre to see the Panto, without May, of course. When asked why she was not included in the party, she was told by Mabel. "Oh, we wouldn't want to interrupt your studies with a boring old visit to the panto!"

May did not do well in her first exam and with failure came frustration and an increase in her bouts of temper. It was no longer possible to hide her sulky moods from Phyllis, who tried to be supportive in her difficult times. But May had had enough of nursing and began to cry and wail complaining that the worry was giving her migraines. She said that she wanted to quit nursing.

After much tantrums and tears Jack and Phyl finally agreed that she might as well give up if she wasn't happy. Un-beknownst to them May had been informed that she could now have student accommodation, and she certainly didn't want to leave Mayon now. So it was imperative that she leave the hospital.

Jack and Phyl were not the sort of people to make any-one continue doing anything which did not make them happy. So at the end of the month May had her final week at the hospital and returned home. A considerable financial loss was incurred selling her uniform and books but May did not concern herself with that ; she was free of that hateful place. She had made no friends amongst the other student nurses, indeed they were glad to see her go. She had been far too superior and moody to make any attempt at friendship.

Back at home Jack and Phyl wondered what would be the best thing to do with her. Of course she must get a job. Perhaps a course at shorthand and typing would be a good idea. May reluctantly agreed, realizing that she couldn't get away with doing nothing. So she trotted off to Pitmans and joined a secretarial course. Her mood improved for a while but even here she became quickly bored and irritated with her fellow students. She thought them far too common and made no attempt, once again, to make any friends. Phyllis suggested that she might like to have some of them home for tea but May did not take up the offer.

During the Easter holidays Pam's cousin Eric got married and all the other girl cousins were bridesmaids including his sister Jean of course.

One weekend shortly after, there was a phone call from Pam's cousin Jean, the daughter of Phyllis's brother Cecil, asking if Pam would be interested in joining the Saturday night youth club which was being run by a Mrs Barrow and her son Andy. it was held in the canteen of Farley's Rusks factory and subsidized by the council. Cecil said that Pam could stay the night with them and come home after lunch on the Sundays. Pam thought this sounded like a great idea and her mum and dad agreed that she should go. So the following Saturday Pam caught the number two bus to Peverell corner where she met her cousin Jean and they went up to her house first to drop off her overnight bag and put on a bit of lipstick before setting off.

Outside the hall was a queue of young people between the ages of fifteen and eighteen waiting to pay their two and six-pence to enter. Mrs Barrow sat at a table in the doorway collecting the money and signing up new members. Jean introduced Pam who was made welcome and then taken in to meet some of Jean's friends. As they were chatting the band started up. It was a small trio with Andy at the piano, Chris on drums and Brian playing a guitar. They were very good and played all the latest popular tunes to which the young coupled danced.

Pam thoroughly enjoyed herself and was asked to dance several times. She soon got friendly with Jean's friends who mainly lived near her. There were two Malcolms, Ian, and Barry who all went to Devonport High School, and Norma., Jean's neighbour. In the interval they all went through into the kitchen where they could buy lemonade and crisps. The dancing soon started up again and one or two of the members got up and sang. The evening was such fun it flew by and ten o'clock seemed to come before any time at all. The group all walked back home together and said they would all meet up again in the morning down in the park. Pam and Jean went to bed and chatted until they fell asleep.

Jean's Mother Rene had died some months before and her brother Eric and his new wife Ilene, had come to live with them. While she was cooking the lunch Jean and Pam went down to the park where they met some of the crowd from the social, gathering together laughing and chating; some of them pairing up and strolling away on their own. They returned for their lunch and then Pam caught the bus back home.

Her parents were delighted to hear that she had had such a good time, and agreed that she should go every Saturday if she wanted to, and why not invite them to Mayon some time?

As time went on May found herself quite enjoying her course at Pitmans. She was often offered temporary work in different offices when their own staff were on holiday or on Maternity leave. So her bad moods were less frequent and with Pam forming her own friendships they did not clash so often. May certainly didn't need to study evenings anymore and started taking an interest in helping Phyllis with the cooking at weekends when Pam was away.

The time approached for Jack to go to London for Harris's, to the Trades and Industries Fair. He announced that this year he was taking some holiday time and would take them all with him. Everyone was very excited, except

May. She didn't want to go, she said it would be tiresome and boring. But Phyllis said that after all the problems over her nursing, she needed a holiday, it would do her good. She reluctantly agreed but made it clear that she was not keen. Of course, Pam was overjoyed. She could hardly wait for the time to come. it was during the Easter holidays so there was no need to ask for time off school. The arrangements were made. They were to stay in a boarding house just off Baker Street. Pam rushed around helping her mother pack and annoyed May all the more with her excitement. Nothing about this trip seemed to please her. It was as though the routine of her work which had settled her down, was to be disrupted and that brought on her irritable moods once again. Nothing anyone did these days seemed to please her.

On the morning the taxi came to take them to the station May held them up until the last minute searching for her watch which was in her pocket all the time. They just got to the station in time and bundled into the carriage as the guard blew his whistle. it was not a pleasant journey as May found something to moan about at every opportunity.

When they reached the boarding house they were all very tired but it was only tea time so Jack was anxious to show them the sights. "Lets catch a bus and go down to Trafalgar Square! We can see Nelson's Column and I'll take you all into Lyons Corner house where I bought those things you liked last year!" "Oh! Wondercake!" Pam shouted. "Oh for God's sake can't you control this child?" complained May. "I don't want to go out now, I'm too tired." "but it's only a quarter to six May, and we have to eat." Coaxed Phyllis. After some persuasion she put on her coat and they hurried down the street before she could change her mind. Pam was much too excited to be put off by May's tantrums. That first look at London thrilled them. They were, of course, shocked to see the amount of bomb damage everywhere, but as Plymothians they took it in their stride.

The Corner House was very busy and it took a while queueing for a table; more for May to moan about; but it was worth while. A trio was playing music on a little stage. The lady violinist was dressed in a black evening dress and the gentleman at the piano was in an evening suit and black tie. Another lady sat by his side playing a cello, also in a black dress. The waitresses wore black silk dresses and pretty little white aprons and cute little hat things. They ordered sardines on toast and they finished with wonder cake! Then May started. She spilt her tea all over the table-cloth and declared it was the waitresses fault. She said she had brushed past and knocked her elbow. The tea tipped down over her skirt and they had to leave. May insisted we return to the boarding house immediately so that she could get out of her wet clothes. It wasn't really very wet, she had drunk most of her tea before it happened, and Pam swore that the waitress had not come anywhere near enough to May to cause the accident. However, they did leave and queued for a bus. May tried to insist that Jack get a taxi back, but he wouldn't hear of the expense. Anyhow, they caught the next bus which took them back the long way so that they had an upstairs round trip of the city driving past Buckingham Palace on the way.

The next day Jack went off to the fair on business and left them to visit Madame Tussauds Waxworks Museum which was near enough to their lodgings for them to walk. Jack said he would meet them back at the boarding house at three o'clock. May moaned about how far it was to walk there. It really wasn't any distance at all really., but in her mood any distance would have been too far. When they arrived there, they paid to go in and started to look around the main hall using the catalogue to see who all these famous waxwork figures were. There was an attendant standing very still at the foot of the stairs, so Phyllis asked Pam to go and ask him where the cloakrooms were. Pam did as she asked and fell about laughing when she got no reply on finding that he was a waxwork figure too! May found this very embarrassing.

They began to look around the different rooms looking at the displays. After about fifteen minutes May began to complain of being tired. Phyllis said that they would stop for some tea after they had followed the guided route a little further. Again, just a few minutes passed before she began to sigh and huff saying she was bored. Pam was having a great time walking up and down finding the famous people she recognized. She called out to them to hurry when she found the royal family exhibit which was truly amazing. Her mother joined her and smiled with pleasure at the detail in the costumes and the clever models of the two princesses. They looked so like the time when they had seen them when they came to Plymouth after the blitz.

May however was not impressed. "They don't look at all like them. They just look like shop dressed dummies. I really don't see what all the fuss is about. I've seen enough, let's get some tea." "But we haven't been in the chamber of horrors yet!" Pam certainly didn't want to miss that. "Come on May." She said, "Don't be mean. Let's go down to see Jack the Ripper and all that." "Oh really Mother, what have you brought up? A positive little monster with a sick mind!" "Don't be silly May, it's only a bit of fun. Come on, it won't take long and it's on the way to the cafeteria." Said Phyllis. May grumbled some more then reluctantly followed them down the stairs. Phyllis read the map and read out the details from the catalogue as they reached each gruesome display But the further they went the more sarcastic May's remarks became. Pam was squealing with delight at being scared of each dark display. Then suddenly May grabbed Pam hard by the arm and hissed, "Will you kindly shut up! You are making an exhibition of yourself and embarrassing your Mother and me!" Pam cried out in pain as May pinched her arm then she pushed Pam into a chair. Phyllis turned angrily to May and ordered her to stop bossing Pam around. "If Pam needs controlling I can do it myself, thank you May. She's not doing any harm. Other young people are squealing and reacting to the gory models, that's what they are supposed to make you feel like. Why don't you relax and enjoy it too?" "I can't see what all the fuss over such poorly made figures is all about. I've had enough. I'm going on to have a cup of tea. You can catch me up when that child had finished making a fool of herself." And she turned on her heels and walked off towards the exit. "Never mind Pam, you carry on looking at the rest of the things and we'll meet up with her later." Phyllis was very cross with May, spoiling their visit like that. They spent another twenty minutes looking around then they went on to find May. They had a drink and something to eat then started back to the boarding house where they were to get changed ready to go out with Jack when he returned from his visit to the fair. May declared that the outing had given her a headache and she went to lie down in her bedroom. Jack came back and told them what a busy day he had had and said that he was looking forward to a meal out before going to the Theatre. They had tickets to see "Bless the Bride" a new musical in town. Phyl told Jack briefly about their visit to Madame Tussauds. And that May was lying down. He said, "Well, if we are to eat before the show we really ought to be going soon." Phyl went to see if May was feeling better. When she came back she reported that May did not feel any better and did not want to go out and eat. So Phyllis arranged for them to eat in the boarding house instead, then they could go straight to the Theatre afterwards. The meal was very nice even though it was prepared at short notice by Mrs Kennedy, the landlady.

May picked at her food and said she didn't feel like going out. Jack very firmly explained that he could not afford to waste the price of the tickets as they were very expensive, so surely she could take a couple of pills, then she would feel better. May reluctantly agreed but took far too long getting dressed and the taxi had arrived to take them to the show long before she was ready. Jack tried not to lose his temper as he did not want to contribute to spoiling their first ever night out to a London Show. He suggested that Phyllis and Pam go ahead in the taxi with their tickets and he would follow in another when May was ready.

This was what they did. Phyllis and Pam got to the Theatre in plenty of time, bought a programme and waited as long as they could in the foyer but the others did not come. A bell sounded and they were obliged to go on in to their seats. They had no idea what was taking the others so long. Just as the overture was ending and the lights had been dimmed Jack and May slipped into their seats just as the curtain was about to rise. Jack must have been very firm with May on the journey as she made no word of complaint for the rest of the evening and indeed for the whole of the next day she behaved as if nothing had happened. Jack was able to spend that day with them and they visited the Tower of London and had a boat trip on the river. That evening they ate in a Lyons Corner House once again where they listened to some lovely music played by a pianist as they enjoyed their meal.

Things were not to stay quiet for long however.

The next day, once again Jack had to go back to the trades Fair so Phyllis decided to spend the day in Regents Park Zoo. No sooner had she paid to go in than May began to find fault. It was smelly; she didn't like reptiles; she thought the elephants were ugly; she did not want to see the lions being fed as she thought the raw meat was attracting the flies; and she simply would not walk the hundred yards to see the penguins at feeding time as her legs hurt.

Pam felt so sorry for her Mother because she really tried to please May by placating her where ever possible but it was hopeless. Fortunately Pam was old enough to be told to go ahead wherever she liked and enjoy herself and if they got separated to meet at the monkey enclosure which was more or less in the centre.

When Pam returned to the meeting point she was surprised to see Phyllis alone and looking worried. "Have you seen May anywhere Pam dear?" she asked. "No Mummy, I thought she was with you. "No. She hasn't been here with me for quite some time." They began to look for her together, after searching everywhere they could think of they stopped to ask a keeper if he had seen her." "Was she dressed in a brown coat and a red beret, did you say? Well I saw a young lady like that leaving through the main gate about half an hour ago. The girl at the turnstile will have seen her too if you ask her." Phyllis thanked the keeper and sank down on a bench. "Why on earth did she leave like that without saying anything? Surely she knew I would be worried?" They checked at the gate, then Phyllis decided that the best thing to do would be to go back to the lodgings and hope that May would return safely, after all she was not a child.

When they got back May had not yet returned. Shortly afterwards Jack came back from the Fair, and Phyllis explained what had happened. Just as they were wondering whether they should contact the police May walked in.

"Where on earth have you been May? Why did you go off like that?" demanded Phyllis.

"What do you mean? You went off without me!" she replied." I went to the ladies toilets and when I came back you were gone. I was so worried, I didn't know what to do so I made my own way back here. I got lost twice before I caught the right bus, that's why it took me so long."

Phyllis was very angry. "You are lying. Two people at the zoo saw you leave through the main gate long before us. Why did you go?" "No I didn't! Why would I leave you when Pam was having such a lovely time?" declared May sarcastically. "Now I know you're lying." Jack said. "You've done everything you could to disrupt this holiday, especially to try and spoil Pam's fun. Well, I've had enough. My work at the Fair is finished. We shall be going home in the morning. This evening we are going to the west end to a show I have tickets for and you will not attempt any more of your nonsense, do you hear? I have had enough!"

May was wise enough to keep quiet and just nodded.

They all went to their rooms to change then they set off to catch a bus to the West End where they had a meal in a little restaurant next to the Theatre. They saw Vic Oliver in "Starlit Roof" with a young girl in it about Pam's age who sang with such a beautiful voice. Her name was Julie Andrews.

May behaved very quietly for the rest of the day and the next, when they caught the train home.

That evening when Jack was out feeding the rabbits, May cried and said how sorry she was to Phyllis.

"I love you all so much and I really don't mean to be a trouble but I just don't know what made me do it. I promise not to ever do it again! Oh, please forgive me!" she wailed. Pam and Charlotte were out in the kitchen wiping the dishes and heard every word. "And what has that young lady been up to?" she whispered. Pam promised to tell her later, which she did when she went upstairs to give them

213

the little presents of model animals which she had bought for them. Afterwards Mabel said, "Well, I'm not one to say I told you so but, I knew that young woman would cause trouble. Mark my words, this is not over. I do wish Phyllis would not be so soft hearted."

On returning to school for the summer term, Pam was given a note to take home to her parents from the Sister Superior. She had no idea what it could be about and that evening when it was read out they were really none the wiser. The Sister merely asked if Pam's parents would make an appointment at their convenience to discuss Pam's future. There was no indication as to the nature of this meeting but of course Jack and Phyllis made an appointment for the following Wednesday afternoon as it was early closing for Phyllis's business. Jack, being the manager could more or less give himself the time off when he chose.

The appointment was made for two o'clock and when they arrived Pam was called from her French lessons to attend. She was only too pleased to miss that particular lesson whatever the reason and went along to the secretary's office. She was told to wait there until she was called in. Her parents were already inside the Sister's sanctum.

After about ten minutes Pam was called in to join them. her Mother was smiling so she relaxed a little. It seemed that it would not be bad news. She had obviously not committed another expulsion offence. "Sit down please Pamela." said Sister Mary Gerda. " I have been explaining to your parents that whilst you are a willing and mainly a hard working student you are not academically gifted. In other words, my dear, I fear that you are unlikely to pass your school certificate and I cannot justify continuing to take fees for your education which, I'm afraid, would be a waste of your parents money. However, we all know that artistically, you are very gifted. Miss Wright tells me that your art work is exceptional and your needlework also is more than praise-worthy. Therefore, I have suggested that your time would be better spent attending the Plymouth School of Art where I have no doubt Mr Lewis, the Principal, would turn your present raw talents into some form of shape whereby you could earn a decent living in that field. What would you think of that?" Pam's first reaction, after the initial shock, blurted out, "Gosh! No more French! I could draw all day long without being told off!" "Precisely!" laughed the Sister Superior." So, do you think you would like that?" "Oh yes please!" she declared with great enthusiasm. "Well, run along back to your lessons. You'll still have to finish out your time here first, including the end of year exams." She warned. Pam gave her mother a quick hug and hurried back to her classroom. The girls were just coming out for the afternoon break so she was able to share her excitement with her friends. She couldn't tell them much except that her wildest dreams seemed to be about to come true. She knew that Sister Mary Gerda was right, she had very little chance, if any, of passing the school certificate which would mean at least another two years at school for probably nothing. Would she really be able to start Art School right away she wondered. She hardly dared to hope and was delighted to find her parents waiting outside in the car when school was over for the day. As they drove home they explained to her that the Sister Superior was going to write to the principal of the Plymouth College of Art to tell him about her and to recommend her as a student. This would probably be followed by an interview with him. Jack said, "the most important thing for you to do right away is to go through all your drawings and find enough good ones to make up a port folio to show what you can do." She panicked for a moment thinking that she would have nothing good enough. "Don't worry darling," he said, "I am sure with Miss Wright's help we will find plenty amongst your sketch books and paintings to show him, and you will have time to knock up a few more before then." When she got home she rushed in to tell Mabel and Charlotte the news, they were delighted. "Your Grandfather would have been so proud. Henry was an excellent artist himself. you've seen those lovely etchings of Windsor Chapel that he did haven't you? And he did lots more. you'll have to ask Aunt Ethel if she will show some to you."

Pam rushed off to her room to turn out her drawings. When her dad came in from work he came up and helped her sort through them. She had lots of dress designs that she had copied from fashion magazines. And many sketches of the rabbits and their dog Rex. There were quite a lot that wee too tatty to be used in a folder of such importance and she was very disappointed that one of her favourites was badly torn and grotty. So she got out her big new sketch pad which she had been given on her birthday and began some fresh ones. She drew Mabel and Charlotte cooking in the kitchen. Then some of the house from the back garden with Grandpa Baker weeding.

About ten days later a letter came with the much awaited appointment. It too was on a Wednesday afternoon. Of course, she was excused from school for the day and tried her best to look grown up and not too nervous, but of course she was, never the less. May had been very quiet about the whole thing. After the London episode she felt that any negativity on her part would not be tolerated so she just muttered "Good luck" as they set off.

The college of Art was a very old Victorian building in the centre of the town opposite the library. Jack parked the car around the side then they walked around to the front entrance and up the impressive flight of stone steps. The building had several different departments including the upstairs where the Architecture department resided. They were directed to the right into the corridor through a set of double doors. They continued down to the end where a door marked Secretary stood open. On entering they were greeted by a very friendly middle aged lady who asked them to sit and wait. Pam sat clutching her brand new port folio with white knuckles hardly daring to breathe in case they were told that the principal would not be able to see them today. But she need not have worried. The door on their left opened after only a few minutes and a very kindly looking gentleman in his late fifties came out and introduced himself as Mr Lewis. They stood up and followed him back into his office each shaking hands as they passed him. After they were seated he directed his questions to Pam asking a few questions about St. Dunstans Abbey and about her favourite lessons. She eagerly told him about her lessons with Miss Wright and how much she enjoyed helping make and paint scenery for the school plays and helping to make costumes as well. Her Mother proudly interjected that she was good with her needle and had made the blouse she had on. He kindly admired it and said that he had had a long chat with Miss Wright whom he knew quite well as she herself had been a pupil here.

He expressed some concern about her age and that she was not yet sixteen, which was the minimum age of entry at the college, but after browsing through her port folio expressed his surprise at her ability and thought that as her birthday was in January just before the Spring term commenced, he would be willing to bend the rules this once. He finally said that Pam could start as a first year student this September.

Pam could have burst with joy. She was going to be a real art student! She was going to be able to draw all day long! The formalities passed over her head as the Principal explained that she had been awarded a free place for four years, provided she passed her end of first year exams with a satisfactory set of marks.

As they departed, the secretary took some details from her father and she gave him a list of things she would need to know and equipment she would need to supply.

Pam traveled home on cloud nine. She could not sleep that night for reliving the day over and over.

When she returned to school she could not wait to tell her friends of her good fortune. she just had time before assembly to tell Miss Wright who was delighted for her. But Sister Eileen Mary brought her firmly down to earth explaining that she still had the rest of the summer term to work at what was left of her feeble education and reminded her that it would not all be drawing. She would have lots of homework on such things as the history of Architecture and such like. But she didn't care. She would soon be free from French and Chemistry and P.E! No more sports, just cycling to college. How great that sounded. No more wearing school uniform either!

As her farewell gift to the school Jack and Pam offered to put on a display of their rabbits and guinea pigs at the end of year summer fete. The Sister Superior was delighted with the idea and gave them the use of one of the smaller gardens next to the tennis court. For the fete they took along about twenty hutches and grass runs so that the girls could come in and pick them up if they wanted to. It was a great success and the voluntary collection box had almost £50 in it by the end of the day, which was joined with other moneys given to charity.

This day of the fete was to be her last day at the Abbey school. It felt very strange walking away for the last time, with no ceremony or farewells to speak of. Oh, of course the sisters came and saw the animals and wished her well at the Art college but never the less, knowing that she would never be a pupil there again was a very odd feeling indeed. Her school friends promised to keep in touch but she knew that except for the one who lived nearest they would soon fade in to memory.

The summer was a very happy one for Pam, she had so much to look forward to at Art College and she had her new friends at the Saturday social club. She often had some of them around to her house to play music on the gramophone or to sing around the piano. She re-met an old friend from infant school named Alan Penman who played the double base. They had been to school together at Somerset Place and he was now one of the boys who regularly came to Farleys. A crowd of them would often go into town and buy sheet music and the latest records and then come back to Mayon and play them. An old school friend of her father's named Albert Ford had a music shop in the centre of town in one of the Nissan hut shops temporarily created to house businesses whilst the new city centre was being built. He said that Pam could come and work for him in the December holidays selling sheet music as it got very busy in the run up to Christmas.

The chums also spent a lot of time at the Mount Wise swimming pool. One of the Malcolms, Venn, was a very good swimmer and competed in many competitions. He also played water polo which all them loved to go and watch. Another swimming friend was Margerite Hill, she had been in the girl guides with Pam and they often went to church at Stoke Damerel together. All in all they were a really jolly bunch and, as Charlotte said, "Brightened up the house with their music and laughter."

May wasn't too happy but that was not unusual. Her term at Pitmans came to an end and it was time for her to look for a permanent job. While she was looking she did a few temporary spells in different offices helping out while someone was sick or on holiday, but she really needed something more regular.

Jack and Phyllis had two very good friends named Edwin and Elsie Broad. They met through their common interest in local politics. They all worked for the Conservative party especially during local elections, indeed Edwin, or Ned as they called him was a local parish councillor. They also shared another common interest in the game of bridge and played together quite regularly. They lived nearby so were often in each other's company. Ned was a solicitor, and one evening in conversation he mentioned tht his secretary was soon to retire and he would have to get a replacement broken in well before she actually left. Jack told him about May. "I must be honest with you Ned, whilst she may be trained to Pitman's standards she herself is a problem." He tried to tell him about her strange moods and the problems they had had on their holiday in London. "So you see Ned, I would be deceiving you if I did not tell you about this side of her. Personally I feel that if she had a good steady job and gained some self esteem she would be a different girl." They talked more about May over supper with the two wives, and finally Ned and Elsie generously agreed to give May a chance as assistant secretary and see how she got on. Jack and Phyllis were very grateful and apologized for presuming on their friendship but Elsie said, " don't feel embarrassed Phyllis dear, if we can't help one another now and then what sort of friends would we be?"

On the following Monday Jack took May along to Ned's office in Albert Road and left her there on her own to talk about the work. She came back that evening quite optimistic and, for her, quite cheerful. Phyllis sighed with relief, perhaps things would get better now. She and May went out shopping that Saturday and bought her a brown costume and a cream blouse, suitable for office work.

In July Jack and Phyllis had their fourteenth wedding anniversary. Jack came in from work carrying a huge bunch of flowers and a box, and when Phyllis opened it there was a lovely cameo brooch inside. She was absolutely delighted with it and they hugged and kissed. Then she jumped up and fetched her present for him. He opened it and took out a new real skin brief case. Again they hugged and kissed. Pam said "Oi! You two, you are embarrassing us innocent young things!" She laughed but May was not laughing. In fact she left the room saying she heard someone at the door. But there was no one there. Later Jack and Phyllis went out to dinner with Ned and Elsie. As Charlotte, May and Pam were clearing up the tea things and Phyllis was upstairs dressing to go out, Pam said "Isn't it lovely when they kiss and cuddle like that after being married all this time. Real romantic, like in the movies!" "Oh, shut up!" responded May. "It's positively obscene at their age." And stormed out into the garden. "Typical. She really has a problem with real affection. I don't think she can have had much of it in her life poor thing." Charlotte said in a sad voice. She was closer to the truth than she knew.

Everything seemed to settle down quietly for a while, then one evening May certainly found a way to shatter the family peace.

Phyllis found May slumped in a corner sobbing with a handkerchief over her eyes.

"What ever is the matter May, my dear. Is the job not going well?" she asked. May shook her head and said nothing. "Well don't you think you should tell me what's troubling you?"

May cried harder and buried her face in Phyllis's shoulder. "Oh! It's awful! I don't know what to do!" she wailed.

"Well, I can't help if you don't stop sobbing and speak up." Phyllis tried to calm her. After a pause while she stopped sobbing she said, "It's Father. He, he touched me. Then he tried to kiss me, out in the rabbit house!"

Phyllis didn't know what to say. She frowned and then she thought hard before she spoke. "You must have been mistaken my dear. My husband would never do a thing like that. I know him, he wouldn't, he couldn't." Never for a moment did Phyllis doubt him. She trusted him completely and her love for him never wavered for one split second. "I am quite sure you've made some mistake May. Think about it sensibly." "He did! He did!" she persisted.

As Phyllis looked at her she could see that there was a lot of noise but no real tears. She began to suspect that this was another of May's ploys to gain attention. May certainly seemed to need to cause such scenes when ever anyone else held Phyllis's affections, and Jack and Phyllis had certainly been very close lately, especially on the day of their wedding anniversary.

"Now I'm going to say this to you May; this kind of accusation is very serious and it is not something to make up stories about. I know my husband as I have said, and I would take his word over yours any day. So, while I go out and talk to him, I want you to think carefully." She got up and left a very quiet May to do some serious thinking.

When Phyllis went out to the rabbit house, Jack looked up and smiled as she went over to him and put her arms around him. "What have I done to deserve this?" he asked giving her a peck on the cheek. "Just tell me you love me and I'll tell you." She said. "I'm a bit mucky right now but, I love you sweetheart and I'll show you how much later, how's that?" "Fine" she laughed rather seriously he thought. "Something the matter old girl?" he asked. "Yes. I'm afraid so. May has been telling me a big story of how you touched her and tried to kiss her." He stopped feeding the rabbit he was holding and shouted," What? Good heavens what will that girl think of next! It would be funny if it werent' so bloody serious! You know I didn't do any such thing don't you?" he asked. very concerned She put her arms around him, " Don't worry darling, of course I didn't believe it, not for a second. We vowed, long ago always to trust one another and I do trust you. My god, I know you! You aren't capable of such rubbish!" "You don't know how glad I am to hear you say that darling. What the hell are we going to do about it? Eigh?" Phyllis thought for a moment." Let her stew upon it for a bit. it won't hurt her. We have to make her understand that she won't gain my affection by attacking everyone I love. you and Pammy have been very patient but I do feel sorry for her, She is disturbed and needs us. Though I don't suppose you feel that way right now." "I feel like throwing her out! That's what I feel!" Jack said, but calmed down after a bit and they went back indoors.

May finally admitted that she had lied and only said it because she was afraid Phyllis wouldn't love her any more. She cried and said she was sorry over and over. Phyllis said firmly, "You'll stop me loving you at all if you don't stop this nonsense!" This hit home hard and May began to realize that she had gone too far and they might turn her out.

Of course everyone in the house had heard it all and Mabel and Charlotte felt that it was the time to send her packing but Phyllis was not one to hold a grudge indeed she felt sorry for May and told her she could stay if she promised to try and control these mad desires to disrupt the family.

On reflection Jack took it fairly lightly and put it down to an attack to hormones.

SEPTEMBER 1948

On the day that Pam was to start her first term at the Art College, it was pouring with rain, but it did not dampen her spirits as her father helped her load her stuff into his car. She waved goodbye and they set off to the centre of town and round to the back door of the College. She struggled out with her board and bags and waved as best she could as she climbed the short flight of steps into the back door where the corridor was in chaos. a teacher with glasses perched on the end of his nose, was trying to gather the new students and direct them into the large classroom on the right. Pam followed as he called out "That's right all first year students in here please. Once they were inside and he had counted to check there were twenty present, he then led them through a second door at the other end back into the corridor but turned right into a small passage way which held several lockers. "these lockers are for the use of you first years. They are not kept locked so do not leave any valuables in them. They are just meant for coats, wet shoes and working smocks and overalls. On this other wall you will notice this large very long cupboard with slits in it. These slits are designed to hold your drawing boards and any port folios you may wish to put in them. Be sure you have your name clearly on everything!" He then waited as they took the opportunity of taking off their coats and putting their boards into the slots. Then he led them back to the room from which they came and told them to sit at the tables.

Some other adults were standing by the blackboard, "Right every one quiet please. My name is Mister Herman and I am your year Mentor. I also will be teaching you Modelling and Pottery at our annex at Sutton Road school across town. Don't worry when you go there tomorrow you will be going together by bus from here". He then indicated the lady by his side. She was tall and thin and had dark hair tied back in a bun. She had bright eyes and a smiling face. "This is Miss Reed. She teaches mainly in this room. As you see there are several looms around the walls so no marks for guessing that she teaches weaving. Also dress design and fabric dying and printing." He then turned as an elderly lady entered the room. She looked very old indeed to the students, indeed she was very close to retirement. She walked with a stoop but like her colleague, gave them a beaming smile. "This dear lady is Miss Pierce. Her room is just across the hall which faces out on to the street. You will be with her every Monday morning drawing plants and other things. "Next he turned to the other lady who was well into middle age and graying but she was very upright and looked more somber than the other two ladies. "Mrs Williams works down in the basement where you will study the history of architecture, and also calligraphy "next came a tall gentleman in his thirties. His hair was slightly balding at the back. He was slim and looked very energetic. "This gentleman is Mister Mann. He teaches screen printing downstairs in the room next to this and upstairs he teaches life drawing." The teachers nodded and then left to go to their respective rooms to begin teaching. "Now before you wonder where you are to go , I will give you your timetables and we will take it a step at a time." From then on everything seemed to move very fast. Collecting papers, finding the way to the first lesson, finding the coffee machine at breaktime and before she knew it, it was lunch time. Most of her fellow students had brought sandwiches as had she so they went out the back door and, now that the weather had brightened up they eat them sitting on the steps or on the grass verge opposite. Some had gone across the road to the pastry shop and bought something to eat. They sighed and chatted about their morning whilst they exchanged information of their names and where they came from. Pam sat next to the girl she had been with in the classroom where they had drawn leaves with Miss Pearce. Julie had been a Saturday morning student for a whole year so she was very confident and knew her way around. She was on good terms with all the tutors too. "Mister Herman lives near me so we often walk home together. Of course this is my second choice as a career as originally I wanted to be a ballet dancer, but I was too tall." She certainly was tall but looked exactly like Alice in Wonderland. She had long straight blonde hair hanging down her back kept tidy by a wide red alice band. She also wore a frilly blouse and a multicoloured skirt. She obviously liked bright colours, thought Pam. They got on well together and were soon chatting to several others. The youngest besides herself, was a young man who was to be known as Kerley. His first name was Francis but he hated it, so insisted everyone use his sir name. Mister Herman took a while to get used to it though. The afternoon was spent in the basement with Mrs Williams learning the rudiments of Caligraphy. Something which Pam took to right away as she had been good at writing at school, it seemed to come easy to her.

The day was gone in a flash and a very tired Pamela crossed the road at four o'clock and lined up for the number fourteen bus which would take her back to Ford Hill, just a stroll from Penlee Road and home. Everyone was diying to hear how her first day had gone. She told them about it over supper and went to bed early as she was really tired, but very happy, it had really begun, this new wonderful experience of being an Art student.

On the Tuesday morning they were taken by Mister Herman down the road and were shown the correct bus stop to catch the number twenty two down to the Sutton Road annex.

They would be expected to find their own way there each Tuesday and would be expected to arrive no later than nine fifteen. They spent the day learning about modelling clay and how to look after it and not let it dry out but keep it in bins with very wet cloths over them. They had overalls available so they didn't get their clothes too dirty but it soon became clear that old clothes were the order of the day on Tuesdays.

And so the first week passed getting into the routine of finding their way around and getting used to each teacher's little ways. Miss Reed was very easy going most of the time but did not suffer late comers lightly. Mister Mann however was the most strict. He was the assistant head so his responsibilities were more pressing on occasion so that they often had to be left to work without him and woe betide anyone who abused his trust by larking about.

Their first life class on the Friday afternoon caused many giggles as they wondered if they were really going to have naked people to draw. But this was not to be the case for the mere first years. They had a very nice lady fully dressed sitting for them. The boys looked disappointed which made all the girls laugh. During the following weeks Pam got on well with all her fellow students but Julie, Kerley and a girl named Gwen were her best friends. Julie, or as she was better know at home as Julia Lethbridge, invited her back to tea at half term and they discovered their joint love of music. Pam played the piano and Julie danced. Pam was quite surprised how good Julie was and realized how disappointed she must have been to have grown too tall. but it did not stop her dancing just for her own pleasure.

On November 5th it was May's 18th birthday and Jack and Phyllis took her out for a meal, without Pam, who realized that taking her too would not have made it so special. May was on her best behaviour and enjoyed it very much. That night she vowed to try very hard to keep her jealousy under control though she still found it difficult at times. She seemed to get fits of depression for no reason at all when she least expected it. Sometimes she wondered if there was really something wrong with her.

Everyone was talking about the pending royal wedding. The princess Elizabeth was going to be married to her Prince Philip on November 20th. And it would be shown on television.

Not many people had television sets yet and those that did only received a very poor quality picture. But of course, everyone wanted to see it. So those who had sets were arranging parties so that their friends and neighbours could come and watch it.

A good friend of Jack's lived not far away and invited them all to come and watch it at his house. Mabel and Charlotte refused and May was going to see it as her office collegue's house, so about fifteen people crowded into the sittingroom to watch. Some sitting on the floor as every seat was taken and as it was to be a long day of watching, both the journey from the palace, the service and the return journey through the cheering London crowds, refreshments were continually being passed around during the day. Everyone who came had contributed biscuits, buns and sandwiches not to mention several kinds of drinks from lemonade for the children to things stronger for the adults; and of course plenty of tea being brewed for the ladies.

The picture on the small television set was very cloudy and difficult to see at times but noone minded. They were actually seeing it all as it happened and David Dimbleby's commentary was so moving. It was certainly a day to re-member. Charlotte and Mabel listened to it on their radio and enjoyed imagining it. The papers next day gave them beautiful pictures which they folded away and saved very carefully.

Just as the first year students were settling down to the routine of their various lessons they were told that on the last day of term there would be a Costume ball. Everyone was very excited and begin to talk about the different fancy dress costumes they might wear. Pam invited her cousin Jean to come too and Jean decided to make a bo-peep cos-tume using her bridesmaid's dress which she had for her brother's wedding, adding a flounce on the hips and a bon-net and shepherd's crook. Pam made herself a midnight blue long dress with a net overlay covered with shiny stars and a head-dress shaped like the moon to represent night. They told no-one else of course. Part of the fun was guess-ing what each other was going to wear.

The large central classroom had a glass room divider which usually separated it into two classrooms. This was now folded back to make one large room. The looms were moved into Miss Pearce's room across the hall and a stage was erected at the end for the dance band. Decorations and balloons were hung everywhere. Then, on the last day every-one left early to get ready. Pam rushed home on the number fourteen bus and had a quick tea before getting herself all dressed up. Jack had arranged to drive via Peverell to pick up Jean and then on to the college. They gave him a hug and started to get out as he told them he would be back for them at midnight.

They hurried up the back steps and into the hallway which was crowded with students and friends anxiously examining each other's costumes. Julie had come dressed as a ballerina and Kerley, the devil, all in red with a pointed beard complete with horns a tail and a pitch fork. But Pam thought that Gwen's was the best. She was dressed as a doll, in a frilly white skirt with a red velvet bodice edged with fur and a pill box hat to match, long bloomers, white stockings and pumps. Her face was painted just like a doll with round rosy cheeks and long lashes. As the students gathered in the main room they saw that their tutors had dressed up too. Mister Herman came in an artist's smock with a beret and a palette. Mister Mann came as a sheik and Miss Reed as a Japanese girl in an authentic Kimono. At Eight o'clock the principal and his wife arrived. They were both dressed as Romans in togas. They circulated and chatted to the more senior students and the teachers then at half past the hall was called to order and Mister and misses Lewis were lead up to the stage where they sat on two decorated 'thrones'. Then everyone in costume paraded around the room for them to choose their favourite. They chose one of the older students called June who had come as Ophelia, in a white flowing gown draped with wild flowers and weeds; it was beautifully done and everyone applauded their choice. She was then crowned Queen of the Ball and led the dance.

The principal and his wife did not stay long, they knew that their presence would inhibit the young people so departed soon after nine, then the band struck up some very lively music and the dancing began, as did the drinking.

The whole evening went with a bang especially when the balloons were released from a net in the ceiling. Midnight came all too soon for our girls and they were surprised when

Jack's head appeared round the door to collect them. Pam had to prize Jean out of the arms of an architect student and they fell laughing into the car to be driven home the way they came. Pam was almost asleep when the car drew up at the door so apart from a sleepy 'goodnight', she left the telling until next day.

In the morning she returned to the college to help clear up the empty bottles, streamers and sad deflated balloons. Then suddenly they all heard a groaning coming from behind the stage. They discovered a drunken senior student, Jeff, upside down with his head stuck between the pipes. They hauled him out and he curled himself into a ball and went back to sleep.

The next day the headlines in the local paper read, "STUDENT PRANKSTERS STRIKE AGAIN" with a picture of the flagpole outside the guildhall with a top hat on the top. Apparently, at the end of the party, about three o'clock a gang of very drunk students went into the town and one of them climbed the very high pole and planted the hat. This was an annual tradition which no self respecting art student would let go by with out a token prank.

Grandpa Baker had been very lonely without Grandma and to try and cheer him up Phyllis put up a bed in the front room and had him to stay at Mayon for Christmas. So it would be a quieter festive occasion this year. Not that it was that quiet for Pam. She had lots of new friends who invited her to their parties as well as the Christmas party at the youth social club. May didn't mind a quiet Christmas. She had been rather dreading nosiy parties with Pam's friends dropping in. But that was to wait until her birthday.

On New Year's Day after a lovely lunch, they were sitting by the fire when Jack, unwittingly, dropped a bomb. After sighing and rubbing his tummy he first congratulated

Charlotte and Phyl on a beautiful meal, then after a pause he said, "Well, what a year it has been. Pammy almost sixteen and an art student, and May, now eighteen years old and a secretary. You'll be wanting to leave us soon I expect and have a flat, a home of your own."

The room went very quiet. Charlotte and Mabel looked at eachother and Phyllis froze, wondering just what May was thinking. Jack had spoken in all innocence, not meaning, 'when are you leaving?' or anything; he just was pointing out her reaching the age of consent when she was free to do as she liked with her life. But sadly, May did not see it that way. Phyllis could tell by her face. The lower lip was trembling and May was building up for a good cry. She jumped up from the table and rushed upstairs to her room, slammed the door behind her and flung herself on her bed.

"Now look what you've done Jack!" scolded Phyllis. "What did I say? I only meant she was a grown woman now, that's all.!" "It sounded more like you were hoping the time had come for her to leave!" "Well, I certainly didn't mean it to sound like that!" "Perhaps you subconsciously do want her to go." said Mabel, and Charlotte nodded. "I don't see what the fuss is about. Surely May is bound to move on some time isn't she?" Pam said, not really sure whether she really wanted it to be true or not. A buzz of conversation ensued. Many home truths were spoken and a few regrets too. Whatever the outcome Phyllis new that she would have to go upstairs and try to calm the situation.

She climbed the stairs and knocked at the closed door. There was no response so Phyllis opened the door and walked over to May's bed. "Men can be the clumsiest creatures sometimes with absolutely no tact at all!" she said as she stroked May's hair. "Don't cry my dear. He only meant that you should be pleased to have reached the age when you are a woman at last. He didn't mean he wants you to leave right now!" "But he does want me to leave doesn't he!" wailed the sobbing girl. "Of course you'll leave one day. We took you into our family to help you get on your feet. Naturally our hope is that when you are ready you will go out into the world on your own. We will say the same to Pammy one day."

"But I don't want to leave you! I want to stay here with you. You understand me. Nobody else does. I know Mabel and Charlotte hate me!"

"What nonsense May! No-one hates you. Now stop feeling sorry for yourself and come down for coffee. Be sensible and cheer up, it's New Year. Who knows what opportunities will come for you this year?"

But May would not come downstairs again. She lay there in the dark convincing herself that no one wanted her. Not even Phyllis. What could she do to make sure she could stay here, in this house where there was so much love to spare. She wanted some of it so much but didn't know how to get it.

JANUARY 1949

This year, on January the ninth, it was Pam's sixteenth birthday and she was allowed to have a really grown-up party with boys and girls. She invited Julie and Kerley from her new art school friends and her cousins Mary and Jean, her 'aunts', the twins, Betty and Joan, and from the youth club friends, The two Malcolms and Ruth, Malcolm Davey's girlfriend, Barry Ian and Alan and her own new boyfriend, Robert. They had a great time playing records and dancing, singing around the piano, and, of course, some kissing games like postman's knock. Phyllis put on a lovely supper and Pam blew out the candles on her birthday cake. After supper they played a game of Murder in the dark, which got the girls screaming, much to the boy's delight. Then came a very special game which had just been invented by one of the boys. All the boys lined up along the darkened passage and each girl in turn was to come out and kiss each boy in turn, then at the end they were pushed into the bathroom where, when the light was turned on they were faced with Malcolm Venn supposedly having a bubble bath. There reactions were noted. Most of them screamed, of course, except the trainee nurse, Betty, who offered to scrub his back! The biggest joke, however, was that Jack joined in and stood in the passage with the other boys getting a kiss. When Ruth came along, she thought it was her boyfriend and gave him a big kiss and sighed, saying, "Oh, Malcolm!" which gave everyone a great laugh. Jack said he enjoyed it very much indeed. Phyllis teased him about it for some time afterwards. Pam's parents were very relaxed about these, in the dark kissing games, and one of the boys said that they were great to be so 'with it'. But Phyllis and Jack said that young people would find somewhere to kiss and cuddle anyway, so why not let them do it where they could be supervised so that nothing went too far. The girls all agreed that it was a pity most parents were not so understanding. Jack drove most of them home after eleven o'clock to make sure they all got home safely.

May had been away for that weekend staying with a girl she had met at Pitmans. When she returned they told her all about the jolly party Pam had had and Phyllis did not miss the opportunity of teasing Jack once again. When she heard about his antics she was quite shocked and let them know in no uncertain terms that she thought it disgusting and childish, to say the least.

May was sullen all the following week and went about the house complaining at every opportunity. On Friday night she took to her bed after supper complaining of a stomach ache. She blamed Charlotte's cooking and just after she got into bed, had to rush down to the bathroom to be sick. Phyllis did not know, of course that May had put her finger down her throat and made herself vomit. She returned to bed and was given some medicine to settle her stomach, but at two o'clock in the morning she did it again, disrupting everyone's night sleep. She would not eat all the next day insisting that Charlotte was trying to poison her. Under her bed she had several packets of biscuits and whilst lying down for a rest, consumed a full packet, making it possible for her to force herself to vomit once more. By Monday morning she was too 'poorly' to go to work and stayed in bed until lunchtime when she came downstairs declaring herself much better. When Phyllis and Jack came home from work she was able to eat her supper, picking at it cautiously, much to Charlotte's annoyance. "It's only sausage and mash, I can't do much to that! Though you'd better not have any trifle, it's got rum in it, to disguise the taste of the arsenic!" Everyone laughed except May, of course, who would dearly have loved to have some of Charlotte's delicious trifle, but stormed out without having any.

So this particular tantrum gained her nothing so she had to try something much more serious next time. A couple of weeks later, when May did not come to supper one Saturday, Phyllis went up to see what was the matter and found May lying on her bed seemingly unconscious with a half empty bottle of pills lying on it's side on her bedside locker. She tried to waken May but could not, so she called Jack who tried to awaken her by shaking her firmly. When this didn't seem to work he slapped her face. Instead of the expected response of perhaps groaning and waking up, she opened her eyes wide and yelled out. It was quite clear then, that she was faking. "I thought so.!" Said Jack. "This is your latest trick is it? Trying to attract attention. Well you're doing that alright young lady! If you do that again I'll give you attention!" and he stormed out. May sobbed and said she was sorry, hugging Phyllis and asking for her forgiveness. Phyllis was at a loss what to do about it. After May calmed down she went downstairs to talk about it with Jack. They had never experienced anything like this before and didn't know where to turn.

At their next bridge evening with Ned and Elsie Broad, during a coffee break they shared their problem. "I'm sorry, Ned, this must have effected you too as May ahs missed some worktime hasn't she?" asked Jack. "More than you know, I'm afraid. I was going to bring the subject up myself. Hardly a week goes by without she takes a day off for something, claiming a visit to the dentist or the doctor or some such excuse. You are correct, it is effecting my office routine."

"I'm dreadfully sorry Ned; we had no idea. Look we will quite understand if you want to sack her. She really is a problem, we don't really know where to turn for advice." said Jack. "I won't sack her just yet, though I do intend to give her a warning. Why don't you have a chat with your doctor, Phyllis? It may be that she needs some treatment." replied Ned. "We'll give it some thought, thank you; and thank you for being so patient with her." Phyllis said.

That night, in bed, they talked quietly about what they should do. They finally decided that a talk with their doctor might be a good idea.

The following week Phyllis made the time to visit Doctor Reeves, who had been their physician and friend for several years. "Well, Phyllis," he said after hearing the story of May's strange fits and tantrums. "You seem to have a very mixed up child on your hands, though at eighteen she is hardly a child. Frankly, I don't think there is much you can do. She is of age and you would not be able to insist she see a specialist; though you might like to suggest that she consult me herself and I could advise her accordingly. You see, she is not your child. You did not adopt her, and frankly, by the sound of it, it's a good job you didn't; though perhaps I shouldn't say that." "No Doctor Reeves, I agree with you. Though we did consider doing so at the beginning. The problem is I feel sorry for her and cannot bring myself to just turn her out. "replied Phyllis. "You have a good heart my dear; many would have, I am sure. However, have a talk with her and see if she will come to me on her own. She must know something is wrong, and would be glad of some expert advice."

At the next opportunity Phyllis had a talk with May, but when May realized that Phyllis had been to the Doctor behind her back she got very angry. "How dare you talk about me to that man without asking me first! I'm not ill! Nor am I going insane! Though if you go on treating me like this I may well go mad!" She got up and grabbing her coat and fled out of the house. Phyllis ran after her but May was already half way down the street. She didn't return that night but came back at seven o'clock the next morning looking dreadful. She had clearly stayed out all night somewhere and Phyllis was just getting ready for work. "I can't stop her with you May. You'll have to look after yourself. Have a bath and go to bed. I'll ring your boss and tell him you won't be in."

May didn't answer but turned her head to the wall until Phyllis left. Charlotte was not happy being left alone with the girl but stayed in her own room until she heard May go to her own bedroom and go to sleep.

That evening the atmosphere in the house was strained. After the meal was over Jack took May aside. "Have you thought about what the Doctor said? I know you are angry at Phyllis for going to see him, but you clearly need help." There was a pause for several minutes before May answered." No I am not going to see any Doctor. I know what you are all trying to do; you want to put me in a sanitarium like they put my Mother in. Oh. I know you hate me. But Phyllis loves me, I know she does."

Jack did not know what to say. He threw up his hands.

"Fine. Think what you like. But if you don't stop all this, I am going to help you find somewhere else to live, do you understand me? This nonsense can't go on. It's wearing Phyllis out, and I won't have her upset any more. So, it's up to you." And he left her to ponder on his words.

She was verly quiet for a couple of weeks and went to work regularly, but her quiet moods continued. She only spoke when spoken to and was often heard weeping in her room whenever Pam was out with her friends. Indeed, Phyllis was thankful that Pam was very busy with her Art school work and her spare time was filled with her music and her friends both at the swimming pool and at the social group at Peverell. She continued to stay over at Jean's every Saturday night. At least she seemed unaffected by May's tantrums.

The resentment over the visit to the Doctor continued to fester and May was trying to think up some way to disturb the family further. One evening Phyllis walked into the bathroom only to find May sitting on a chair with her wrists in a sink of water coloured with blood. May's arms were smeared with blood and there were cuts on her wrists. Phyllis yelled for Jack as she wrapped a towel around May's arms and made her walk back into the diningroom. When Jack came in they got out the medicine box ready to bandage her wrists but on closer inspection Phyllis realized that May had not actually cut her veins. Yes she had slashed her arm but certainly not anywhere near the artery.

Jack stood back with a sigh." First you pretend to take pills now you pretend to cut your wrists! What is the matter with you? This has got to stop, do you hear?"

"I'm not going to any Doctor! I won't and you can't make me. If you try I really will cut my wrists next time!" she screamed at them then ran upstairs slamming the door.

"I'm sorry Phyllis, this can't go on. That girl is more than we can handle and I don't think I can bear seeing what it's doing to you my darling. You are trying to be kind but nothing seems to please her and I've had enough quite frankly. I'm going to look for a flat for her, she can't stay here any more."

Phyllis knew Jack well enough to know when not to

argue with him and in her heart she knew he was right. Whatever it was that May needed it was not something that they could give her. She was old enough to stand on her own two feet and decide for herself what she really wanted. Never the less when Jack came in a couple of days later and said that he had found a nice flat in Albert Road not far from Ned's office she did not know how May would react when they told her.

They waited until after supper when Pam had gone out and the aunts had gone to their room before they talked to May.

Jack began," May, you remember I said the other day that it would be best if you lived somewhere else, well I've found a very nice flat near your work which will be vacant from Saturday next. Would you like to go and see it?" May looked at Phyllis with a pleading look. "It's no use looking at Phyllis. We have made up our minds because no matter how much we have tried you have not been happy here, so it's for the best that you move on." She looked again at Phyllis who just nodded to show that she was in agreement with her husband. "Please. You can't really want me to go. Can't you let me try again? I know you care about me! I haven't got anyone else." she pleaded.

"Don't make it harder for us all May. Just say you'll agree and make the best of it. Please." Phyllis looked at May sadly but got no help from May. She was determined to fight all the way, but Jack was addiment. "It's for the best as I said, so you'd better start packing your things together." No more was said and May realized she was losing her battle so retreated to get out her suitcase from under the stairs. After she left the room Phyllis let the tears fall. "Don't cry darling" said Jack softly. "It's your happiness I care about and I can't see any other way. I haven't seen you smile for a long time." He held her close and she sighed. "Oh Jack.

It's just that I feel such a failure. Why couldn't we make her happy here with us?" "That girl has had a hard life losing first her father and then her mother and Lord knows how deep all that ran in her mind. She just saw Pammy within a happy family here and wanted some of it but went about getting some the wrong way. Now it's too late. We could never go back. I'm sorry too but she's got to go. You know I'm right. Let's just hope she'll find happiness somewhere soon." On the Saturday Jack took May around to the flat. It had been lived in by a young girl who had left to get married. She obviously had good taste for the flat was bright a cheerful and well decorated. It was a furnished rental so May would not need to spend any money on it; everything was there that she would need bar groceries of course. She actually quite liked it and agreed to move in the next day. But when it came time to leave Mayon she suddenly clung to the front door jamb and shouted, "No! I won't go! You can't make me!" But Jack was firm and told everyone to go away and leave it to him. When her 'audience' had gone into other rooms and shut the doors May gave in and walked quietly to the car. She looked back to the windows but noone was in sight. Jack drove her to Albert Road and carried a box of groceries in which Phyllis had insisted on providing her with to get started. Then once everything was inside he turned away to his car and got in, giving her a small wave and a smile. "Good luck" he said as he drove away.

Fortunately Phyllis had a busy time ahead of her with changing her job. Her friend who owned the shop in Union Street was opening another one on Peverell Corner and asked Phyllis to manage it for her. It was a much nicer district than Union Street and opening a new shop was exciting. It too was a hardware store, not as large as the other but well stocked with all types of kitchen utensils, crockery and cutlery, as well as other sundry household goods. This shop was no nearer to home but it gave her two half days a week instead of one as this shop did not open on Saturday afternoons or Wednesdays. She and Jack were also getting more and more involved with politics. It was known that there would be a general election the next spring and it would take a lot of preparation for the Devonport division of the Conservative party to get organized. At a special meeting it was agreed that Phyllis would run the campaign office which would be situated in the ground floor of a large house in Tavistock Road, near the Technical college; and Jack would be the events co-ordinator including rallies and large campaign meetings. The candidate had not been selected yet but rumours were floating around. One of which was that it would be Winston Churchill's son Randolf. But it was too soon to know yet for sure. There would certainly have to be a strong candidate to have a chance of beating the present M.P. Micheal Foot.

After one of their campaign planning meetings which involved the councillors of the party, Ned Broad took the chance to speak to Phyl and Jack in a quiet corner.

"I'm afraid I have some unpleasant news for you; I had to give May Evans the sack. She came to work the worse for drink and was rather rude. I regret to give you this news and hope that your sympathies will not tempt you to get in touch with her again. She is her own worst enemy I fear."

Jack and Phyllis were indeed very distressed to receive this news but Jack was firm when he saw Phyllis wavering towards seeing May.

She did as Jack said and tried not to worry about what might happen to May now she was presumably out of work.

On the following Saturday evening as they were sitting by the fire listening to the radio, there was a heavy ganging on the front door. As Jack went to see what all the fuss was about he was met at the bottom of the stairs by Mabel.

"It's May, Jack. Don't open the door." He waited, but the banging continued as Phyllis joined him. Charlotte stood above on the stairs as Jack made the decision to open it "The neighbours will be complaining if I don't open the door." he said as he went forward then opened it half way only to have if flung wider by the weight of May falling in, half drunk.

"Let me in! Let me come back please or I really will slash my wrists! Look I've got a knife here and I'll do it! I will!" She struggled to her feet and leant against the door. She looked a mess, untidy with lipstick smudged over her face and eye make-up the like of which she had never used before. "For God's sake May, get a hold of yourself!" cried Jack. "This won't do you any good. You can't come here behaving like this, I won't have my wife upset any more do you understand? Now go away!" "No! I'm going to do it!" she grabbed the knife out of her jacket and started to try and damage herself with it. Jack and Phyllis struggled to stop her and in the fracas Mabel got knocked to the ground and when Charlotte tried to help, May's fist caught her in the face. By then Jack had managed to take the knife away from her and pushed her outside the door. He managed to shut it only to have May banging on it peering through the glass panels shouting and crying out.

"It's no use we'll have to call the police." said Jack as he went to the end of the hall and picked up the phone and dialed 999.

Only a few minutes later a police car arrived outside and quickly assessed the situation. As one lady constable bundled May into the back of the car the other came into the house to gather the details. Jack explained briefly and then the policeman left saying he would return to talk some more after they had dealt appropriately with May.

It all seemed never ending. Just as they thought that the problem had gone away, this had to happen. When the policeman came back they told him May's story in detail starting from the time when she first came to help Pammy with her French. At the end of the policeman taking lots of notes he said that it would be up to the magistrate now, but it may be that she would be sent back to Guernsey to live with her family there. They would certainly give her a restraining order to stop her coming to their house again. And so it was. A few weeks later the policeman returned informing them that she had been sent back to the Channel Islands where her Grandmother had agreed to take care of her. He agreed that if she had been prepared to see a Doctor earlier things might have been different but in his opinion her problems were very deep rooted and would take a long time to improve.

The forthcoming election proved to be very time consuming and the announcement on December 22nd that it would indeed be Randolph Churchill who would be running against Micheal Foot in the February. When they heard that he would be coming to Devonport to meet his campaign team, Phyllis offered their frontroom as the venue for this meeting. Everyone at Mayon bustled about getting prepared. First, giving the room a good spring clean. Not that it needed it as Jack had recently decorated, but it made the women feel better. At the next committee meeting they decided how many could be there allowing for the fact that absolutely everyone wanted to meet him. Phyllis said that ten would be a good number to accommodate so the list was made with the chairman's decision as final. Of course there would be those who were not chosen who would protest but they were promised that if there were any drop outs, there might be a chance for them.

The best three piece suite would hold five and the four diningroom chairs plus a stool from the bedroom leaving a chair for Randolph himself. He was a big man like his father so they didn't want to make a mistake and put him on something too flimsy or indeed too small. Ned came to the rescue and offered his leather office chair which they brought round at the weekend.

It was very cold that December so a fire was laid in the grate and the coal bucket filled and put in the corner. Then Phyllis and Charlotte considered what they should prepare for refreshments. Sandwiches perhaps but what sort? And a sponge cake. Charlotte made beautiful sponges and said she would be honoured to cook one for such an important gentleman. After some discussion they decided on ham for the sandwiches and added shortbread biscuits as an after thought. Tea and coffee of course but should they provide Whiskey or Brandy? As Jack was a tea-totaller, they did not keep any such drinks in the house and decided to ask Ned about that; and he thought that they had better not as this was an official meeting. Everything they could think of was done and the day arrived.

Jack lit the fire in plenty of time to be sure the room was comfortable. The ladies fussed about plumping the cushions and placing the chairs. they put the special chair in the centre of the room with it's back towards the fireplace.

Ned and Elsie were the first to arrive followed quickly by the other chosen members of the committee. Sir Clifford Tozer was to be bringing Mister Churchill in his car. Shortly after eight o'clock, the car drove up and everyone stood up expectantly. Jack was at the door with Phyllis to greet him and he came in shaking hands with everyone as they were introduced. Then he was invited to sit. As he did so he slid the chair backwards somewhat, so that he could see everyone. The problem with that was, as time went on he got very hot at his back and began to perspire. Jack could see the problem and quickly put a fire screen which Pam had embroidered at college, behind the chair. Then he left the door open to cool the room a bit.

The initial meeting went quite well, Phyllis thought; they talked about his family and when they would be joining him and a rough plan of the campaign which they assured him was well in hand. He announced that his father, Sir Winston himself, would be coming down to give him support and would like four big rallies arranged. This would be Jack's job, and venues were discussed. After refreshments the meeting drew to a close and Mister Churchill shook everyone's hand and wished them all a merry Xmas before driving off with Sir Clifford. Everyone sighed with relief that everything had gone off so well. After the guests had left they cleared up and went off to bed, well satisfied with how it had gone. There was that embarrassing moment when the poor man was nearly roasted but Pam's fire screen came to the rescue.

Christmas went quite quickly as everyone was anxious to get to grips with the political campaign which would swing into action as soon as the New year celebrations were over. Jack and Sir Clifford Tozer fixed two of the rally sites quite easily. The first would be in the car park of Argyll Football ground. As he was Chairman of the club, that was not a problem. The second was Saltrum House just outside of town near Plymstock which would be housed in a large marquee. The third was the Forum Cinema in Fore Street Devonport which they were sure they would be able to rent for an afternoon. As it turned out they were told that Sir Winston Churchill would only be able to spare three days so a fourth venue was no longer needed which was just as well as they had drawn a blank for a suitable place for it.

Once January began, Randolf and his family moved into their temporary accommodation near the office where his personal agent and Phyllis would work. This had a large outer room where volunteers were contantly working folding leaflets and filling envelopes with pamphlets. Pam was a member of the young conservatives who also were kept busy running errands and doing deliveries of the mail and so forth. Jack checked that the marquees were ordered along with all the folding chairs etc.

Phyllis dealt with the press and advertising, which was a full time job. This meant that her friend let her have as much time off as she needed from the shop at Peverell.

Grandad Baker was very keen to help all he could. He had been involved in local politics all his life and loved the hustle and bustle of electioneering. His experience of running door to door campaigning was invaluable to Phyllis whose business it was to see that each ward in Devonport had empty shops and such like buildings were made available for the week of the voting and check that they were strategically near to the polling stations.

Her own office and indeed the central office for Devonport division was near Devonport park and was a hive of industry every day with volunteers dealing with postal votes, pamphlets and folding literature to be mailed to voters. One morning after Randolph and his family were settled in, he called into the office to check the post. As he walked through the room where the ladies were busy, they all called out "Good morning Mister Churchill.", he continued into Phylliss's office and closed the door. She got up from her desk and said, "Mister Churchill, may I say something? I have noticed that, not for the first time, you came through the outer office past your workers who greeted you saying 'good morning' and you did not reply to them. You just walked by and came in here without even a nod or a smile. I have to tell you that it just won't do. You cannot afford to ignore these willing volunteers like that. A little bit of courtesy goes a long way. Now, if you want them to vote for you may I suggest you back out there and give them your appreciation of their work, please." He looked at her for a moment, then, without a word he turned around and went out to the outer office and said 'good morning' then circulated amongst them asking how they all were before returning to Phyllis's room and continued surveying his post. When she told Jack about it that night he laughed. "Good for you darling. It had to be said by somebody. He's so busy he's forgetting to be sociable, you're absolutely right. He won't win votes if he doesn't learn the art of being a politician. That means wooing your voters and he's not quite got the hang of it yet. You keep reminding him love, he certainly respects your opinions." She felt better after that but had to admit she had taken a risk speaking out.

Pam and her young conservative friends loved going to the opposition meetings and heckling Micheal Foot as did their young people at Randolph's meetings. They wore rosettes and carried banners shouting and singing having a great time.

The day finally came when Sir Winston Churchill came to the three big rallies. He arrived at Plymouth railway station where he and his entourage were driven swiftly off to Saltram where, unfortunately, it was teeming down with rain. It had started about one o'clock, thankfully after all the audience had arrived and found their seats. The entertainment began with a parade by the Dagenham Girl Pipers and finished with the beautiful singing by the coloured singer, Elizabeth Walsh. Then everyone waited for the main event, the arrival of the Churchill family with Sir Winston at their head. The crowd rose and cheered him as he made his way to the stage. He began by thanking the Plymouth and Devonport people for their courage and bravery during the Blitz. The whole tent erupted with cheering and someone started 'for he's a jolly good fellow', and the audience joined in to a man. Once the uproar had subsided, he began his campaign speech demanding that the electorate do all they could to elect a new Conservative Government. Naturally, most of the listeners were of the party so needless to say it was received with great cheering. His son followed with his own speech, promising the electors his full support. Finally the rain stopped as the cavalcade of Churchills left followed by the public who all agreed it had been an exciting day.

The next day the same enthusiasm was shown at the second rally held in the car park of Argyll Football ground. A covered stage had been erected and voters were first entertained and then listened to the political speeches. Once again Winston was cheered. Another successful meeting, well organized by Jack. He just hoped that the third rrally would go as well.

He was particularly anxious, for his wife who was going to make a speech. When the time came, Winston Churchill was cheered as before and all the speeches went well. finally it was Phyllis's turn. She looked so small on that huge stage but when she stepped up to the mike, her voice was clear and strong as she thanked all the workers and hoped to see them all in the days to come, out there campaigning for all they were worth! They cheered her too. No-one louder than her daughter. As the meeting ended, Jack was privileged to walk down the steps of the Forum cinema side by side with Winston who shook his hand and complemented him on his good organization of the three rallies. The press were there, of course and the family were very excited to see a photo of Jack shaking Winston's hand in the next copy of the Morning News.

Many other political collegues came down from London to support Randolph at the meetings that followed almost daily. Members of parliament such as Brendan Brackan and Lord Balfour, Lord Hailsham and Anthony Eden.

Pam had been busy with her autograph book and got the names of most of these in her book, of which she was very proud.

When the week of the election arrived there was a lot of door to door canvassing to do and Randolph soon realized that his opponent was a very popular man and his name alone was not going to make the winning easy. All the preparations were in place. Each ward had a polling office close to the school where the voting was to take place Phyllis would remain in the central office whilst Grandad Baker ran the Stoke ward office from a corner house in Molesworth Road near the top of the hill. Jack would be busy with other men with cars transporting elderly and infirm people to the polling stations, whilst Pam and some other young conservatives would act as runners, or rather with their bicycles where possible, collecting the slips of numbers from the station back to the nearest relevant poling office so that they could be checked off on the electoral roll thereby making sure that the definite conservatives would be sure to get to the polls. It would be a long day and every vote would count.

The morning went swiftly by as the shoppers stopped off to vote and Jack was kept busy driving people to and fro. They stopped for a quick lunch of a sandwich and tea before starting off again, collecting addresses from the Stoke office every now and then. Just about two o'clock Pam was cycling up to the Ford Hill crossroads when she saw her father's car a couple of hundred yards in front of her when suddenly, at the junction just as Jack was signaling to turn right, May rushed out of the corner shop and grabbed the door handle of the front passenger's side and hung on as Jack began to accelerate. He braked. She shouted for him to let her get in. He shook his head and told her to get away. He tried to shake her off as he slowly moved forward. A bus was coming up the hill on his right hand side. May fell to the ground almost under it's wheels but the bus driver managed to stop before hitting her. As Pam came up Jack got out of his car at the same time as the bus driver got down from his cab. All the passengers were staring out of the windows wondering what had happened. May was yelling at Jack to please let her come home with him, and he was trying to calm her down when a police car arrived and two policemen came over. "Come along gentlemen, you're blocking the road. What's been going on here?" Everyone talked at once and eventually one policeman persuaded the bus driver to move the bus over to the bus stop then took his statement. The other policeman came over to Jack and May who were arguing. "Now then. Can we get some order here? What's going on please? Your names first, if you don't mind." May panicked and started to run off but the policeman was too quick for her and grabbed her by her elbow. She struggled and fell down on the pavement. He then told Jack to park safely and come and give a statement. When Jack explained their family situation and that there was a restraining order on May not to contact his family again the policeman put May into his car and took her away after taking Jack's address.

Everything then returned to the business of the election. Jack called Pam over and said, "Don't tell your Mother what happened here this afternoon. She's got enough to worry about today. We'll tell her later when the polls are closed.

Finally everyone who was going to vote had done so. There was nothing more to do except wait. It would take some time for all of the votes to be counted. Several hours in fact. They all went home for a rest and something to eat before going to the Devonport Guildhall where the count was taking place. At home after supper Jack told the family what had happened that afternoon. "Oh, my God Jack, you could have been patrolling the polling stations." "And how was May?" Phyllis asked softly. "Wild!" Pam replied. "She looked crazy and scruffy too." "Poor child" murmoured Phyllis. "I wish there was something we could do for her." "No!" everyone said in chorus. "No Phyl," said Jack. "You've done all you could for that girl. You gave her a home and love. The sad thing was she didn't know what to do with it. Maybe she will learn to love someday." "At least learn to accept love when it's offered with an open heart." said wise old Charlotte.

The policeman came just then and explained that May would be held in custody until she could be put on the next ferry to Guernsey where she would get medical help.

They all attended the count at eleven o'clock and chatted to all the workers as well as Randolph and his family. It took until the early hours of the morning before the count was finally in. Randolph Churchill had lost. The ballet was clearly for Micheal Foot, the local boy had won once again.

So it was all over. The election, and the problem that was May. But life would go on. Pammy with her Art School and it's future and Phyllis with her very own business soon, and she and Jack shared their close married life for many many years to come.

And May? They never saw or heard from her again.

Lightning Source UK Ltd.
Milton Keynes UK
171221UK00001B/2/P